T0114187

THE MONSTER GAME
BY PRECIA DAVIDSON

Trafford rev. 03/23/2012

 www.trafford.com

North America & international
toll-free: 1 888 232 4444 (USA & Canada)
phone: 250 383 6864 ♦ fax: 812 355 4082

PART ONE

CHAPTER ONE

It was him, the one who wore the black cape. But it wasn't the normal black that you and I see, no, it was darker than the darkest night. The cape held something evil; a red, human-like object with scaly skin and two sharp, long horns that curved around. They were also black, though not like the cape, and drawn with fine thin lines. The eyes were aglow, almost red except for the reflection of something it was holding.

A rainbow of colours escaped from his clawed hand, as pure and beautiful as a drop of golden sun and he grasped it tightly. He wanted it for something, which was certain from the way he hurried. He walked quickly along a sidewalk somewhere, his cape ruffling silently as it blew in the wind. He gazed straight ahead, his eyes unblinking, unmoving.

A castle arose out of seemingly nowhere, surrounded by a dense eerie fog. It was night and not the moon nor stars dared to peek through the gathering clouds. A silence fell over the castle, suspended in the cool night air. Crack! Thunder roared across the sky and the wind, as strong and fast as a train, sent the rain hurtling at me with powerful force.

The castle was black with sharp points jabbing fiercely out of the walls in all directions. It was tall, reaching high up into the clouds and the odd window placed at the front was drawn with black curtains. There was a small door, surprisingly, and only one person would be able to fit through at a time. I wondered then if he could change his size, but the creature simply walked in.

I heard and saw nothing after that. The wind had picked up even more and its whistle in my ears was deafening. The rain continued to shoot at me from behind the bushes where I crouched. I tried desperately to stand but the wind knocked me down with a hard blow. I tried to cry out but the wind, rain and thunder drowned out my voice.

Why did you follow him, I thought, why didn't you think of the danger? I tried to crawl but the weight of my drenched clothes made it impossible. I was stranded in a place I did not recognize with… what lived in the castle? A monster, I decided, and then a thought struck me. How long would I be there? Days, weeks, years perhaps? By the time morning came, the monster would probably find me and take me prisoner. I cringed at the thought.

I had to escape, but to where? Not to the castle at least. There was no possible way to escape, at night anyway. I would have to take my chances. In the morning I would leave and hopefully find my way back home.

A light; I looked up quickly. There was a little light, glowing brighter as it neared. I waved my arms in the air weakly. It was coming towards me! I felt a tinge of excitement hoping that whoever it was had seen me. There was a bright flash of lightning and it blinded me. I helplessly reached out my hand catching nothing but air. The light was gone when I looked again and I began to lose hope. I was sure that they would help me. I cradled my legs in close to my body for warmth. Slowly, very slowly so that I didn't miss the light if it returned, I closed my eyes…

Something rang loudly and my eyes shot open. Sunlight poured through my window, snaking around my cream coloured curtain and gently resting on my face. I touched my bed with my warm pink blanket upon it, confused at first, but then I remembered. That dream; I had dreamt of that castle, that monster, the scenery. I had had the same dream twice before and could make no sense of it. It was so real, so real that I could even feel the weight of the pounding rain. It meant something, don't all dreams? But what?

§

"Come on Kay, you know that it isn't real," Rob laughed, nudging me with his elbow. I knew that it would happen this way; I would go to school, tell him about my dream and he would laugh at me. Actually, it was a bit funny and I smiled a little.

"Yes, I know that it isn't real, but-" I began. Rob cut me off.

"-Good, then that settles it. It was fake and next time you dream of it, just remind yourself."

Rob always had a way of convincing me that what I believed to be true really wasn't.

"You're right," I replied, "I was silly to think that it was real."

Rob smiled as though he'd just accomplished some heroic action.

"Right," he said in agreement, yet I'd had a thought just then. When I walked home from school I'd take a short cut through the forest. I'd suddenly felt a long forgotten need for adventure and had never taken that path before, never actually seen those woods up close, so I asked Rob to go with me. The moment our day had ended, we set out.

Excitement grew in every step closer we came to the forest. The large patch of dense trees were unevenly arranged and much too close together. Some were falling down and painfully bent, others were upright in all colours, sizes and varieties. My favourite was the birch, one in particular, standing taller than the rest like a ghost against the autumn sky. I went to it and gently rubbed the cold, smooth trunk. Rob did the same, carefully peeling off a piece of loose papery bark.

"What," he asked, reading my questioning glance, "I'm just gathering some paper in case we become stranded and need to write a note home."

He was always saying crazy things like that.

"Rob," I commented, and he looked up at me, "we're not even in the woods yet."

What a worrier! He quickly dropped the paper and I watched it gently flutter to the ground, almost like a delicate snowflake, until it finally settled on a patch of soft green grass.

We made our way through rows and rows of trees whose tops were so clustered that they blocked out the sun. Darkness had settled and I was ready to turn around. The wind picked up and the lowest, probably the sharpest branches bowed down, smacking me in the face and pulling at my sleeves. I looked back to see Rob cautiously following behind me.

Suddenly something sharp jabbed painfully into my left leg and I pulled back quickly, almost taking a fall. My head spun back around to see a patch of thistles, as sharp as swords and as tall as my height, framing the border of the trees. Rob saw them too and without speaking, we both turned around to journey back out.

The trees were blocking the path. I frantically tried to squeeze through but couldn't. The trees had not been there before. We were trapped! Our only chance was through the woods. I took a sharp stick and flattened the thistles down. Rob did the same until we'd cleared a path and walked quickly through it, the surrounding thistles scratching our legs as they blew in the quickening wind. I let out a sigh. We'd come to a clearing in the forest but there was no longer a path to follow. We were on our own.

"Kay, look," Rob exclaimed, pointing to the thistles. They were all in straight lines, rows of hundreds as though someone had planted them there, but why? Maybe, and horror struck me, maybe to keep us out.

§

It was strange, the set up of these woods. The darkness and gloom no longer lingered, it was instead filled with light. Trees with multi-coloured leaves were planted neatly alongside all varieties and colours of wildflowers ever imaginable. A feeling of peace and comfort washed over me at its beauty. The odd rose bush grew sweet and beautiful, yet its thorns never cut.

I picked up a wonderful rose and gently stroked its silky petals in my hand. Something rolled out of it; two little berries, soft and green, something I had never seen in a rose before. I touched my finger to my lips and a sweet full taste entered my mouth; the berry juice. I had learned that if a berry were poisonous it would taste bitter. I decided to try it, it wouldn't hurt to have one.

"Try one of these, they're not poisonous," I told Rob, "go ahead."

I popped one into my mouth and offered him the other. He carefully took it and dropped it into his mouth. I could feel the sweet juice squeezing out of the berry and running down the back of my throat. I closed my eyes, savouring the taste. I rolled it from side to side, eventually crushing the thin skin with my teeth. Little seeds were inside and I easily broke them. I swallowed it softly, opening my eyes, and jumped back because I didn't know where I was.

The forest around us had completely changed. I quickly shut my eyes again. I was imagining and I automatically thought of the berries. They had been poisonous all along, what other explanation could there be for what I saw? I opened my eyes and looked at Rob. He saw it too; little beings flying around, fairies.

There were hundreds of them fluttering around not too far away. They appeared as little people with delicate wings, some having a hint of blue, yellow, or even pink to them. All wore flowing garments of fine linens and silks with hundreds of colours all spiraling in and out from flower to flower. It was amazing watching them work. They would take pollen and dust their wings; like butterflies, I thought, enchanting.

I heard a gentle humming like the music notes of a low tune and it grew nearer. I could soon see a little light approaching until it was in front of me. A fairy, the height of my thumb and almost as wide, rested on the tip of my outstretched hand. His blonde hair shone, he wore white pants and a matching shirt with a crown embroidered in gold on its right, and his wings were a brilliant yellow dotted with blue. He looked up at me and smiled, his green eyes sparkling brightly.

"My name is Frendall," he explained and I almost dropped him. He could talk!

"I work at the castle as well as the palace, which is why I'm wearing this."

He pointed at the embroidered crown proudly and his smile widened.

"It is a pleasure to meet you Kay," he said, shaking my finger as though it were a hand.

"You too Rob," he added, looking over at him. Rob stared forward, unmoving.

"Welcome to Fairyland. Follow me," Frendall told us before flying off of my finger. That's when I noticed his shoes. They were pointed at the toes and green, looking as though they had belonged to an elf at one point, but they hadn't. They had been made by hand out of painted rose petals.

"Follow me," called Frendall in a louder voice. He thought that because we were not following him, we had not heard him. This wasn't so. I was staring in awe at the land that stretched before us with its breathtaking view and beauty. Somehow I gained a sense of trust and though my legs felt like rubber I reluctantly followed and Rob slowly walked after me.

Everything suddenly fell silent like the calm before a storm. Nothing moved except for the pairs of little eyes watching our every move, all bright and shining like moons. Some fairies wore glasses woven of a fine material and I noticed that many were young. Few fairies had white or grey hair, or even a wrinkled face. The whole swarm of them burst into yells and shouts of joy. There was much clapping as more and more fairies cleared the way before us. They were harder to see as many landed on the ground and began bowing to us. Soon we had passed the patches of flowers and came to yet another clearing in which trees, mostly evergreens, surrounded the back half ahead of us.

It was a fairy village with tiny brick houses, rows of them, built by little hands. There were a great deal more fairies there, all bowing as the others had done, yet I still could not make out what they were saying. Then in the centre of it all stood a great castle, or what appeared much larger compared to the houses and it was glistening in pure white diamonds. One of the diamonds caught a drop of sun and turned golden. It shot through to all of the others until a rainbow of colours encircled the structure. I gasped at how perfectly the jewels reflected the light just right, so that it would hit and pour out colourful beams.

"Wow," I whispered under my breath. I had never seen something so beautiful. I was so relaxed that when I heard a response, I was almost startled.

"Why, thank you," I heard, and yet another fairy came to rest atop my finger. She was very pretty and had a long face. Her cheeks puffed out ever so slightly under her bright blue eyes. She laughed a raspy laugh and I could see that the skin on her throat was beginning to fold. Her dress was as yellow as a buttercup, reaching down just below her knees, giving way to blue wings powdered with soft pink pollen. Brown hair curled nicely around her face, not too tightly, and hung about her shoulders with a crown of roses gently resting on the top of her head.

"This is for you," she explained softly and flew up to place the crown of roses on my head. I was confused, why would she give it to me?

"I was the Queen of Fairyland," she said, coming back in front of me, "who do you suppose it is now?"

But the crown didn't fit me and I was a human so I couldn't become a Queen, could I? I was even more confused and I knew that the Queen could sense this. She took the crown off of my head.

"First, come inside and we will talk," she told us, flying down to the ground. I nearly started to walk in but the door was much too tiny. Frendall flew up to me and handed me a paper. I took a magnifying glass from my pocket and read the tiny lettering.

The note was written in fine gold ink. I looked over to see that Rob had received one also. It told of a promise to the fairies. The only words upon it were, 'you must never tell anyone about Fairyland'.

"To sign your name," called the Queen in her raspy voice, "one must only run their finger across the page."

Without knowing what was going to happen we both ran a finger over the page. We hadn't looked on the back or we might have seen the few little words appearing much smaller than on the front; 'if you intend to play the game by signing this sheet, if it may arise within your time, you must finish it'.

CHAPTER TWO

Either we were shrinking or everything was growing. The castle was soon a grand structure reaching high above us. If one of the diamonds were to fall, I realized, it would splinter into millions of sharp slivers of light. The fairies had grown too. Frendall was slightly taller than me. He was amazing! His face was round and pale, and his nose was only a small dot upon his face. His green eyes lit up with a glow when he smiled and his smile was warm and comforting. I felt safe around him.

The Queen appeared mostly the same, however, she was slightly more hunched than how she'd looked when I first saw her. Her fiery blue eyes were full of kindness and when she smiled her face became tightly wrinkled. I would have guessed her to be about sixty years old if not for her brown hair. She gently reached up and placed the crown of roses upon my head.

"It suits you," she said. I raised my arms to grasp it and suddenly discovered something moving on my back. I spun around but nothing was there. When it appeared again and I saw it out of the corner of my eye, I turned my head slowly. There behind me was a delicate pair of silvered wings. They were long, heart shaped and attached to, or maybe coming out of, a beautiful flowing pink dress. It didn't take very long to realize that I was wearing that pink dress and that those were my wings. I was a fairy.

I thought of Rob and automatically jumped when I realized that he had been turned into a fairy also. His brown hair was the same but his brown eyes had a glow to them just like the Queen and Frendall. He wore blue pants and a shirt lined with silver. Then, behind him, I saw it. Two wings, *his* wings, and they were clear. They looked like stained glass edged with a hint of green and as pure as water. The sun caught one of them and made it appear golden. The Queen gave him a crown of roses like mine.

"I'm sorry that the King is not with us, so he couldn't crown you," the Queen apologized to Rob, "he will be home around suppertime. Right now he's out hunting."

I could suddenly picture it. He would stuff berries into roses so that we could see his kingdom, then go out hunting... for humans! He'd be home around suppertime and we would be the meal.

"We can't stay for supper," I said, my voice shaking. I made sure that my grip on Rob's arm was tight and then I ran, faster than I'd ever run before, dragging him along. I ran away from the castle and past the houses, large and spacious now, and into the flowers. It was obvious that Rob was quite confused, looking bewildered as he trailed beside me. I was not going to look back.

I continued through the flowers and roses so quickly that they were a blur of colours all mixing together, until I looked upon something that stopped me dead in my tracks. There was something up ahead far off in the distance that I had not seen before. It was a castle.

"What is that?"

Rob was standing beside me hardly moving, speechless. He had spoken only those three words before becoming completely consumed by fear. It looked so familiar, like I'd seen it somewhere before. The black castle stood tall and menacing with sharp points jabbing fiercely out of the walls in all directions.

It was my dream! I was about to tell Rob this when I heard a rustling to my left and my head snapped in the direction of the noise. I saw nothing but an old log cabin, enormous, much larger than even the castle in Fairyland, with enough room to fit a couple of human sized people. A crooked chimney made of stones was attached to the side of the house. I figured that it was abandoned because faded curtains hung in the windows and the rose garden out front grew wild. Vines reached up the side wall and wound themselves chokingly around the chimney.

The chimney; I hadn't realized the little puffs of grey smoke slowly rising out of it, lingering in the air and then being caught and taken by the breeze. The smoke floated up into the sky, becoming lighter as it rose until finally it vanished altogether. There was someone living there after all. The front door knob jiggled and then the door opened. I stood frozen, unable to run or even move as it emerged.

It was like something from a nightmare. A monster, exactly like the one in my dream, stood only a few steps away from us. If he wanted to, with only a leap he could capture us and pull us into his cabin. We would be his prisoners! He was like a giant and could step on me very easily. Maybe he wouldn't see us, we were probably like mice to him. I slowly started to inch away but he did look. He'd seen me but his eyes were a soft green, not red and instead of wearing a black cape he wore a white one. He started to lean down towards me when a sudden gust of wind came up. It caught one of my wings and I was tossed into the air like a leaf. I was rushing back, spinning and hurtling backwards, being tossed from side to side! Soon the castle was just a speck of black in the distance.

All at once the flowers and the village poured out before me as I began to gain speed. I turned my head as far as it would go but all that came into view was the white fairy castle with its glistening diamonds. I was going to crash into it, I was on a direct path! I turned again to see the village moving away from me and I closed my eyes. I was going to hit it any minute and I was expecting to feel a searing pain cut sharply into my back and sides, but it didn't. Instead, I felt something soft and frail catch me. I was being gently lowered to the ground and I didn't have to open my eyes to find out who had saved me.

§

Rob began shivering and the Queen wrapped a warm blanket around him. We were inside the castle now and it was just as beautiful as the outside. Silk wallpaper lined the walls with matching red velvet bedspreads draped across the gold and white furniture. There were chairs and tables, and a hallway that led to many rooms under the marble staircase. Chandeliers hung with amazing teardrops glittering from golden strings like drops of dew.

The Queen had just finished telling us what had happened. The gust had thrown me back and she had caught me just before I would have slammed into the wall. She had set me on the ground and I was so dizzy and overwhelmed that I had lost track of Rob. What I didn't know was that, only seconds later, Rob had come hurtling back after me. Frendall had taken me inside just before the rain hit. It pounded Rob to the ground until the Queen carried him inside. By then he was very weak and starting to shiver. The only thing that I had suffered from was fear.

The door swung open and I looked away from the chandelier, turning my attention to what stood there. It was still raining outside and no sooner did the door open than it closed again. At first I didn't think that anyone was there until I saw two puddles on the floor. They slowly neared, leaving behind a small discoloured spot on the carpet as water dripped from nowhere. The sun was setting quickly and I knew what that meant; it was almost suppertime, time for the King fairy to return home from his hunting trip.

"Henry, you're still invisible," the Queen laughed. Her face lit up and I smiled. I felt safer since she'd saved our lives and in a sense, I trusted her.

"So I am," a hearty laugh escaped from somewhere above the puddles and I jumped. So the King was old too, I could tell by his voice. Then everything rushed back to me at once; how we'd found our way into Fairyland, how we'd been turned into fairies. The monster in the log cabin was my most vivid memory. 'Who lives there, what is this, let me go home', I tried to choke out, but no words came. Finally I turned to Frendall.

"I need to lie down," I said, but my voice came out as a whisper. I felt weak and as much as I tried to stay awake, it was impossible. I soon gave into exhaustion and sank into sleep as I listened to a faraway voice.

"She'll make a fine Queen," it seemed to say, then it trailed off and I heard nothing more. I found myself in sweet dreams just then but they were soon disturbed by monsters. My mind flashed back to the one in the black cape. This time I watched him from a distance. He was laughing as he held a large chain. My eyes fearfully followed his every move. He walked up to a house of some sort, but it was night in my dream and I couldn't tell what it was.

Another monster came out of the house, one that was more hunched than the first, and the two suddenly began fighting. Lights and smoke, both red and green, were thrown back and forth and fireballs came out of nowhere. The hunched one was bound in chains. A white cape, I noticed, swirled around him.

"Save the village," he shouted and I realized that he was looking at me. He was the one that I'd seen I thought, as I began to drift into wakefulness and now as I looked at the house it wasn't a house at all. It was a log cabin...

I jumped and opened my eyes. I was in a large bedroom with a pine dresser dotted with pink and splashed with gold. A heart shaped mirror hung above another smaller table. On the dresser I noticed, rubbing the sleep from my eyes, sat a very large book. It was very old because the pages were wrinkled and yellowing, and the leather cover was curling and thin. Sunlight crept in through a window behind me and beamed upon it, making gold lettering appear. I walked over, sitting down in the comforts of an old wooden chair at its side and read it aloud.

"The Book of Fairies," I read. I ran my finger over the delicate words that would be forever embedded in the cover. A line of roses ran along its outer edge, faded now, the paint chipping away where they twisted around each other. I glanced at the spine and there hung a little gold key, tiny and frail, with a piece of red ribbon attaching it to the book.

"Hello Kay," I heard a deep soothing voice and at first I thought it might have come from the book. Recognizing the voice, I turned around to see Henry in the doorway dressed thickly in furs.

"Very cold out today," Henry commented, a smile crossing his face, "here, take this."

He threw me a fur coat, real fur, as white as new snow and the softness of it was wonderful.

"You gave us quite a scare last night," his smile faded into concern, "are you well today?"

I nodded, still unsure of what to think. His smile returned as he walked over to the table. He reached out towards me but his hand passed me and touched the book. He grasped it tightly, holding it to his chest and then slowly he opened it to the very first page.

"Here," he offered, extending the book towards me, "read it."

I took it slowly, holding it just as he had and peered down at the tiny gold writing. Suddenly, as if taken by the wind, the pages turned slowly at first then sped so quickly that the writing could no longer be seen. I looked at Henry.

"How do I make it stop?!"

It stopped just as I had spoken these words and I looked at the page it had turned to, I looked again. I had to look several times before I believed what I saw. In the same tiny gold lettering at the top of the page was written 'Kay'.

"What is this," I exclaimed, dropping the book to the floor. There had to be some sort of logical explanation for what I was seeing, but then again what was logical about any of this? Perhaps it was a blank book I decided, a guest book and whoever came to visit would have their name printed in it. Afraid, I backed away. Henry looked at the book, appearing dead now as it lay on the floor painfully bent open, and then back up at me. His face was old, much like the Queen's but pale like Frendall's. He was much taller than me and stood very straight. He quietly turned and left the room, and I feared that in some way I might have offended him. But the Queen entered the room now, coming closer until I looked up and our eyes met.

"Don't worry, Henry just went out to visit the palace," she explained kindly, as if reading my mind. Now I pictured the palace; it would be as wonderful as the castle, only smaller. Where was the palace, I wondered, who lived there?

"Have you read the book," she asked, referring to 'the book' as though there were no other. I almost asked which one she meant then I remembered. The Book of Fairies which now rested on the floor, the one that had said my name, the one that flipped its own pages. I shook my head as she gently lifted the book and set it on my lap.

"Read this," she explained, "and you will understand much about our world."

She left the room as Frendall entered. He set down a bowl of oatmeal, full and steaming. It had been a long time since I'd had anything to eat and my stomach growled. Frendall nodded, then left. I sat on the edge of my bed and ate. It was as sweet as the berry had been when we'd first entered the woods and very filling. Once I was content I slowly opened the book a little ways, then flung it fully open. I closed my eyes and opened them again. Nothing happened, it remained on the first page I had opened it to, so slowly I set it down in front of me. I lifted my feet off of the soft carpet and flung my legs onto the bed. When at last I was in a comfortable position, afraid yet excited I read this:

There is good and there is evil. The Fairy Book, also known as the 'Book of Fairies' was made very long ago in the age of the fairies when the magic first came. The good came before the evil. A boy on Earth found this very forest and in the centre planted a rose, which began our enchanted world.

Winters came, harsh and long and the boy became ill. He could no longer care for the rose and didn't have a chance to see that the snow never touched it, it never died. But the boy did; he passed away that spring, the spring when a wonderful thing happened. A winged wonder arose from the rose. It was George, the first fairy born. It is not known what happened to the boy...

I stopped for a moment. It is not known what happened to the boy? What did it mean, I thought it said that he had died. I continued curiously.

Christopher was his name. It is thought that that he became a fairy, although this is not certain.

A fairy, I thought in amazement. He turned into a fairy?!

More than one event took place that day. The petals became the fairies and the healthy leaves became this book. The brown, crisp leaves became the Book of Monsters and the thorns became the monsters, which will be mentioned further on.

I stopped again. The monsters, like the ones in my dreams? They were here in this very land and they had their own book like this one?

George was greeted by Marianne, another fairy who came from the rose. The rose is like no other, you shall know it if ever you see it. It lies in the exact centre of Fairyland Old. Fairyland was once the entire land where George and Marianne ruled with their two children, Paul and Mary. They ruled over four monsters; a mud monster (Cookstone), a ghost (Woo) and two scale skins, Amile and Hesman.

The monsters turned against the fairies and left to another part of Fairyland. It took them three days and once they arrived, a castle was built and the land proclaimed 'Monsterland'. A curse was laid upon it that if a fairy entered, they would be forced out. Capes were given to the scale skins, appearing on their backs according to the strength of their powers. Evil was red, somewhat kind hearted was deep pink.

The scale skins built a log cabin almost borderline between Monsterland and Fairyland. This was the house in which their son was born and grew to become King.

The book closed tightly after I had finished reading the last line and it would not open. I had found out some but not enough. Even so, it seemed important, so I kept it tucked away in the back of my mind.

I wandered into the long hallway bearing golden wallpaper etched with roses and continued down the stairs. I moved along slowly, brushing the marble staircase with one hand and holding the Book of Fairies in the other.

Rob ran towards me as I reached the bottom of the stairs. Startled, I dropped it on the soft carpet. The pages flipped open as it lay there, then the cover came together and it closed once more.

"They're gone," Rob explained, sounding worried. I gave him a questioning look and he continued, "the Queen and Henry. They went to some palace to visit someone named George."

Rob shrugged as Frendall stepped out from behind him. His gaze dropped until all of us looked upon the book. It hadn't closed all the way, it had remained open just barely a crack to one page. I lifted it and spread it out as Rob came over. We read together.

King Monster became King around two hundred years ago. He was feared by many, as his cape started out pink and then turned white. No other monster had a white cape and so, as he was marked differently, he was made King. His parents lived in the castle, however, he lived alone in the log cabin. The fairies heard of this and in turn the palace was built. It housed the King and Queen, George and Marianne, yet their two children remained behind in the castle. They recorded rules with a golden pen, using petals as paper. This is how the ten rules of fairies came to be.

The Ten Rules Of Fairies (as recorded by Paul and Mary)

1. *Fairies are granted powers to do good and as self defense only if necessary.*
2. *Fairies are granted eternal life.*
3. *A new generation of fairy royalty must be a human one.*
4. *Fairies will never become ill.*
5. *Fairies will never grow old.*
6. *Fairies are granted the power of free will.*
7. *If a fairy makes a promise, they must keep it.*
8. *Royalty are granted the ability to move the land and all which rests upon it.*
9. *Fairies are granted wings for the ability to fly.*
10. *If you begin the game, if it may arise within your time, you must finish it.*

The book closed and I looked up. Henry and the Queen were back, I watched them enter through the front door. I had so many questions to ask them!

CHAPTER THREE

"Let us all be seated, then we may begin," the Queen spoke softly. Rob sat on a chair edged with delicate and gentle lace while I sat on a couch beside the Queen. The King leaned back in a rocking chair directly across from me while Frendall found comfort on a wooden stool.

"I am aware that you have many questions," she continued, warbling and clearing her throat. A glass of pure water appeared in her hand.

"Thank you Frendall," she exclaimed, sipping at it lightly. I gasped, nearly falling off of the couch in surprise. Frendall had made it appear! The fairies had magical powers! Then I remembered the first rule of fairies and fell silent. The Queen turned to me quickly then directed her attention towards Rob.

"You will have one hour of questions and answers every day. But for now you will learn about your powers. If all goes well, we may begin on flying lessons. I am under the assumption that you have read some of the book, correct?"

Rob and I nodded. Suddenly the Queen whipped her glass at me. It rushed towards my face and I fearfully covered my eyes with my hands, but nothing happened. I opened my eyes and could see the cup, water and all, hanging in mid-air before me. When I moved my hand, the glass moved with it. Water had come out of the glass in a spray but the beads of liquid were suspended in their places. I moved my other hand and the water moved with it. One hand moved the glass and the other moved the liquid, I had figured it out! Soon I had replaced all of the drink, tipped the cup upright and rested it on the table in front of us. The Queen beamed with pride.

"How did you do that, why did you do that," I sputtered.

"In your fairy life," she began, "there will be tests for various skills. You must put all that you have into passing them. This was one of those tests. I was prepared to help you if you were in need but I didn't have to. You did that by yourself, with your magic."

The Queen's face lit up and her eyes glowed even brighter. I took her extended hand.

"You passed," she confirmed, shaking it heartily. I decided not to ask questions, perhaps I would wait until tomorrow. There was plenty of time.

I was very relieved when it was time to go upstairs for the night. I was very tired and quickly changed into my patterned nightgown. I could see an orange glow in the hall followed by a head peering in through the doorway. It was Frendall carrying a tall candle. With a smile and a nod, his way of saying goodnight, he moved something over to the dresser. He progressed down the hall, the candlelight growing fainter until it disappeared altogether. The moon provided light but only enough to see that what he had placed on the dresser was the Book of Fairies.

I did not dream of monsters that night, but of something else. Those words rang in my ears and echoed through my mind all night. It was the second rule of fairies, 'fairies are granted eternal life'. I had often wondered what it would be like to continue on forever; to see the future, to *live* it, hundreds of years later. But soon the thought escaped my mind as a far off noise pulled me from my sleep.

It was still dark outside when I awoke hearing faint whisperings in the hallway. I made my way towards the door, stumbling in the dark room. At first I could see nothing, then slowly a little light started to appear at the end of the long hall. Drowsy, I simply figured that it was Frendall but as it drew nearer I wasn't so certain.

The outline of some being, what it was I didn't know as I couldn't make it out clearly, slowly drifted towards me like a shadow among the shadows. It sent chills up my spine how it lingered about and I had an odd sense now that it wasn't Frendall at all. An eerie glow surrounded the figure, partly from a dim candle it held but also from itself. I noticed that the glow had turned green by this time and that it was quickening its pace. I grasped the cold hard doorknob and carefully pulled it towards me.

A faint creak escaped from deep inside one of the door's brass hinges. The figure made a dead stop in the middle of the hall, its head appearing to turn from side to side until it fixed its attention on my doorway. I silently flung myself behind the door, barely breathing, the blackness of the night swallowing me. The candle was so close now that its light filtered in through the crack. I grasped the handle tighter, my palms sweating as it stationed itself at the doorway. I plunged forward, thrusting my weight upon the door until it latched itself with a loud chirp and was locked beyond opening. I heard heavy breathing on the other side and froze, fear pulsing through me. I fell to the floor with my legs feeling as though they were tied down with heavy weights, my arms hanging loose and limp at my sides and my head spinning crazily.

"Help me," I cried weakly to no one in particular. The knob turned slowly, met by the grind of hinges moving over each other. Someone was entering by magic, the situation was becoming desperate. I called louder, hearing another noise now of quick footsteps hurrying down the hall. The figure fled, I listened as it scurried down the stairs and when the door opened wide at last it was Frendall who stood there.

"What's going on, are you alright," he exclaimed, extending a hand towards me. I grasped it and he pulled me off of the floor.

"I saw something in the hall," I exclaimed, out of breath from the shock. He took my comment lightly.

"It was probably just me," he chuckled, "I walked by earlier."

"No," I argued, "just now. Someone was out there just now and I heard them flee down the staircase at the same time I heard you coming down the hall."

He pondered this for a moment, looking around curiously.

"I don't see anything Kay," he explained kindly, "it was probably just a dream. Don't worry, go back to sleep now."

"But-" I began helplessly, realizing that there was no proof it had happened. No one had seen it and it had left once Frendall came. Maybe there was no threat after all, I decided.

"Ok," I finally agreed as Frendall left the room. I peeked out again just to be sure but saw nothing and the night became silent once more. I calmly returned to my bed.

I slept for quite awhile after that and when I awoke the sun had risen high in the sky, signaling the start of another day. I yawned and climbed out of bed, my feet welcoming the warmth of the floor. I crept to my open door and gazed out into the hall; everything was white and golden and beautiful. I headed downstairs still admiring the beauty of the castle in the silence of the morning. There were so many rooms circling around the downstairs corridor, some fancier than others, all with clear or golden handles. I returned upstairs and hammered on one of the doors. I heard a groan and the popping of springs, then a sleepy eyed Rob appeared at the doorway.

"Time to get up," I called impatiently, making my way downstairs yet again but still I heard nothing. Where was everyone? I turned towards the kitchen at my left and walked in. No one was there, the stove was bare and the tea kettle remained empty. Then, hardly noticeable, I discovered a tiny door at the back of the room.

"They want to see you, you know."

I was startled by the sudden noise but automatically knew that it was the Queen.

"Who," I asked, turning around to face her. She smiled.

"George, Marianne, Paul, Mary," she replied, "they wanted to see you before you even came."

Before I came! But how would they know I was coming?

"We are going to the palace today," the Queen continued excitedly and as soon as Rob came down the stairs, we headed out.

Rob dragged his feet as we walked along. I nudged him and he seemed to get the point, for fairy shoes are very fragile and can easily be torn. We followed the Queen behind the castle into the surrounding forest. As we neared, we could make out quiet voices ahead and once we travelled through the final patch of birches and pines, it came into view. The palace was a brick building with a grey roof. My hopes sank, I had expected it to be as glorious as the castle. It looked so hard and cold and empty.

"They are here, they've come! Look, just look at them George! I've always waited for this day," a voice spoke out from deep inside the structure, yet they sounded close as though they were standing beside me. There was silence until another voice sounded.

"Yes, I do agree that they will make fine royalty," a male voice seemed to say, "soon they will be able to rule the land by themselves."

This would have been George then, I figured, and the first one would have been Marianne.

"Oh, do look," the woman gawked once more, "Kay and Rob are here! Mary, Paul! Come see them!"

"How do you know our names," I blurted out, astonished. The voices were still once more and for an instant I was afraid that I may have offended them in some way, but soon she answered.

"The Book of Fairies foretold of your arrival and so you have come at last," she replied kindly with a hint of excitement in her voice. So that's how they knew, the book had had my name within it after all!

"How do you enter the palace," Rob questioned noticing that, surprisingly, there was no door.

"There is a way in," a younger man said softly, "you shall know and come to understand its purpose in time. We are very grateful for your visit and shall tell you more next time. Goodbye."

As quickly as the meeting began it ended now and we were led back to the castle to have a meal with the King and Frendall.

"You're going around town today," the King instructed without hesitation once we were gathered at the kitchen table, "you must learn what to do when we are gone."

I gasped, not knowing what he meant. When they were *gone*? What was he talking about?

"But we just got here," I stammered, "what do you mean, you'll be gone?"

He waved the thought away with his hand.

"We won't worry about that right now," he offered, passing out plates stacked with some sort of bread. I crunched down on it but it wouldn't rip. I tugged it and rolled it but it kept its shape. Although I was only able to nibble small bits of it, it was the most delicious bread I had ever tasted, lavished with rich creamy butter. I ran my knife across it but it was like rubber. The King let out a hearty laugh and soon we were all laughing with him.

"This is my custom, I call it 'chew bread'," he exclaimed, grinning, then addressed my question seeing that I was still troubled by it.

"Anyway, we will soon live in the palace. Once a new generation of royalty comes, the old one moves away. That's what I meant by leaving."

There was a hint of sadness in his voice but soon he began to laugh again, leaving us still trying to figure out how to eat our chew bread!

After we were finished eating, I took out the fur coat that Henry had presented me with on the second day that I was in Fairyland. It had been a wonderful gift and I wrapped it around me. I adjusted my crown atop my head, then we were ready to walk about the town.

Rob opened the door and we went out, leaving Henry, Frendall and the Queen behind. It was a strange feeling venturing out on our own in such an unknown land but once I saw the sight before us, my feeling turned to joy. The door, once opened, felt as though it led to another world within Fairyland. Fairies were hurrying about carrying all sorts of parcels and goods in sparkling rainbow colours. They seemed to come in all shapes and sizes, being carried to and from a row of buildings bearing tidy signs. They were stores.

The first one I noticed was a bakery. Good smells wafted out of it and the chimney was busily puffing out clouds of white smoke. I ran over and looked into its front window display filled with royal cakes, cookies and all of the types of candy ever imaginable. I was pulled inside by an invisible force; my hunger. Hunger was different for fairies, I realized, feeling my stomach grow warmer and warmer until I decided I had to have one of the treats. My eyes came to rest on a glistening glazed candy on a stick. It was golden yellow in colour, spiraling up from the stick like a drill. I reached for it but my hand did not grasp it. Instead, I found myself shaking hands with the kind baker who worked there.

"You seemed to have your eye on those honey sticks over there," he laughed, "why don't you take one?"

The baker took two down from the shelf, handing one to Rob and I. We thanked him. He walked a ways then turned and motioned us to follow. We entered into a back hall with a plain white door that simply read 'berries'. The room was completely white and empty except for a little brown table in the centre of the beige floor.

"In this room, the bakers and I sift out the berries, separating the bad from the good," the baker exclaimed, pointing to a medium sized bowl on the table. I peered into it to find it filled with fuzzy green berries. They looked so familiar, where had I seen them before?

"Do you have a name for this type of berry," I asked. He nodded.

"Fairy berries. They grow on a special tree behind the castle. If eaten by a fairy, they are a dessert most cherished and can be consumed in great numbers. If a human eats a fairy berry, however, it allows them to see our world."

It all made sense now, so that's why Rob and I could see the fairies! We had eaten fairy berries that were tucked into the roses! We thanked him once again and left to explore more of Fairyland.

As we pushed ahead, already the sun was sinking lower and the trees were turning pink in the hues of dusk. I was confused, we had only been in the bakery a short while, how could night have fallen so quickly? I realized now how long I had slept that morning. It wasn't morning when I awoke, it had really been afternoon. I decided that we needed to head back to the castle.

"We need to go home," I called out to Rob in front of me, suddenly catching myself and stopping dead in my tracks. How could we go home? Exactly how far away were we? I was startled to find that I had called the castle 'home', for it wasn't, and I felt terrible for the mistake. Rob caught it too but said nothing and quietly walked beside me. Behind us, the fairy houses were all aglow and the stars were coming out one by one. Somehow I had a feeling that someone was watching us, but all stood quiet and still. When I saw a figure move into the shadows and caught a glimpse of white, however, my feeling became stronger. It had come from the cabin, I realized, that marked the borderline between Fairyland and Monsterland, good and evil, as though it were in the very centre of Fairyland Old.

Frendall greeted us when we arrived back at the castle and we followed him into the kitchen. I took the honey stick out of my pocket and began crunching it in my mouth, savouring the sweetness, when something caught my eye near the stove. It was that little door I'd noticed earlier before leaving for the palace. It was open a crack, just enough to see the pure light escaping through it. Frendall shut it by magic from where he sat.

"Don't look in there," he advised harshly, motioning Rob and I out of the kitchen. As we walked up the stairs we glanced at each other in shock. Frendall had almost seemed angry!

"I'm sure he didn't mean it, he's probably just tired," Rob said, still a little confused. I entered my room, pretending to be asleep when Frendall walked by. He nodded goodnight, I could tell through my slightly open lids and I watched until the glow of his candle faded. Once I knew that he was gone I sat up, smiling to myself. My brilliant plan would work. It would be a good night in deed, especially when I found out what hid behind that door.

§

I glanced around. Everything was quiet and I could see Frendall way down the hall with his back facing me. He was wearing a blue shirt and baggy blue pants with a matching grey cap, a change from his usual white clothes.

I silently made my way down the stairs. One step let out a faint squeak and I shrank against the side of the staircase. I could see an orange glow fill the hall and I knew instantly that Frendall would see me! But the light stopped and faded away once more; he had decided not to walk as far as where I stood and I was thankful. Soon I had reached the bottom of the stairs to the right of the kitchen, appearing like a large hole in the wall with the room's insides displayed for all to see. I entered.

Light flooded out from all around the door in a rainbow of pure colours. I reached for it, a little further, further… someone was advancing towards the kitchen and I froze again. A light turned on in the living room where Henry and the Queen stood. The Queen was hurrying towards the kitchen, towards *me*, and I knew at last that I was caught when the kitchen light came on. The Queen regarded me sleepily, extending an arm as if to grab me and push me off to bed. I was horrified thinking of what she would do if she found me and how disappointed she would be. What was she going to do?

She wandered past me, grasping a cup on the counter and taking it to Henry. The light in the kitchen went off and when my attention turned towards the door again, it was no longer glowing. Once I'd come to the conclusion that I was invisible I decided to sneak back upstairs. Perhaps it was not right to find something that wasn't meant to be found. I ran across the living room and up the stairs as quickly as I could.

Once I'd reached my bedroom I could hear Frendall approaching. I threw the covers over my legs and pretended to be asleep yet again.

"I don't think they saw you, pretty close though. Here," Frendall said, tossing me a hand bag, "don't open this until tomorrow, your birthday."

I shyly nodded as he left, blushing because he knew that I was wide awake and because he had made me invisible so that Henry and the Queen would not see me. I somehow knew that this would be our secret and that he found it humorous. I carefully tucked the package under the edge of the bed. But wait, my birthday wasn't until next month! Besides, how would they know that my birthday was near? I decided to wait until the next day to ask and to open my gift. I had already learned my lesson well.

CHAPTER FOUR

I ran down the stairs with the gift in my hand, very excited about what it could be. Frendall and the others were sitting around the kitchen table when I came to join them.

"Happy birthday Queen fairy," the Queen said. She was talking to me and I shook my head.

"You are the Queen," I said, looking deep into the eyes of the old fairy.

"No, you are," she replied, "from now on, just call me Sheena. This is my real name."

"Open your gift, let us not keep you waiting," Henry urged eagerly, so I did. I gently pulled the tassels at the end of the bag. It was silk and nestled in my palm but I set it down before I could see what waited inside.

"It's not my birthday," I broke the news, "my birthday is a month away. I'm sorry, I can't open it."

Frendall sat straighter in his chair.

"One day in Fairyland is a month in the human world," he explained, "so today is your birthday in this world."

I looked over at Rob, watching his brown eyes glowing brighter as I reached for the gift. I pulled the tassels a little more until the end of the sack opened, revealing a light bursting through it. I jumped, dropping it on the table. The light went rolling out, eventually coming to rest in front of Sheena. I leaned closer to it; it was a pure, white, clear stone of some sort with rainbow colours all throughout it.

"It is the Rainbow Crystal. It has belonged to every generation of royal fairies, the King or Queen, but not both. It is the one who has a pure heart, which was meant to have it by the book," Sheena explained.

"It has powers," Henry continued, "but not what you might think. It has the power to keep whoever owns it safe. You will know of its other purpose in time."

I clutched it and held it in my hand. The crystal was cool to the touch and very round and smooth. I dropped it into my pocket.

"In return, you must keep it safe," Frendall told me, removing it from my pocket and placing it safely back behind the little door.

"We mustn't let anything happen to it," he said solemnly, "ever."

By the way he looked at me, I could tell that he meant it. He really meant it.

"Delivery," I heard from the front door of the castle. I hopped out of my chair to see who it was but when I opened the door, no one was there. I closed the door and shrugged. The voice had sounded like a deep growling rumble and I wondered if it had just been the wind. Sheena and Henry smiled at me as I explained that I saw nothing there. The same rumble soon came again and I ran to the door once more, determined to find out who it was. When I realized that a monster stood in front of me I screamed and slammed the door, running to Henry.

"Monster, help," I screamed. He or she, or whatever the monster was, was made entirely of caked mud with hollow, formed eyes and a mouth. Why it was at the castle I was uncertain. Surprisingly, Sheena and Henry did not seem at all frightened.

"Enter, Letterman and bring the mail," Sheena exclaimed, opening the door from where she sat. The monster entered, looking rather tired, holding a parcel in the creases of his hands. He was dark brown in colour like a tree trunk and slightly shorter than me.

"Deliver to the Queen on her birthday," he announced, reading a small card neatly attached to the top of the parcel, "some day you will know what to do with this book."

He then pushed a clipboard towards me with a narrow strip of paper attached to it.

"Sign here," he rumbled deeply, pointing to the paper.

"I, I need a pen," I stumbled. He sighed and gently touched my finger, pressing it to the paper and running it across.

"There, you've signed. Have a good day," he concluded, handing me the present with the note still attached. Then he left and, gazing down at the note, I realized that the birthday greeting was written in black ink with sharp points at the ends of the letters.

"Who is this from," I asked once the monster was gone, "who was that?"

"The mail monster, Letterman," Henry spoke, "he delivers any mail we may receive, but he is the only monster allowed into Fairyland and only for that purpose. Since it has no return address, you cannot find out who sent it."

Who would have sent me a package and why? Who else knew that it was my birthday?

"We are waiting for you to open it," Frendall said anxiously and his eyes flared up fiery green. I shook the neatly wrapped parcel with uncertainty. If there was no return address it could be from anyone, anywhere. What if it was a trap? The fairies were magical, I remembered, they could help me if I were in trouble. I carefully removed the little attached card. So, it was a book then? I tore open the package along its edges and, sure enough, found a book inside.

The pages were empty when I opened it. It had a red leather cover which read 'diary' on the front in scroll and it was large in size. In towards the middle was a beautiful brass pen with a fine tip for writing. It was heavy and seemed to go along with the book. I was meant to write something in it. I tucked the little card inside the front cover and set it on the table.

Rob finally smiled, which hadn't happened in long time, as he handed me a gift. It was wrapped in fine paper bound with ribbon, all of which was white.

"It's from all of us," he explained as I carefully undid the paper finding yet another book, also a diary though it did not say so, but I knew because the pages were blank. It was small and white as well.

"Thank you everyone," I exclaimed, looking up into their warm faces. Rob was thoughtful, Frendall was excited, Sheena and Henry were beaming with happiness. It was as if everyone around me were kind and caring and gave me the acceptance I had searched for in my life back in the Human World. I felt a joy inside that I had never felt before. Then, suddenly, it dawned on me. Whatever it was called when you were sheltered and loved and respected, that's where I was. I was home.

§

"These are the one hundred rooms," Sheena explained, pointing to a roughly sketched map that she had crafted. It was a draft of the Fairyland castle with all of the rooms labeled. One hundred boxes were drawn neatly on the sheet of paper, some upstairs and some down. Rob and I stared in amazement.

"There are really one hundred rooms in the castle," Rob asked excitedly and Sheena nodded. I could not have ever imagined that the castle had so many rooms! The only rooms that Rob and I knew of were the living room, the kitchen, my room, Rob's room, Frendall's room, Sheena's room and Henry's room. That only made seven, so the thought of ninety three other rooms existing that we were unaware of was a shocking one. Looking at the map, the rooms didn't make sense. Ten pie rooms, ten colour rooms, ten game rooms, three storage rooms? Five flying rooms, five testing rooms, ten wish rooms, twenty study rooms?

Finally, as shown on the map, there were twenty empty ones, their purpose to be decided at a later date. Since the castle had existed the one hundred rooms had been there, some being able to be freely entered, some being entered only by way of a key and others only able to be accessed through secret passageways and steps. Sheena told us of a crawlspace beneath the castle, so small that you could only crawl through it but it was not considered to be a dwelling place and had not been placed on the map. Since the reign of Paul and Mary, Sheena went on to explain, she and Henry had filled the twenty study and five flying rooms which had beforehand been empty. Just the same as the twenty empty rooms that were now left up to Rob and I to fill. Even after George and Marianne, their two children who had come before Sheena and Henry had filled the ten game and wish rooms which had been empty after their parent's reign.

Rob and I took the map, then made our way down the long hallway leading off of the living room. It was straight and narrow with a crystal chandelier placed here and there to light the way and wooden doors with shiny brass knobs stood beckoning at either side. We entered the first chamber, which was about the size of my bedroom, slightly smaller than the kitchen. The pastel green walls gave way to a window that viewed the small houses and the cabin. The room was completely empty with the window being the only source of outside light, shining dimly on the green floor. It was a colour room. Rob and I went out of it and then into another, zigzagging back and forth through the hall until we had covered all of them.

The colour rooms were all the same size with plain coloured walls and matching floors, all of which were empty. Some had windows while in others light filtered through by way of a stained glass domed ceiling, which was in fact the same colour as the rest of the room. After we had toured the green room we went through the orange, pink, yellow, purple, blue, red, grey, silver and gold ones. When we reached the gold one a door stood to the side of the room, built into the wall so that it was flush against it and barely visible except for the tiny keyhole. Luckily Sheena had given us the key, a golden skeleton one, and with a click the door opened to another hallway. We continued.

We entered into the pie rooms shaped like pies; apple, rhubarb, lemon, strawberry, cherry, pumpkin, raisin, pecan, raspberry and fairy berry. There were pies in boxes stacked against the wall and the smells were wonderful. The game rooms were for fun and enjoyment with marbles, colourful balls and playgrounds with swings! The storage rooms were rather boring really, with musty old furniture stored within them in the same style as we used now. The testing rooms were empty for the most part and led upstairs. In them, tables had been set up with glass cups filled with bright liquids that mixed to become different colours. The ten wish rooms had stars sprawled out on the floor with moons on the ceiling and were neatly attached to form one big room with dividers.

The twenty study rooms led down a straight path through door after door. They were filled with desks, and books thick with pages sat upon dusty shelves. So many titles, so many subjects, how could anyone have time to read them all? We continued through the empty rooms. What would we make of them? They were spacious and could be turned into anything. Our last stop was to the flying chambers. They were large rooms filled with various currents of air to strengthen our wings and teach us to fly in many weather conditions. We wandered out to find ourselves in the same place standing before Sheena, excitedly going on about all that we had seen. She already knew as she'd been in those very rooms before, but she still listened with a warm gentle smile.

After some wonderful chew bread complete with honeysuckle syrup, I went upstairs to my room. Lying on my stomach upon the bed, I opened the little diary that Rob had presented me with. I removed the brass pen from the red diary and touched it to the paper of the white one, pulling back to discover that it had left a small gold dot of ink on the page. I grasped it tightly, as it was cold and slippery, then I began.

After much reading and conversation I am beginning to discover my purpose for being in Fairyland. I was taken from the Human World awhile ago, I've lost track of time since I've been here. All I know is that they need me, these fairies, they need me for something. It was because of magical berries that I was able to see this world and I was made Queen. Today is my birthday in Fairyland. I received a Rainbow Crystal but do not yet know of its powers. I have had many adventures already; I have been to the palace, have toured the one hundred hidden rooms of the castle. I have seen a monster in the cabin and have watched the menacing black castle of Monsterland off in the distance. How long will I be here? I have no idea.

I stopped at this. Perhaps I should have written more but I was too excited and overwhelmed. I had been on so many adventures already and I knew I had left out a few. I set the pen beside the Book of Fairies on my dresser and closing the diary, I laid it there also.

I stared at the Book of Fairies now. What secrets did it hold, what would it reveal to me? I reached towards it when Frendall called me from downstairs. I decided to return later.

"Let's go to town," Frendall told me when I arrived at the front door where he stood, "you spend way too much time in this castle. You should get to know your fairies, the land and our history. That is the only way to truly know how much responsibility you have and what you need to earn."

"I need my coat," I said, tapping my finger on the door. Suddenly the coat appeared hanging over my shoulder. I gasped, then my surprise turned to laughter.

"Thank you Frendall," I said. He was beaming with pride and it took a minute to realize that I had somehow made my coat appear on my shoulder by magic.

"I could teach you how to fly," he said with a twinkle in his eye. I smiled, excitedly throwing my coat on and walking out the door with Rob trailing behind me.

"We'll fly to the village," Frendall yelled over his shoulder. He raised his arms to the sky, his wings humming as he flew high above the castle. Unfortunately I was afraid of heights and just watching him made me dizzy. Frendall returned to the ground in front of us.

"It's really quite fun, try it," he urged. I backed away and Frendall realized my fear.

"What if you could fly with someone helping you and you didn't have to go very high? Would you," Frendall asked kindly, awaiting an answer, but I had no idea how to answer him. Yes, no?

"Then hold on tight," he said before I answered and he took my hands into his. Before I fully understood what was happening my feet were off of the ground. I felt very light and the delicate humming of Frendall's wings calmed me. Suddenly there was another humming of wings, different than his. It followed a steady rhythm and I was startled to find that it was coming from behind me. I glanced back to see my heart shaped wings flapping quickly.

"Take me down to the ground," I yelped. He quickly lowered me to the ground, appearing concerned. I felt awful.

"I'm sorry Frendall, it's just that I can't help but remember when I was thrown into the air and forced back to the castle. I don't mean to upset you."

"It's ok. You're not ready to fly yet, neither was I at first. You can always try again later," he tried, "so, where do you want to go?"

I was glad that he didn't look disappointed, but I was. I could feel tears welling in my eyes.

"I'm sorry, I need to be alone with my thoughts," I explained softly. Letting go of his hands, I ran back to the castle and continued into the woods beyond.

There was a large clearing in the middle of the trees. The forest was old with fallen trees and many evergreens giving the appearance of depth and shadows. I walked out further under the grey sky. When I turned and looked behind me through the dense trees, I could only make out the top of the Fairyland castle. It didn't look like I was in Fairyland anymore.

I jumped and my mouth gaped when I faced forward again. The ground was covered with a thick blanket of snow and there were tracks leading towards me. I was scared beyond reason. I shook with fright as my stomach tied in painful knots and my head spun with jumbled thoughts. It frightened me even more that something was with me, or some*one*, using the power of invisibility. Out of the corner of my eye, something moved. It was brown but I couldn't make out any more details as it disappeared when I turned towards it. This happened four more times until I began to become crazy. I tried to run but tripped and fell on uneven ground beneath the snow as it grew deeper and deeper. A wild storm was whipping around me, cutting through me like a knife. I'd twisted my foot and couldn't get up! I called out for help but the rushing snow took my breath away. Something was approaching and I desperately reached out my hand.

A warm hand grasped mine and pulled me up out of the snow. I opened my eyes but whoever it was still remained unseen. My foot was shooting pain up my leg and I cringed. Something warm touched my foot and the pain was automatically gone.

"You must leave, you're not supposed to be here. Don't you know that you're in evil," a soft voice rumbled in front of me. Who was there, I wondered, did they intend to hurt me?

"What, where," I asked. I knew what evil meant, but how could someone be *in* evil? Where was I? I knew that it wasn't Fairyland for certain now, because the only trees they had were colourful and there was no snow in Fairyland.

"You're in evil, the main village in Monsterland," the rumble came again and that is when I saw the little white sign, tacked to the top of a leaning wooden stake, with points at the ends of the letters. It read 'E-ville'. So it wasn't 'evil' after all, then, it was 'E-*ville*'. Then the lettering caught my eye. I'd seen it somewhere before, black lettering with points at the ends, on a card or something.

"Do you promise not to scream if I show myself," the rumble continued, "because I am not a fairy."

I was somewhat surprised, but agreed. The snow was slowing down when he came into view. He was a mud monster, nothing too interesting to look at, although he was smiling nicely. He stood, towering over me at about twice my height but I remained calm. He handed me a rough leather bag with black string tied around the top.

"Here, for your birthday," he trailed off as he walked away, "my gift to you. Open it when you return to the castle."

He pointed behind me and disappeared once more. I could still see the top of the castle looming above the trees. I walked towards it, all the while wondering who he was and why he had saved me, and how he knew it was my birthday. That's when the trees started closing in on me. They went slowly at first, shifting out of the ground, becoming so dense that I couldn't get out. The sky darkened and the snow came again, still deepening.

The top of the castle, the white castle of Fairyland, I knew I had to get there. I stretched out my arms and concentrated. A wonderful melody filled the air as my wings flapped steadily, quickly, as they had when Frendall took me into the air. Suddenly I lifted from the ground, raising my arms higher. The higher I raised them, the higher

I would go. The more I kicked my feet, the faster I would go. Soon I was racing towards the castle not daring to look down.

Before I knew it I was there. The huge point of the castle stood before me within my reach. I had escaped Monsterland but why was the main city there in the first place? Wasn't this Fairyland? I began to feel dizzy so I stood up in mid-air, the breezes rustling my hair, until I had lowered to the ground and crept around the castle's side to its entrance. When I looked back to the woods beyond I saw only the densely packed trees of E-ville from which I had escaped by myself, by flying.

CHAPTER FIVE

"Yes, gone without a trace. She was upset and ran behind the castle," Frendall explained hurriedly.

"Don't be alarmed, many of the good forest animals will guide her unless-" it was Sheena's voice this time.

"You don't think," Frendall gasped, "that they dare move their territory onto ours?!"

"I don't know," Sheena whispered, "but if they did..." Her voice faded away.

"No," Frendall cried in devastation, "surely she was captured!"

They were going crazy! I had crawled to the door of the castle and opened it a crack. It had been just enough to hear and still I was shocked at how worried they sounded. I felt guilty listening in and not making them aware that I was safe, but I felt that I needed to hear more. I opened the door a little further and continued listening.

"I'm going out to find her," Frendall concluded, "I should have followed her when she ran."

He edged towards the door, walking backwards, still focusing on Sheena.

"No, Frendall," Sheena argued, full of concern, "if they have moved their territory onto ours, I would be the right fairy to rescue her."

From his now half turned position, I could see Frendall's mouth gaping and his eyes opening wide.

"You don't mean, they wouldn't move," Frendall whined, "Jaypen? Jaypen! What if she said its name?!"

Frendall was screeching by the time that he had completed the sentence.

"I must save her," he continued. I was frightened, I'd never seen him like that before. His face was burning red with fear and anger.

"No," Sheena yelled and an orange bolt of power flew from her hand, smashing the door shut. I was sent flying back onto the hard ground from the force of it closing. I was so overwhelmed that I sat there for a moment, then sprang up and ran back to the door. I yanked and clawed at the handle but it was locked tight. Looking up, I noticed a small window. It was open a little ways and if I could fly up there, I knew that I could get inside.

As I concentrated on it, my wings began to hum. I stretched my arms upwards, slowly lifting off of the ground when the door suddenly opened. I turned towards it, lowering myself to the ground in time to see two fairies walking out together.

§

Once I was inside, even after two hours of sitting on the couch, I was still not ready to tell any of them where I had been. They overwhelmed me with questions at first but soon they wanted only for me to be comfortable. They gave me honeysuckle tea and chew bread with fairy berries on the side. The tea warmed me nicely, the berries were as delicious as always and the chew bread was chewier than ever.

"Are you ready to tell us yet, Kay," Sheena asked gently, "where have you been?"

The kindness and excitement in her voice made me feel comfortable.

"I was in the woods," I began, "behind the castle. It was snowing and pulling me in, but I couldn't escape because I had twisted my ankle and was unable to walk. A mud monster healed me and told me that I was in E-ville. He gave me something in a leather bag for my birthday, which I was supposed to open once I arrived at the castle. The trees began to close in on me, and that's when-"

I stopped. Did I want them to know yet that I had flown? Why should I hide it? Yet I wanted to keep it a secret all to myself, something I knew that no one else did.

"What happened next," Sheena asked gently, laying her hand on my shoulder.

"I flew," I admitted quietly. Sheena looked at me warmly, her blue eyes shining and sparkling.

"Did you say you flew, dear," Sheena asked sweetly, "I couldn't hear you very well. Go on."

"Yes, that's right, I flew out of the trees," I repeated softly, slightly louder than I had before. Sheena glanced at Frendall, then back at me.

"What I mean is," I stumbled, not ready to admit it yet, "I ran quickly. As in, I *flew* out of the woods." I nervously looked at the pairs of eyes focused on me. Finally, Frendall laughed.

"For a minute there, I actually thought you knew how to fly," he chuckled.

I grew worried once the laughter had died down that they would figure out my secret. Their eyes continued to stare at me and I became frightened. I began to shift uneasily on the couch, my every move being carefully watched, but soon I sighed in relief. Frendall, Henry, Sheena and Rob were looking at the bag upon my lap, not at me. They were waiting for me to open it.

I picked it up and nestled it in my palm, the tough cracked leather feeling sand papery in my hand. I had to tug the string to remove it as the knot was too tight to undo. An elaborate ring fell into my hand, bound of polished marble with inlaid precious stones. It was cold and heavy, and absolutely extraordinary! I carefully slipped it onto my finger. It was a perfect fit, as though it had been made just for me and I marvelled at its beauty. I'd never owned or seen anything like it before. Roses were formed from rose quartz and the leaves from emeralds. A diamond was placed in the middle of one huge rose, looking very proud, in the centre of the ring.

I remembered just then that on our first day in Fairyland, I had read the tiny lettering of the agreement with a magnifying glass. I wondered if I still had it. Reaching into a small pocket of my dress, I retrieved it and when I pulled it out and held it over the ring, fine lettering appeared. Deeply engraved into the interior was the name 'Cookstone'.

"He's a ring maker," Sheena explained, "a very good one indeed. However, you must remember that he is a monster. He cannot fully be trusted. We don't trust him especially, for in the very beginning he betrayed us."

"But Sheena, he saved my life," I objected. She half smiled.

"If he 'saved' you, then how come fairies have eternal life," she gawked, "it should never have happened in the first place."

"What," I asked, seeing that she was upset, "what shouldn't have happened?"

Sheena's face held a blank expression.

"Just don't trust them, don't ever trust a monster. It's dangerous," she explained, leaving the living room and Henry followed. Frendall stared forward, Rob gave me a sympathetic look. I lifted myself from the couch and silently headed upstairs straight to my room. I admired the ring once more, then sat on my bed staring out the window.

One by one the stars were coming out and the sky was growing still darker as I looked behind the castle. I happened to see a bit of movement but I couldn't tell what it was. It fled into the darkness and somehow I knew that it was Cookstone, the one who had made my ring, the one I was warned to avoid. Somehow I cared about him and longed to see him again. I felt that I could trust him. I knew that he was a monster but something about him was different, kind hearted almost. I wanted to go outside to talk to him about how I'd come from the Human World and to ask him questions. I was part of the fairy people, but what about them? Didn't I need to discover their world as well? Perhaps we would be friends, I thought. He may not have saved my life but he had helped me. I decided that I would see him again.

I realized I had fallen asleep when I woke up and it was early morning. I slowly advanced down the dark staircase towards the living room. I went to the front door and touched the knob. My ring from Cookstone, I could see, was glowing and lighting my way. I let go of the knob; instead of opening the door with my hand, I pointed at it with my index finger and whispered, 'open'. The door didn't move. I focused on it, watching it swing open in my mind, the land pouring out before me under a moonlit sky. Before I knew it, the door really did open just as I had imagined.

The sky was full of stars and silvered by the moon. The same constellations existed in Fairyland as they did in the Human World. The moon had a haze of cloud around it and I frowned as, in the Human World, it signaled rain ahead.

"Beautiful! Let's go out and look."

I jumped at hearing a voice in the silence. Sheena walked up beside me and covered me with the warm coat that Henry had given me. We walked out into the crisp autumn air and she shut the door behind us.

"Look at the land before you and your fairies. I know that you're ready to rule, or that you will be when the time comes. You have much to learn yet, Kay. You have the title of Queen but are not yet ready to lead the people on your own. There are three stages you must go through in order to be ready. Right now, you're only a first stage ruler and are unable to make the decisions that I am. Even if you did, you couldn't act upon them. You've not yet learned to fly or fully use your powers."

"What are the other two stages," I asked her.

"Young ruler and then full leader," Sheena answered, then continued, "I will leave with Henry someday and Frendall will remain. We will leave when you are ready. We will leave unexpectedly."

The sun was rising and lights in the little brick houses were coming on, bringing them to life. I knew that it was soon time for the stores to open and Sheena guided me away. We found ourselves behind the castle looking at a tree. It was different from all others and I knew that we were not in E-ville.

"Why isn't this E-ville," I asked Sheena, "besides, why is E-ville here anyway? If it's the main village in Monsterland, how can they move their territory onto ours?"

"Who told you it was the main village and that they moved their territory onto ours," Sheena questioned, stopping in her tracks.

"Cookstone," I said, "why?"

Sheena smiled and her hair bobbed up and down in the wind.

"You also listened to Frendall and I talk, we knew that you were there," she scoffed, then began to laugh. I laughed as well.

"You see," Sheena explained sadly, "there are good forest animals who live here and help us. If we are lost or hurt they are very kind-" I cut her off.

"-Then why does Henry hunt," I cried and she assured me soothingly.

"He hunts in the Human World," she explained, "he takes the scraps of meat they don't use."

I gasped at this. Henry travelled to the Human World!

"Where do the fur coats come from," I asked, calming down a little.

"He gathers scraps of fur as well," she told me, "and they cut and sew it here in Fairyland. He is invisible and besides, fairies have eternal life. I wouldn't worry about him too much."

There was a pause.

"Frendall and I didn't know what happened to you," she continued, changing the subject, "you see, entire lands can be moved; by the person in power, of course. We could move all of Fairyland to another location if myself, or anyone at the palace said so. You can also move one village. If I wanted to move all of the houses, or even just one, I could do so. It is written as rule eight of the ten rules of fairies."

"Why did they move E-ville, who moved E-ville," I asked quietly.

"Either King Monster or his parents, Amile and Hesman. They are granted the power to move their property just as we are. They could have moved it for a number of reasons. Perhaps they needed more space for renovations, or so that they can rebuild. They've never done this before but don't be alarmed, I'm sure it's only temporary."

It made me feel very uneasy, then I remembered what Sheena and Frendall had said.

"What right do they have to move their territory onto ours," I questioned, anxious to hear more, "how did you know they might have? What is Jaypen?"

"Dear young one," Sheena sighed, with a hint of excitement in her voice that she was able to retell her story from what she had learned, "there is no law stating that they can't move their territory onto ours and no law stating that they can. The Book of Fairies holds the laws of the fairies within it and this is mentioned as an undecided law. It also does not state if we can or cannot force them out. Fairyland only goes back so far, then it is the woodland animals' territory and they must decide. I figured the monsters would do this because it is undecided and though one half is on our land, the other is on the woodlands."

"What about Jaypen," I mentioned again excitedly.

"Goodness me," Sheena called, putting a hand on her head and then letting it drop to her side like a rope, "Rob must hear this as well. We had best head back to the castle."

I turned to take one last look at the special tree, whatever it was, that grew in the forest by itself.

§

"Are we all comfortably seated," Sheena asked when we arrived at the castle and took our places in the living room. Rob and I nodded. Henry brought us honeysuckle tea, as we were very thirsty and we set them on our laps. Honeysuckle, I remembered, tasted like nothing more than a mixture of cream, sugar and honey. Sheena took her place on the couch and began.

"There is a way into Monsterland," Sheena began, shifting her gaze between Rob and I. Frendall joined the meeting by quietly making his way over to the rocking chair.

"You are able to enter, if need be, only in absolute emergencies where another is at risk," Sheena continued, "there is only one way of arriving at the castle; through Jaypen. Jaypen is a curse."

Sheena was staring at us as she spoke and I cast my eyes downward at my creamy yellow tea.

"A curse surrounds Monsterland, a curse drives you out of Monsterland. The first is a force field. Upon entering, you will be forced out. The only way to enter is around the outside, deep in the forest where strange and dangerous creatures live. The curse is not as strong there but there is no path to follow. You would fly for two days and arrive at the castle on the third. That's when you hit the second curse."

She paused and took a breath.

"Another curse surrounds the castle. It is called Jaypen. There would be a sign, much like 'E-ville', but it would be written in the monster tongue. The 'e' in Jaypen is an 'o' in the monster language. There are invisible guards that you must get past. Once you passed them, you would come upon a monster. The monster would ask you where you are. Answer 'Jaypen', for that is the name of the curse in fairy language. Never answer or speak the name in monster, or they will imprison you for speaking their tongue. They will let you pass into the city if you answer 'Jaypen'."

"You didn't answer my question," I said aloud, surprised at the harshness of the monster rules. Sheena's eyes met mine thoughtfully.

"What question is that," she asked in her melodical voice. I blushed slightly at my sudden outburst.

"When we were behind the castle today, why wasn't it E-ville," I asked shyly and Sheena answered me.

§

After we were done talking, I returned upstairs to my room once more. I felt satisfied, as all of my questions had been quenched with answers. The woodland, I learned, was divided into three sections; the fields and property surrounding the palace (fairy territory), the bush (fairy and woodland territory) and the clearing (woodland animal territory). E-ville had been placed in the bush, but Sheena and I had been in a different section by the fields, so we hadn't come across it. I had asked Sheena why it was snowing in E-ville but yet the rest of Monsterland that stretched on beyond the cabin appeared to have no snow at all. She explained that monster towns could experience different weather conditions at the same time; while it appeared dry and cool in one part of Monsterland, it could be cold and damp in another.

I found myself standing at my window now. The sun was high in the sky, nearly at noon, but way back on the horizon the clouds were gathering. I picked up my diary and opened it to see the gold writing I had placed on the page. I took the cap off of the pen with a snap, deciding to write in it again. I decided to document everything I had done so that I could look back upon it and remember it in the future. I began right after the last sheet I had written on.

I had a dream about a monster with a black cape, when I was still a human. He held something shining brightly and entered into a black castle. When I told Rob about it the next day, he thought that it wasn't real. The thought was soon replaced by the excitement of taking a new path home through the woods.

We had to fight our way through horrific thistles to enter. That's when we came here, after eating magical berries. Fairyland is a beautiful, wonderful place with a diamond castle and tiny brick houses. Rob and I are the King and Queen. There's Frendall, the night hall patroller, Sheena, the old Queen and Henry, the old King and hunter. There are also monsters in this magical world and they live in Monsterland. Rob and I saw a monster with a white cape.

I stopped and read the sentence again. 'A white cape' caught my eye. Who had a white cape? Hadn't I read about a special monster who others feared and so made him King? We'd seen King Monster! I dropped the brass pen and it rolled across the carpeted floor.

I jumped off of the bed so quickly that the movement was followed by the noise of popping springs. I ran to the dresser and gently lifted the Book of Fairies from it. I opened it, or else it opened itself, to the very page I was looking for! I read once more;

The scale skins built a log cabin almost borderline between Monsterland and Fairyland. This was the house in which their son was born and grew to become King.

I read further down.

King Monster became King around two hundred years ago. He was feared by many, as his cape started out pink and then turned white.

I retrieved my pen from its place on the floor and by this time the Book of Fairies had closed. I returned it to its rightful place on the dresser and continued with my writing. *We saw King Monster*, I wrote, crossing out the last line. Then after I set the diary on the dresser as well, I climbed down the stairs and I did not return to my room until that evening.

It rained that night. The drops came down heavily, making tings as they bounced off of the diamonds. I listened to the steady dripping and my thoughts turned to home. What was my family doing right now? Were they sick with worry? I saw the fairies differently then. Was I in fact a prisoner and they didn't want me to know? I felt terrible thinking that such kind fairies as they could be lying to me. I decided I would ask them why I was here another day, tomorrow perhaps, so that I would know what to say as not to offend them. With that thought and the quiet comfort of the rain, I closed my eyes softly.

§

King Monster stood outside of his cabin between Fairyland and Monsterland. His white cape looked like a star among the darkness of the night. He looked at me, locking his eyes on me, beckoning me. He reached out a scaley hand, bringing it closer.

"I know the way," he begged, "Kay, follow me."

I looked into his deep green eyes. They looked so sympathetic, so desperate, that in an instant I found myself reaching towards him, our hands almost touching...

I was being continuously tapped on the shoulder.

"Kay, wake up," I heard, "it's me, Frendall."

The voice of Frendall sounded far away as I was half awake and half asleep, yet still the words of King Monster resounded in my head, 'come, come'.

I came into wakefulness suddenly, still dazed by the dream and I flung myself into a sitting position, scrambling to throw my legs over the side of the bed. Frendall came into view with his large eyes and open mouth. His hands rested on his knees and he looked rather silly, I think I would have laughed at the sight if I weren't so afraid.

"King Monster," I gasped between quick breaths, "I need to see King Monster!"

Frendall stared at me bewildered, his eyes shining like moons in the light of his candle. As he sat there I watched the colour drain from his face and his mouth curled into a tight knot.

"I need to see him," I cried again, laying my hands on Frendall's shoulders, "please, please let me see him."

Frendall didn't move, he just stared at me, trance like. But soon the trance was broken and he spoke softly.

"Kay," he explained kindly, "you've had a bad dream, everything is fine. I'll tell you about King Monster and we'll see if you want to visit him."

He said the last line harshly, as though King Monster were an enemy and I began to have second thoughts. I let go of his shoulders and nodded, suddenly remembering how responsible he'd felt when I was lost and how kind he'd been. Even how he was willing to risk being captured just to save me. I decided that what I'd thought before I'd fallen asleep wasn't altogether true. I wasn't a prisoner, but I did wonder why the fairies kept me. Maybe…I was important to them. At that thought, a wonderful thing happened. I felt a joyous feeling inside and at that moment I knew that the fairies had found a place in my heart to fill. Those wonderful fairies that lived in a beautiful place called Fairyland, at peace with the magical world, the palace and the woods beyond.

"Let me tell you a little about King Monster," Frendall continued solemnly, "he was born in the cabin between Monsterland and Fairyland. Have you read about him?"

I nodded and he went on.

"Anyway, legend has it that he owns the Lost Book," Frendall scoffed, shaking his head. I was filled with excitement at hearing this, the way he said it made it sound so mystical.

"Oh, Frendall," I blurted out, "tell me all about it!"

He stopped mid sentence, startled at my outburst, but smiled when he realized how interested I was.

"Yes," he sighed, "the Lost Book. It is told that when the Book of Fairies and the Book of Monsters came from the rose, so did a third book. Marianne and George were the first owners of the Book of Fairies and Amile and Hesman owned the Book of Monsters. We passed our book to Paul and Mary, then to Sheena and Henry, and now to you."

"The Book of Monsters went on to King Monster. It is said that the Lost Book also went on to him, although there are others who believe it fell away and will never be found. The Lost Book is said to have a blue leather cover with a gold rose impressed on the front."

Frendall stopped and looked at the dresser.

"Speaking of books," he laughed, "how is your diary coming along?"

"Great," I answered, "would you like to see my writing? I've tried to keep it neat."

I climbed off of my bed to show him and we peered down at the book, half by the light of the moon and half by the dim light that Frendall's candle provided. I opened it wider and wider until the light hit the full page.

I jumped and rubbed my eyes at what stood before me. The light that had fallen upon the page revealed that it was empty! All of the writing I had done, all of the time and effort that I had spent was wasted! That's when Frendall started to laugh. He shook and clutched his stomach.

"What- did you- use- Kay," he gasped for air between laughs. Finally, after a couple of minutes of rolling on the floor, the laughter subsided and a calmer Frendall took his place.

"You're supposed to write it in the fairy way. Did you run your finger across the page or did you use a pen?"

Before I had a chance to answer, his eyes ran up and down the dresser, resting on the piece of dull brass.

"This is very, very old," he said with wonder in his voice and eyes. He picked it up, mesmerized by it, holding it close to the flame to examine it. In a flash, he threw it down to the floor with a hard smack. His eyes followed it.

"Come apart," Frendall boomed, his green eyes glowing furiously as a blue bolt escaped from his fingertips and turned the pen a fiery red. Automatically everything stopped as quickly as it had started. The pen died down to its normal colour and Frendall still stood glaring at it. I backed against the wall. Frendall pulled his eyes from the pen and looked at me.

"It is from hundreds of years ago," Frendall said quietly in his normal voice, "from the time of Paul and Mary or before. It was used to write the Book of Fairies. We don't use pens anymore, we write by running our fingers over the page. That was a test, the pen used to write the Book of Fairies was indestructible. It might work, but it will only truly stay on the page in the Human World."

"It came in a package with a book," I explained, "so someone intended me to write with it, whoever it's from."

There was a pause.

"Does this mean I'm going back home," I asked cautiously, "ever?"

Frendall eyed me carefully.

"I couldn't say," he whispered as he walked out of the room and entered the hall, "I'll simply say that we need you, we really do. For how long, I'm not certain. Maybe a day, a year... or a lifetime."

CHAPTER SIX

"King Monster," Sheena sighed, "you still want to see him?"

It was breakfast time and Sheena had ordered everyone out of the kitchen except for me. She looked me full in the face uncertainly, curiously.

"Yes I do," I answered patiently. She leaned towards me over the table until I could see every sparkle in her eye. Somehow, she seemed upset.

"May I," I asked cautiously and quietly. Sheena leaned back in her chair, remaining so silent and deep in thought that it startled me when she spoke.

"You attended school in the Human World," she explained, "so it would only be right for you to resume your studies here."

"When," I questioned, suddenly becoming interested.

"Today. We'll begin after breakfast, quickly now, eat your meal and be off. Make sure to wear your coat, it is chilly outside, and tell Rob to wear his as well. Perhaps we will begin with a history lesson."

The front door opened to the little fairy houses all in a row. They were covered in flakes of fine frost that looked like tiny diamonds, like tiny Fairyland castles. I started to leave when Sheena called me back inside.

"Be very careful," she warned us. Rob looked at Sheena fearfully, not knowing what would come next.

"Tell me now, do you want to see King Monster," she asked mischievously, "well go ahead, visit him."

We were ushered out. A cold wind swept into the castle and once it had died down I turned once more to look out over the land. A thick fog had risen and I stepped forward into the haze with Rob at my side. There was a heave, a movement of metal hinges, then the door to the castle closed with us trapped outside. Unfortunately, Rob had stepped in the opposite direction and I could not find him. The fog was becoming denser all the while and I didn't know which way I was heading. Aimlessly I reached my arms out in front of me to see if I could find anything. It was hopeless. Just then, I hit something. I felt my way around it, the faint outline of a building coming into view like a picture appearing in a cloud of mist.

"Rob," I yelled, "Rob, where are you?"

Suddenly a hand clamped over my mouth, pulling me to a sitting position on the ground. I tried to scream but the hand clamped even tighter.

"Shh, Kay! I'm right here! Listen," a voice floating out of the fog exclaimed. I was relieved to find that it was Rob. We were before the structure now, which we had come to recognize as the cabin, towering over us like a giant. The fog was clearing and as I looked back at Fairyland, I gasped. Rob turned in concern. All of the houses in Fairyland, those tiny brick ones that I had watched frost form on earlier that very morning... they were gone!

I stood there, frozen stiff as though I were a statue. As still as the log cabin in the parting fog, as if time were passing before me. I felt as though I were a stranger to the land. I felt lost, I felt afraid, I felt sick. Gripping my knotted stomach, I stared in disbelief. Suddenly a thought struck me and I turned to look at the cabin; that confirmed it.

Instead of a pathway of roses built along the outer edge, there was nothing but grass. I started wondering why the roses were not there. The sight had been enough to answer my question; we were not in the time we'd previously been in.

I tapped Rob's leg and he sat down also. We didn't say a word to each other, we only thought about what possibly could have happened. If I didn't know what year it was in Fairyland before, how was I to know what time we were in now? A voice crying out of the cabin caught my attention. Rob heard it also; a wailing, a yelling, and I knew if I could make it to the high cabin window I could find where it was coming from.

I gripped Rob's arm, my wings gently humming. We began to rise into the air, higher and higher, concentrating on the window. Rob wriggled and squirmed, making it hard to hold onto him. We were almost there. I reached out my other hand until I had it! Rob let out a soft whimper as I pulled him up to what I had gripped. We were resting on the windowsill of the cabin, looking through the blurry glass to see something red. It was a clawed hand and it was reaching towards us!

"Stupid windows, they never open!"

I jumped at the roaring voice, almost falling off of the ledge. It rolled on like thunder as I sat paralyzed like a rabbit that sees a hunter. The hand slammed into the window.

"I've got it," I heard the voice of an adult scale skin growl, but it was too late. The window flew open, shooting out a gust of air and sucking us in. I shut my eyes, barely breathing as I was thrust inside the cabin. I heard laughter coming from above me and knew right away that it was a young child. Less afraid, I decided to risk opening my eyes just for a minute, just for a peek.

Above me loomed a giant, but it wasn't as large as the other monsters I'd seen. His black horns were small, his eyes gentle and he appeared to be in some type of low chair. A red jewel edged with gold hung just under his small chin, clasping shut a rosy pink cape.

I heard other voices and turned around. The inside of the cabin was very large but it could only have housed a couple of humans. It was much larger than the castle and palace with walls constructed of massive logs laid on top of each other. In the middle of the room stood a round table with polished wooden legs, bearing a neatly spread black tablecloth. Greyish blue plates spread themselves over the top, filled with food. There was a feast of chicken, peas and potatoes with gravy. Creamed corn was served in a smaller red dish and red napkins were laid out covering silver cutlery.

A stove with a built-in oven stood to the left of the room. It was black and the sweet smell of carrots had risen from a silver pot resting on it. Over to the right was a small door that a fairy could easily fit through. It was open just a crack, just enough to see the outline of it carved into the wood.

The giggling returned once more from behind me and I decided to direct my attention towards the baby monster. The little one's face lit up when he saw us. His grin spread even wider as he leaned down towards me. Rob was slowly backing away but as I inched towards the front door also, the little monster frowned. His eyes welled with tears and he quietly whimpered. I felt myself frown as well. It was a sad sight, watching him. I didn't see him as a monster then, but as a little boy. Perhaps he was young enough not to be dangerous, I wanted to find out.

I slowly walked forward again. He looked down and giggled once I was within reach. In a flash his hand hurried past me, his sharp black claws grazing my wings. I fell to the floor dizzily and very frightened. Perhaps he was the enemy after all, I thought, but when I looked up again he was bouncing up and down.

"Game, game," he laughed. I realized that he wasn't after me at all, he was playing. I decided to watch him from a safe distance so I backed away again. He began to cry.

"It's ok, don't cry," I said softly, "you must be gentle to see a fairy up close."

I realized that he couldn't hear me, I was too small. If I flew up to him, I thought, maybe he could hear me. Rob edged closer to the baby while I flew up to him until I was in front of his eyes. He stared at me, his mouth in an 'o' as though he was blowing an invisible bubble.

"Ooh," he exclaimed in wonder, "pretty!"

He reached an outstretched hand towards me. His claws and fingers were closing together as they came nearer. He was going to capture me! I flew out of his reach. Again, he was upset. I was feeling hopeless, how could I teach him to be gentle? An idea came to my mind but I had to act quickly.

I flew up to him again. As soon as his claws came near, I bolted away. I was tired of going back and forth and up and down, but finally he understood. Instead of clawing his hand, at which I flew away, he spread it out flat. I slowly floated down onto his slimy palm.

He tilted his head and looked at me in total fascination as though he had never seen a fairy before in his life, which I'd guessed he hadn't. He glanced down at the floor and lowered his other hand. Rob hesitated, then smiled and climbed on. The little monster looked at me, then at Rob, then back at me until he gasped and his face lit up.

"Fairthee," he yelled joyfully.

"Stop that racket at once," I heard a voice boom near the table. Out of nowhere an extremely large monster appeared, a fully grown one, with grey eyes and a red cape.

"Fairthee," the little one squealed with delight. The adult scale skin looked thoughtful, slowly coming to understand.

"Fairy," he raged, stopping dead in his tracks once he saw us. His eyes turned fiery red as he ripped a log from the floor.

"Get away from my son," he screamed, raising the log high in the air. I snatched Rob out of the baby's hand and flew faster than I'd ever flown before. The monster slammed the log down that was, in itself, as large as a tree compared to my size and the draft pinned me to the ground!

I flew in a blind daze, completely unaware of where I was and I didn't rest until I was safely outside, laying Rob on the grass. I realized that I had just escaped out the window before it had slammed shut. A cry rang out of the cabin; it was the baby. He missed us already.

"He sure was cute," Rob chuckled once we were far from the cabin, "and totally amazed, even as much as we were when we first saw the fairies ourselves!"

I nodded, breathing a sigh of relief. The houses had, strangely, returned to their proper places in Fairyland. They glistened with the same morning frost and I was overjoyed to see them! We were making our way back to the castle and were nearly there when a young fairy boy stopped us.

"Do you want a paper," he asked kindly, his blue eyes sparkling.

"Of course," I said, reaching for the piece of paper. It was a newspaper! How could Fairyland have a newspaper that we didn't even know about? He pulled back.

"It tells of weather, current events, celebrations and, of course, information about our royalty," he explained further.

"Well, it's your lucky day," I exclaimed, suddenly losing interest in the paper, "because we are the King and Queen."

I expected him to be excited and shake my hand but he didn't. Instead, a large grin came to his face and he began to laugh.

"How can *you* be royalty," he stated, "if our very own King and Queen are in the castle now?"

I was confused at first, but then remembered that perhaps he was thinking of Henry and Sheena. I decided to explain.

"We are first stage fairies," I explained to him. He still remained confused so I continued, "we will fully rule Fairyland someday when Sheena and Henry feel that we are ready-"

He cut me off.

"-Who are Sheena and Henry? What are you talking about?"

I jumped and so did Rob. Entirely baffled and frustrated I wished him a good day, handing the paper back to him, and we walked away. The wind caught a piece of newspaper and it flew towards us. Rob picked it up, ready to return it to the boy, when something caught our eye. Right on the paper, at the beginning of the paragraph on royalty, it read; *'on this day, the royalty switched hands from George and Marianne to Paul and Mary'.*

§

"So, what did you think," Sheena chuckled mischievously. Rob let out a sigh of relief and so did I. Upon seeing the newspaper we had run to the castle out of fear and were greeted, thankfully, by Sheena. We sat in the living room, all in our own chairs and began the conversation.

"Why exactly did you do that and where exactly did we go," Rob questioned, bewildered. Sheena leaned back in her chair, a slow smile lifting the corners of her mouth, threatening to explode at any unknown moment into a large one.

"You went back in time," Sheena explained, smiling broadly now, "for your history lesson."

"Who was that baby monster," I asked her curiously.

"King Monster, only, maybe not as evil as you might have imagined. I'm guessing that you thought him to be cute?"

Rob and I nodded, still baffled.

"How did you send us back in time," I asked in amazement, what had happened slowly etching itself into my mind.

"It was quite difficult. Number five is difficult to land on. Only one other time in my life have I ever had the chance to go, by myself of course. It is even more rare for it to bounce more than once, which it did in your case-"

Sheena stopped mid sentence when she realized that we were staring at her. She let out a light melodic laugh that shook her stomach.

"Silly me, continuing on and you have no idea what I'm talking about! I guess we are on to the next subject in your studies. It is time for you to play the Fairy Game."

We were taken behind the castle yet again, into the dense forest. I thought I noticed that same familiar tree that I had seen last time a ways off, but soon we passed it. We continued to walk until we had found a group of stones, their smoothness carved with various numbers, lined up and embedded in the ground. A flat silver stone laid next to them, hidden in the tall grass. As soon as I had recovered the silver piece and held it, nestled in my palm, the numbers on the stones lit up. They burned with light and as I could now see, were numbered one through ten. They were of different sizes and spaced differently. Some were closer together than others and the smallest one was number five, which appeared only as a tiny strip surrounded by grass.

"This is how the game works," Sheena exclaimed, "you play this not for fun, but for chance. We do not gamble, however, this is safe to play. You can never lose. Monsters are able to play, however, they have no interest. They have their own game, the Monster Game, and the rules are unknown to us."

"It is from pure luck, no magic will change your chances. It is not possible to cheat. Each number stands for something. You throw the silver onto the board and it will land on one of the rocks. If it bounces on the same stone more than once, you receive the prize twice. You'll understand once I explain, now listen carefully."

She then explained what the numbers meant. One was for wishes, two for more power, three for wealth and four was to see the future. Five was to see the past, six was to escape from an enemy, seven, eight and nine were a chance to roll again, and ten granted the ability to pass through the border's force field to enter Monsterland.

Because it had landed and then bounced on five, two people could go back in time. If it landed and then bounced on number one, the player would receive two wishes or a wish for themselves and another. When I looked up, I realized that all eyes were on me and I knew why. Very slowly, afraid yet excited, I lowered the silver and thrust it onto the board.

§

"What are we going to do, are we going to play again tomorrow," Rob asked. We were walking back to the castle with Sheena when Frendall came to join us. Henry had gone to visit the palace.

"All that it landed on were seven and nine, and once on ten. What will that do for me? Why would I want to go to Monsterland," I said glumly, "I guess that it depends on skill."

"Not at all," Frendall piped up, suddenly joining the conversation, "in fact, the silver seems quite content on where it lands. It doesn't matter what you aim for, the board runs itself."

I was amazed and confused. Frendall sensed this.

"By the power of luck, of course," he added quickly, "and fate."

Sheena turned to us with a serious face.

"I shouldn't tell you this," she said plainly, "but there will be a test tomorrow on flying. In your studies you will have times when I will test you. I will not tell you when the tests are going to come after this, but as this is your first time, I wanted to let you know. From now on they will come randomly, some easy and others difficult."

I was nervous. The only ones who knew I could fly were Rob and I.

"We must take this test seriously," Sheena spoke suddenly, making me jump.

"We must try our best," she continued, looking at Rob, "even those who cannot yet fly."

Then a cold chill ran across my skin, making me shiver as Sheena turned to me, ending with, "and those who can."

CHAPTER SEVEN

"I want to see you," he said, the unmistakable voice of Cookstone. In the blink of an eye he was before me; all mud, with two gaping eyes and a narrow slit for his mouth. Then he faded away, becoming a blurred image until he was gone altogether.

"When," I called out to nothing. I heard a faint rumble in the distance.

"Tomorrow," he said, seeming to come from a far place, "tomorrow…"

I woke up. It was hardly dawn yet and the stars were still lining the sky. Down below, the land was still and silent. Those crazy dreams! Perhaps I was afraid of what might come of the flying test. Had Sheena known that I could fly? How? Another thought struck me; was it night or early morning? I suddenly realized that I had no idea. Perhaps in my learning, also, would come fairy time. Maybe you could tell by magic or some sort of secret watches. That would probably come later.

Something moved, I could see it out of the corner of my eye. A shadow moved along the trees, just a faint outline could be seen. It didn't have wings. My throat tightened. What if the Fairy Game had been played and there was some mistake, and now all of Fairyland had been sent back in time again? What dangerous creatures lurked in the shadows awaiting our arrival?

I peered out again but the figure was gone. Fairyland looked the same as it always had, at least the woodlands did anyway, as I couldn't see the houses from my room. I burst into laughter, unable to remember a time when I'd been so nervous! Once I'd calmed down, a strong feeling of drowsiness overtook me. Regardless of what time it was I needed sleep. I was warm under the flannel blankets and comforted by the puffy pillows. I felt safe. I closed my eyes, almost asleep, when a voice inside of me spoke.

'If you had a chance to leave Fairyland today without saying goodbye, and you could go home but never return, would you?' Perhaps I was between awake and asleep, in Fairyland or in my own dream world, but it still shocked me what the answer was. 'No, my place is here and I am needed' another voice within me spoke, and this time I knew that the answer had come from my heart.

The sun was sitting on the horizon when I opened my eyes again, so that only a bright sliver of it could be seen. Above it a dusting of pink and a handful of stars scattered the fading night sky. I gazed at it in awe. Something was odd about it, however. Although the sun was not fully up, my room was glowing with colour. A peach light surrounded me, bouncing off of the pale walls and it didn't take me long to realize where it was coming from; my ring.

It projected light from somewhere deep within it and sprayed it out on the walls from where it sat on my dresser. I crawled to the end of my bed in fear as, on the bare surface of the wall behind me, words began to appear. They appeared in dark pinks, breaking and swirling in the peach hue. Slowly they came into view until they were clear enough to read. The message was in two sentences, 'Kay, meet me after your flying test. By the cabin.'

The room suddenly fell into darkness as soon as I had read the secret message. How and why had the message been sent to me, why 'by the cabin'? Who had sent it and how had they known about my flying test? Cookstone, of course *he'd* sent it. Who else could have, if they hadn't made the ring and known how it worked? I knew that I had to go, I had to see what he wanted to tell me.

§

"Here we are," Henry said happily. We had been led behind the castle and strangely enough, we found a small swing set standing there.

"There are three kinds of tests," Sheena explained, "simulative, application and reality. Simulative is when you are tested in a way that is similar to fairy life, but in which we can know how much you understand without you actually having to do it. Like today, we will test you on your posture and wing movement so you don't have to actually fly, but it is like flying. You have to know how to prepare for flight."

"Application is when you tell us in words only, using your knowledge, how to do something," Henry continued, "you would tell us what the proper posture is for flying and how to do it smoothly."

"Reality is when you do something in real life," Frendall finished, "for example, if you knew how to fly, we would test you by watching you fly. We would see how smooth the flight was and how long you stayed in the air. All you have to do for today is sit upon one of the swings. You may begin."

Cautiously, Rob and I stepped forward towards the swings. It was just an average swing set with a frame made of pastel blue bars on both sides and a steel beam at the top. Two swings with silver linked chains and black rubber seats awaited us. We sat upon them, the cold metal chains touching our arms. Rob stared forward with a confused look on his face, but nothing happened. Nothing moved. I realized that we had to push off of the ground with our feet. Soon the swings had locked into a constant rocking motion and my wings began to hum. I noticed that Rob's wings were blowing in the breeze and that he was rocking with a jerking motion. It was like flying, with the wind moving past us and the way we were able to keep rising higher. After a few minutes the test was complete. We had both passed.

Then they went back to the castle. Frendall, Sheena and Henry were all talking to Rob and they thought that I was following them. I was-that is, until curiosity got the best of me and I decided to head back to the cabin. Rob glanced at me and gave me a questioning look. I waved him away and put a finger to my lips.

"Shh," I warned him. He shrugged, nodded and continued walking alongside the others. I inched towards the cabin, the image becoming clearer as I neared. I passed the little houses, lit up warmly inside with puffs of smoke rising up from their chimneys. Fairy children scattered the dry streets and busy bakers lined the sides steering carts and selling bread.

An eerie shadow loomed over the cabin and I shivered. Should I go further, I wondered to myself, remembering when I had gone back in time. I decided that I should. Soon I was in front of it, remembering how it had looked. Its roof bowed slightly inwards now, whereas before it had an even slope. The chimney had been straighter and there had been no roses winding their way around it.

King Monster, the thought struck me. He would no longer be the little boy that I'd met, the one who was so fascinated by us. He would be an adult. I wondered about him; did he still have beautiful green eyes? Would he still gaze at fairies in wonder?

"So, you received my message, did you," a voice rumbled beside me and at once I knew who it was. Cookstone walked up beside me smiling. He was shorter, I noticed, only slightly taller than I was. When I had first seen him, he had stood high above me.

"You're small," I laughed, then stopped, thinking that I might have upset him. He nodded his head and laughed along with me.

"Yes, I know. We can change our size, I can be as small as you or as tall as a castle. I can even be as flat as the ground so you won't notice me," he explained, then the laughter subsided and his voice took on seriousness.

"But that isn't why I brought you here," he continued, "it's about what I've been hearing lately."

I looked at him, confused.

"He's alive," he whispered excitedly. This confused me more than ever.

"Who's alive," I exclaimed, "fairies, monsters? What?"

The cabin door flew open and a roaring voice boomed, "where is all of that racket coming from?!"

I glanced over dizzily, afraid of what I might see. It was King Monster outside of the cabin, his eyes glaring in fury. Cookstone was gone and I began to panic, backing away. A small light flickered in King Monster's eye and in an instant I saw my reflection in it like a mirror, appearing little and frightened. Soon a hand clamped over me. My wings flapped hard against each other and I felt as though I was going to be crushed. There was no use in trying to escape, he had caught me.

"What are you doing here, annoying fly," King Monster bellowed.

"Actually, I'm a fairy," I explained, feeling very afraid, my voice shaking.

"I know what you are," he growled angrily and I shook at the sharpness of his voice.

"I'm, I'm sorry," I stumbled as he squeezed my wings together harder. I yelped in pain. Saying nothing, he opened the cabin door and threw me inside. I landed on my hands and knees on the table, brushing off my dress and then standing up. The front door locked with a 'click'. I began to cry, burying my face in my hands, too terrified to speak.

"Stop crying," he yelled, covering his ears, "stop!"

This made me cry even harder. He let out an angry roar and turned his back to me, a white cape swirling around him.

"Are you King Monster," I managed to choke between sobs. This time, he turned and eyed me curiously.

"Yes I am," he said in a low voice, then he leaned down towards me, focusing his green eyes on me.

"You are Kay," he exclaimed, "little first stage Kay!"

He was laughing so hard that he clutched his stomach. When I asked him how he knew my name, he told me that the Book of Monsters had foretold of my coming.

"And I entered into the Fairyland castle to see if it were true that a new generation had arrived," he added, chuckling. I gasped! So that's what the light in the hall had been that night, I realized, recalling it like a fuzzy memory. The night when I saw the glowing figure outside of my door and locked myself in my room out of fear. He must have shrunk to fairy size! I was right, it hadn't been Frendall after all. I dried my eyes on the sleeve of my dress and he backed away.

"You are not supposed to be here," he continued impatiently, "don't you know the monster laws? Fairies do not enter property without being wanted there!"

"Cookstone wanted to see me, to talk to me, right here. I didn't mean-" I began.

"Then he is a fool," he growled quietly. Suddenly, his face brightened.

"Or not," he corrected himself, focusing on me again, "he gave me a wonderful idea!"

It had only been a few minutes of sitting on the table with him staring at me until he told me the details of his plan.

"I will take you hostage," he said carefully, still working on a plan, "until Sheena comes to save you."

He paused and appeared thoughtful. He lowered himself into one of the wooden chairs beside the table.

"Tell me how to make fairy berries," he said, coming out of his thoughts. I remained silent.

"Tell me," he raged and I began to shake again.

"I don't know," I said quickly, "they grow on a tree behind the castle, a special tree."

"What does the tree look like," he asked. I fell silent again.

"Answer me," he roared as his eyes flared red like fires.

"I don't know, I'm sorry, I don't know," I screamed over his growl. He stopped, his eyes going back to their regular green irises.

"Then I have no use for you," he said flatly, finally deciding what he was going to do, "you will stay here until Sheena comes with the berries."

§

The sun was setting and the stars were coming out. I could see Fairyland from the cabin window. The lights in the houses were going out one by one as if they had no interest in coming for me, as though they didn't know where I was, as though they didn't care. I sat there, unmoving. What if they couldn't find me? What if Sheena never came? What if I didn't eat? My stomach growled and I realized how hungry I was. I hadn't had anything to eat for awhile and King Monster hadn't attempted to offer me any supper. Would I accept food from him? What if it was poisoned? Would he tie me up? If Sheena didn't give him the berries, would he have *me* for supper instead?!

"Why do you need fairy berries," I asked him cautiously. He turned to look at me again and I shrank down at the grin upon his face.

"So that I can live forever," he explained, followed by a yawn. He was becoming tired.

"I had decided to tie you up, but there's no way to escape so I won't," he continued. I sighed. He wasn't going to tie me up after all! Then I saw it; a small door carved into the side of the cabin, maybe it led out! Once King Monster had turned his head away, I edged towards the end of the table. He caught sight of me and frowned.

"Where are you going," he questioned. I shuttered.

"What's behind that door," I asked, pointing. He hissed, jumping in front of it.

"Nothing, it's empty," he yelled. He extended his claws out in front of him when, suddenly, Frendall flew in and scooped me up in his arms. King Monster cried out in anger as Frendall flew to the front door and opened it by magic, losing his grip on me. I spread my wings and flew out into the cool night air as he slammed the door shut behind us.

"Are you ok," he asked, wide eyed. I nodded.

"What were you doing at the cabin," he questioned harshly. I told him about Cookstone and he listened but did not give a comment.

"You can fly," Frendall exclaimed coming to a dead stop in mid air. He chuckled, "actually, Rob already told me."

I had to laugh too, it was such a typical thing for Rob to do.

§

After I had finished telling them what had happened earlier, we sat down to a turkey supper. I was so thankful to be safe in the castle again. Frendall was beside Rob, I was across from him, and Sheena and Henry were at either end. Henry cut the turkey and gave us each a little apple jelly to go alongside it. The turkey was moist and a juicy taste came from within it. The skin was covered in a rich sauce with a few added spices and the apple jelly was very sweet. I watched it wobble on my plate as I greedily dined on my meal.

"Oh, Henry, this is delicious," I commented, "and the apple jelly is so sweet!"

"You must have some dessert," Sheena urged, making a cream filled pie appear on the table, bearing elegant patterns embedded in the crust.

"It's very nice, but I'm full," I said contently.

"Why did King Monster really want fairy berries? Can he truly live forever by eating them," I asked to no one in particular.

"No one has been able to prove that," Frendall explained, cutting a piece of pie for himself, "besides, monsters cannot even as much as touch any. A fairy must willingly give them to a monster without being threatened and *that* would never happen!"

I understood. Even if I knew where the tree was and had given them to King Monster, they would be useless because he pressured me.

"But, King Monster said-" I argued, remembering something else. He had decided to keep me hostage until Sheena came with the berries. Would she have given him berries, I wondered, to save me? Or was that considered a threat? If they worked, would he live forever?

"Kay," Sheena said softly, interrupting me, "that's what monsters do. They try to confuse you into believing something that isn't true. They lie and try to cheat fairies out of their powers. Some even appear to be kind, although they are not. Like Cookstone, Kay; he thought he could trick you into thinking that he saved your life when he knew that you can live forever."

"What do I do," I asked, fearing monsters more and more.

"Pretend that you are more powerful even if you aren't, you can confuse them this way. Soon they will think you are as powerful as you seem to be and they will not be as willing to bother you. Remember, Kay, sometimes the power of the mind is greater than that of real magic."

"But, Sheena," I gulped in air to calm myself, "Cookstone wouldn't trick me!"

Her face held a serious look.

"He is an example," Sheena scoffed, "of what happens when you trust them. They take advantage of you by moving their land onto yours. They push away any friendship that you offer them. He betrayed us."

I hid my face in my hands.

"Whatever is the matter," Sheena questioned in concern.

"I'm afraid of the monsters," I cried, coming to my feet. Through blurred vision I made my way upstairs. All the while, I heard voices floating up the stairs from the kitchen.

"Poor dear, I didn't mean to frighten her," Sheena spoke with a hint of sadness in her voice.

"Just as well that she knows now rather than later, after what happened today," Henry offered kindly.

"I should have told you," it was Rob's voice now, and I was impressed that he felt a certain amount of responsibility for me. This ended with Frendall,

"I think that we need to tell her more about the Rainbow Crystal."

Sheena entered my room late that evening, but it was no surprise. I knew that one of them would come, it was just a matter of waiting to see which one it would be. I suspected it would be Sheena because of how awful she felt about what had happened.

"Kay," she whispered from the doorway just loud enough for me to hear. I sat up, seeing only her silhouette encased in the light from her candle. She wore a long pink housecoat with a matching bonnet. She asked how I was as she sat on my bed, extending a steaming cup of hot milk towards me. I reached out and took it greedily, sipping the mild flavour. Suddenly I stopped, almost dropping it.

"It's here, in your pocket," I stated without thinking. It startled me when I thrust my hand into her pocket and removed the Rainbow Crystal. I sat back, completely baffled. I hadn't known it was there, but somehow the words had come from my mouth and I had discovered it.

"The crystal let you know that it was here," Sheena explained, "you are the keeper of the crystal. You have a special connection to it and are safe because of it. No matter what life brings, if you are in trouble, you will not be harmed as long as you have it. Henry has explained this to you before, but I feel the need to tell you again."

"Henry also said that I will know its purpose in time," I continued the conversation, recalling what he had told me, "when will I know? Why was it created, and for what?"

Sheena showed me the Book of Fairies, telling me that the answer could be found within its pages. She opened it and I read of the events that had taken place that very day, but when I went to turn the page, the book shut tight.

"Pesky little thing, it tends to like to keep the future all to itself," Sheena chuckled. Somehow at that moment, thinking about the future, the thought of going home filled my mind.

"Sheena," I asked quietly, "are you going to let me go home?"

The grin on her face left and there was a long pause.

"Let me tell you a story," Sheena spoke in a dull, sad tone, "you see, Henry and I were like you and Rob. We, too, were humans at one point. We were brought here when we were a little younger than you, imagine how unsettled we were!"

"Although Paul and Mary were very kind, we were still afraid and confused. Eventually everything became better and Frendall helped us to feel more at ease. He was chosen before we were, how long before I don't know, but a strange thing happened. Frendall was older than we were. Then, one day, he stopped growing although we continued to age. He would be about fifteen years old in the Human World now, and we would be about sixty."

"He refused to tell us where he came from. Anyway, life went on. Then suddenly, Henry found a way into the Human World. He returned to tell me but when we tried to escape, we were caught. After that, Paul and Mary didn't trust us, so they decided as punishment to only let Henry hunt there. Now he goes back to hunt, knowing that no one can see him and that he cannot return to that world again. We will never be able to return."

A long silence hung in the air, thick with sadness.

"Oh, Sheena," I said, at a loss for words, "I'm so sorry."

There was silence again.

"Well," she said after awhile, "it was partly my fault. I chose to leave, so I paid the price."

"I can't believe that Paul and Mary were so cruel," I exclaimed angrily, "you should have been allowed to go back!"

"I felt that way too, at first. But they needed us, that's all and they didn't want us to go. We should not have been so selfish," Sheena explained seriously, "because when you're a ruler, you can't just 'leave'. Lives could be endangered by one person's foolish actions. Sometimes we do not choose to be rulers, but we are chosen because there is a purpose in it, even if we do not understand. I don't want you to leave. You wouldn't leave, would you?"

I gasped, "of course not Sheena! Never, you have my word!"

"It isn't that I don't trust you, it's that once you returned, you would forget us. It happens to all fairies."

"No, never," I argued, "I could never forget you! Isn't there a way for either of us to go back?"

"There is a way," Sheena said thoughtfully, "by the Book of Fairies, other than the pathway we tried, but I'd have no idea how to do it. I'm sorry, I really wish I could help, but I can't. You understand."

Sheena looked out the window.

"Goodness," she cried, "the sun is rising! You'd best get all of the sleep that you can before dawn has fully come."

With that, Sheena left. Regardless of what time it was, I knew that I would get no sleep.

CHAPTER EIGHT

"Oh Rob! I haven't slept a wink all night," I grumbled tiredly. Surprisingly, he appeared that way also.

"I know, did Sheena tell you? I couldn't believe-" he began. I cut him off.

"-Yes she did. Isn't it so sad about Henry and Sheena? You were talking about that weren't you," I asked.

"Yes, yes, of course," Rob exclaimed, nodding vigorously, "I can't even consider the thought of never going back! Do you think?"

He paused, deep in thought. We had met in the hall heading downstairs when we decided to stop and talk. I could tell that he'd had about the same amount of sleep as I had because there were dark bags under his eyes and his eyelids appeared to be heavy. He continuously blinked them as though he would fall asleep if he didn't. Judging by how tired he was, I guessed it was true that the fluttering of his eyelids somehow kept him awake.

"You don't think," he started his thought again, "that if we found the portal to the Human World and weren't caught, we could return?"

I gasped, not expecting him to say that.

"No Rob, it's too risky! Besides, you remember what Sheena said, we'd forget them!"

"Oh, that's right. I forgot," he said, then grew quiet again.

"But wouldn't it be fun to find it and explore it," I burst out, startling myself, "we wouldn't have to enter, we could just take a look, right?"

Rob was smiling by the time that I had finished. I couldn't believe I'd just said that!

"I thought that I heard someone in the hall," a voice called out. It was Frendall and I jumped, desperately hoping that he had not heard anything we said. I cautiously turned towards him. By the look on his face I'd guessed that he hadn't, so I played along.

"Good morning Frendall," Rob and I greeted him. Frendall gestured us down the stairs and we followed him to the kitchen where he proudly displayed plates of pancakes. They were hot and steaming, and covered with sweet clear syrup. Fairy berries decked the side. A thought crossed my mind when I saw them, a crazy thought, and my mind turned to King Monster. He could not have berries without a fairy willingly giving them to him, Frendall had told me that himself. Would King Monster really live forever if he ate them? How many would he have to eat? When no one was looking, I slipped two into my pocket.

"I think that we'll explore E-ville today, just to look. What if the pathway is there, Kay? No one would ever think to look there," Rob asked excitedly. After we had been told to go exploring on our own again, all that I could focus on was the cabin.

"Why don't we go to the cabin," I suggested, "maybe the pathway is there, through that little door in the cabin wall!" Rob shrugged.

All of Fairyland was a flutter of excitement as the street filled with hurrying fairies flying from shop to shop. Although it was a beautiful day in Fairyland, it was a dreary day off in the distant borders of Monsterland.

"It's a little risky," Rob commented, "remember what happened last time you went to the cabin?"

He didn't need to remind me, I remembered all too well.

"Yes I do," I answered, " but I just need some time to think right now, I'll catch up to you later."

Rob walked away. I was relieved because I really did need time to think. What was I going to do with these two berries? I wondered if I should put them into the roses for humans to find. I had soon decided to do what I had thought of earlier and though my legs felt very unsteady, I walked to the cabin.

I flew to the open window and peered in. The cabin looked as it had before; dishes placed neatly on the table, a small stove in the corner and the hidden door still securely in place. He did not appear to be home.

"King Monster," I called out weakly. Nothing moved. I opened my mouth to call again when I saw a flash of white. I stood and listened. Very quietly, from somewhere within the cabin, were footsteps. I heard a faint growl and soon King Monster appeared in full view sitting in a chair by the far wall.

"Who said that," King Monster growled in anger, looking around. I had to force my words out.

"It's Kay, the Queen fairy. I'm-I'm at your window," I said, trying to sound like I wasn't afraid. King Monster turned his head quickly, sending his white cape swirling around his shoulders. Finally spotting me, his eyes narrowed and focused as he snarled.

"What do you want," he demanded, stating sharply, "you have no business being here!"

I tried to stand tall but I was having a difficult time. Sheena had said that if I acted as though I were more powerful, the monsters would begin to believe it. I tried.

"It's not polite to turn a guest away, don't you know what I bring? I have done as you requested, but it comes at a price," I explained. My price, I had decided, would be information. I would give him fairy berries in exchange for him telling me where the portal to the Human World was. I retrieved the two small berries from earlier, displaying them in my hand. I rolled them, taunting him. I acted as though I was more powerful although I knew that, at any time, he could snatch them...and me!

"I should not have to pay anything of any value! I may decide to take you prisoner again because of this," he raged, "I will take them from your hand!"

He rose from his chair, making a slow advance towards me. His claws were extended, ready to clamp down on me!

"You couldn't take them even if you tried, a fairy must willingly give the berries to you," I replied calmly, surprising myself just as much as I did him.

"Then give them to me and leave," he scowled, then grinned, "and if you read that in the Book of Fairies, you're wrong. That rule is not printed in the Book of Monsters, so I'll take them now."

I gasped. What if it were true? What if he took me prisoner again?

"You're lying," I said desperately, trying even harder to steady my voice, "to persuade me. Monsters lie, that's what Sheena told me, and Henry and Frendall agree."

King Monster cringed in anger at the mention of Frendall.

"I did not come here to be badgered! Either give me the berries and leave, or leave me in peace! This is no way to treat a King!"

The entire cabin trembled at his thundering voice. I caught sight of his sharp claws again. His face tightened as I dropped the berries on the window ledge and started my way towards the Fairyland castle. Looking back, I could see King Monster carefully gathering the berries into his hand. I was surprised, as he did not eat them. Instead, he crushed them into juice and dribbled it onto something that waited on the other side of the hidden door.

§

"You really need to teach me the spell of invisibility," I exclaimed once I had caught up to Rob who was walking around looking about. He shrugged.

"Actually, I don't know how to go invisible," Rob explained, "maybe you should ask Frendall."

I had told Rob what had happened and how King Monster was acting strangely. We both agreed that whatever remained hidden behind that secret door was somehow important. The last person I wanted to talk to was Frendall.

"Rob," I whispered, grasping his arm as we neared the castle, "we can't tell Frendall!"

He eyed me curiously.

"You don't want him to know," he confirmed, "because then he will be upset with you and won't trust you anymore, right?"

Rob grinned mischievously and I sighed, agreeing and explaining how King Monster had tensed when I mentioned Frendall. There was silence, then Rob laughed.

"Come on, Kay, you're probably imagining things! I'm sure that King Monster was becoming more upset all of that time and his face just so happened to tighten on his name," Rob suggested. He was probably right, I had said some upsetting things to King Monster and it would make sense that he was becoming angrier the more we had spoken. I nodded in agreement and we made our slow advance towards the Fairyland castle.

Rob and I wandered into the castle to find Sheena, Henry and Frendall gathered in the living room.

"So, where have you been," Frendall asked kindly, smiling up at us, "around the town, I suppose. Did you venture to the bakery again?"

"Um…not exactly," I hesitated, all eyes on me. They sat up straighter, eyeing me suspiciously. What was I going to say, I couldn't tell them where I had really been!

"Could you teach us the spell of invisibility," Rob questioned, "because, when Kay visited King Monster today-oops!"

Frendall leapt from his chair and I caught my breath. His hands flew into the air and he shook his head.

"You can lead them, but they refuse to follow," Frendall scowled, "I can't see why you're so important to Fairyland! All you do is make mistakes when there's no one there to help you make decisions! Some day you really will be on your own, and what then?!"

Frendall strode quickly down the hall until he was gone.

"He's just a little upset right now, it will pass," Sheena said kindly, motioning us to her side. We spent the rest of the day learning about invisibility from Henry and Sheena who remained patient. We did not see Frendall after that and when at last the evening had settled in, he still did not return downstairs. The castle remained silent.

"Frendall, at least say goodnight to Rob and Kay," Henry called out desperately, "Frendall? Where are you?"

Instead of the candle that Frendall always carried lighting the hall, only darkness filled it. Figuring that he had gone to bed, Sheena and Henry bid us well and then left.

Standing at my bedroom window I looked out upon the land, my land, as it stretched far into the distance. Only trees running on for miles were visible under a moonlit sky sprinkled with stars. I thought of home and could almost see it in my mind's eye. How far away was I? To calm myself, I imagined that it was just beyond those trees; Mom and Dad waiting on the grass to welcome me. I would run up to them, telling them how much I had missed them and promising that I would never leave. They were out there, just waiting, beyond the woods…

"This is the sky map," Sheena explained the next day, holding a diagram in front of Rob and I, "it is divided into three sections; the flying zone, the upper level and the furthest reaches."

The map was laid out in a simple way just as she had described, with three different levels clearly labeled on it. There was a sun on one side, a moon on the other and clouds and stars in between. Sheena explained that it could be used in the day or at night for finding our way, or identifying a flying area. Rob and I had been sitting behind the castle that morning trying to learn about maps and landmarks. Sheena had agreed to give us lessons and we were trying to find the locations that she had been describing to us.

"Why would we need to find our way by the sky when we can just look at the land," Rob asked curiously. Sheena continued, telling us that if we were without a map or could not see for some reason, such as fog, that it was wise to use the sky. We would just have to locate where the sun or moon was and then follow the sky levels to where we needed to go.

"I don't see where the flying zone is," I exclaimed, staring up at the sky. Rob did not see it either.

"You cannot see them very well," Sheena chuckled, "because they are just currents of air. The flying zone is a certain level of air currents that are suitable for a fairy to fly in. The flying zone extends from the ground up to the middle of the sky. The upper level is a harder, forcing current. It is still suitable for a fairy to fly in, however, only the strongest and most experienced fairies dare to attempt it. It is very thin, attached to the top of the flying zone and the bottom of the furthest reaches. Its range is as thick as a fairy is tall."

"The furthest reaches stretch on forever. It lays on top of the upper level but no fairy has ever ventured that far or even gone near it, as its borderline currents would pull fairies up into it. You could not survive up there, the currents are strong enough to rip a house apart. Do you understand the sky map now?"

Rob and I nodded, still gazing up. I found myself wondering what was up there and if it were as strong as some claimed it to be. Looking over at Rob and seeing the twinkle in his eyes, I couldn't help but think that he wondered the same.

"I see that the stars are printed on the map," I said, turning my attention towards the diagram that stretched out before us, "and they form the same constellations as in the Human World."

"Indeed they do," Sheena explained, "and if you're lost at night or need help, just follow the North Star to safety."

Rob gasped and I quickly looked up. Far in the distance beyond the busy streets, something white filled the sky. It spiralled down heavily, its edges appearing to be sharp and jagged, swirling through the trees.

"They look like tiny blades," Rob gasped, "we should get away from them, shouldn't we?"

"The 'blades' are hardly as ugly as you make them seem," Sheena replied, "look, as they approach the Fairyland border, something unique happens."

In a burst, all of the fairies in their houses poured out into the street, shouting and yelling in joyous voices. 'They have come,' many called out and, 'they will be flying in any minute now to welcome the celebration'. In some strange way I found myself becoming part of the celebration also, jumping and shouting just as they were. Excitement and merriment had filled the air and despite the cold temperature, whatever it was seemed to delight the fairies and bring them together. Before I realized it, Rob was also jumping up and down with his eyes all lit up.

Suddenly the noise ceased and everything was still. Not a single fairy dared to move as the white blades made it to the borderline of Fairyland.

"Are we to have a good crop this year and enough food to eat for winter? Show us," Frendall called, coming out of the castle in a fur coat. I was somewhat relieved to see him. He stood watching the cabin and the fairies had not seemed to hear him as they continued to watch the cabin as well, but they nodded their heads as though they acknowledged his words. A gust of wind sent the blades swirling around in the air. The sharp points molded together, forming wings, while the other points formed a back, tail and head. The newly formed flakes gently looped and twisted in the air until they came to rest on the ground. I stared in wonder at the shapes. As one came closer I realized that it was a little bird with fluttering white wings. When it touched my hand I felt a tingling and then it disappeared until all that I held was a drop of water. Hooting and hollering erupted as the fairies danced around and jumped up and down again. Frendall smiled and hushed the crowd.

"It is time to go inside and prepare for harvest day tomorrow. Rest up, we have a lot of work ahead of us. The snow doves have come."

After Frendall was done speaking, surprisingly, all of the fairies returned inside until the road remained empty. The flakes, which Frendall had called 'snow doves', littered it and still more flew in.

§

"They were snow doves, a rare sight indeed. Don't forget that you saw them, as they will be gone tomorrow," Sheena exclaimed.

"How could all of this snow just disappear by tomorrow," Rob asked curiously, staring out the window. We had gone inside and we were watching the doves still silently fluttering in the air.

"That's why it's rare," Sheena toned her voice down almost to a whisper, "you see, every year on this October day it snows for the first time in the season, in Fairyland. In Monsterland the snow is always the same, jagged and sharp, representing the evil of all who live there. Once it gets to the borderline, it changes. If it comes over in a heart shape, it will snow all winter and we'll lose most of our crop. We will have to work in the snow to bring the crop in. If it comes as a flock of doves then it means that Fairyland will have a mild winter. The flakes are so light that they melt easily and most of the crops will survive."

"How do you harvest the crops," I asked, "do you use tools?"

Sheena nodded and smiled.

"Follow me to the wheat fields and see," Sheena began merrily, twirling as she walked out the front door, "Henry is out in the fields already."

"That's funny, I haven't seen any fields yet," I whispered to Rob as we, too, walked out the door. Sheena overheard me, correcting me, explaining that we had in fact seen the fields. There was more than one type of crop to be harvested, she explained; wheat, corn, cotton and beans were hidden deep within the forest. Many more types of plants and fruit were harvested, she went on to tell us, but at different times of the year and in smaller amounts. Then there was the fairy berry tree and the rose bushes like the ones we had seen when we first arrived in Fairyland, the ones that the two fuzzy berries had rolled out of.

"Why would you harvest roses," Rob asked, "and wouldn't it take more than one day to harvest everything?"

"No, as there are many different harvests that different fairies do," Sheena explained, "the bakers harvest fairy berries to make desserts. The seamstresses harvest the cotton plants to make clothes and also the rose petals to make shoes."

Rob looked down at his rose petal shoes and blushed.

"The fairies that work in the mills beyond the fields harvest the wheat, beans and corn," Sheena finished with a grin.

"What about the fairies that don't work anywhere," I asked, unsure of the answer.

"Good question," Sheena proclaimed in her melodious voice, "they provide entertainment and food throughout the evening and arrange the dance at night."

I gasped. It all sounded so exciting!

"What do we do," Rob questioned excitedly and I could tell that he was looking forward to the event also.

"Stop asking questions," Sheena chuckled, "and see for yourself!"

The door creaked open and I shivered as we stepped out into the cold.

Behind the castle there were many trees, so many that I had lost count. Some were birch or cedars or evergreens, so many kinds and colours all spiraling up towards the cloudy sky. We were led to a small opening, but it wasn't E-ville. It was a tunnel really, as I noticed that a ceiling of rocks blocked the sky out. It appeared larger as we entered and it was not very long, but wide enough to hold about five fairies. It led to a vast field, or what appeared to be many fields. I saw light at the end and watched little flakes of snow still gently fluttering down. I would have run out to see the crops if it weren't for something I discovered within the tunnel.

One of the small rocks that made up the tunnel wall had a halo of light around it. I figured that it had probably just come loose but when I reached up to touch it, warm humid air began blowing in from all around it, which was strange for it being such a cold day. Sheena and Rob were talking so I decided to take a peek. Slowly I removed the rock. It made little clicking sounds against the others but neither Sheena nor Rob seemed to notice. A flood of light and warm air continued to come through the hole where I had pulled the rock out. I carefully removed three more until I had made a slot big enough to fit my head through.

I hesitated, afraid to look. What was out there? What if I got sucked through and no one ever found me? But the sense of adventure was too great and I had to see. Slowly, I brought myself to look. I shut my eyes, edging to the slot. Suddenly I didn't want to be in the tunnel. Suddenly I thought about it collapsing and all of us being trapped with no food and no air. Suddenly I opened my eyes and fell back onto the soil of the tunnel floor. I rubbed my eyes and then, even more slowly than before, I crept over to the slot again and looked out.

Rob must have seen it too, because he yelled 'Kay' at the moment that I peered out again. I spun around, put a finger to my lips and hissed at him to be quiet. Sheena's back was towards me, but by this time she had stopped talking and was starting to turn my way! I froze and, backing against the wall on wobbly legs, I covered the slot. If I moved a few more stones, there would be enough space for me to squeeze through! But what about Rob, I couldn't just leave him behind, could I? But Sheena would catch me and then...

"Hurry, Kay, you don't want to miss this," Sheena yelled over her shoulder, deciding not to fully turn around. I let my breath out as she turned away and continued to talk to Rob, but Rob was still staring at me.

"Go," I mouthed out, directing him to the end of the tunnel. I began filling the slot with rocks again.

"Is it," he mouthed back to me before turning around. I nodded, a huge smirk coming to my face. Rob smiled widely, then went with Sheena. Before I placed the last rock in, I decided to take another look through the small hole in the wall. Rob and I would be coming back tonight, I had already planned, to escape. I had my final glorious view of my street, my house, Rob's street and Rob's house, before wedging the last stone in so that no light showed. Then, still smiling, I joined up with Rob and Sheena, thinking about the Human World.

CHAPTER NINE

I caught up to them quickly. Many acres of land, mostly flat, stretched before us. Little spindles of green poked up through the white blanket of snow but hardly enough to tell which types of crops they were. There was nothing, as far as I could see, that divided the fields. They all seemed to run into each other and I began to wonder if they were different fields at all, or just one big area of land.

"These are the fields," Sheena pointed, moving her hand over the vast area. As Rob and I ventured nearer she strode ahead of us, dusting the snow off of the delicate plants. Soon she had revealed them, all planted neatly in a row. Suddenly, my mind flashed back to when Rob and I had first entered the woods and how we had moved amongst the thistles, row upon row.

"Do the monsters harvest anything," I asked.

"Yes," Sheena replied simply, "thorns, thistles and sharp branches. They also mine precious stones and metals from the ground."

"Do fairies mine," I questioned, because she had not mentioned it.

"No," she explained, "all jewels and precious metals in Fairyland can only be found deep within the woods, in the land that belongs to the forest animals. We fairies do not believe in mining, it is destructive to the land."

"What about the Rainbow Crystal," Rob stepped into the conversation, "where did it come from, then?"

Sheena turned towards him.

"You must read the Book of Fairies to know. It will answer all of your questions. Until then, follow me to another part of the forest and I will show you more," Sheena concluded. We walked until we had reached another section of woods behind the castle and had come to yet another field. It was smaller this time, with crops bearing long stalks heavy with snow. By the way they appeared, I was sure that they had to be corn. Sheena confirmed it, with a sweep of her hand I watched the snow drop from the slender husks of corn. Rob leaned close, carefully looking at the other crops to find that they were still green!

"These aren't ready to be harvested," Rob exclaimed, bending down to examine a green leaf.

"Yes they are," Sheena laughed, "you see, our crops do not brown, only the plants of the monsters do. Ours stay green even after the harvest so we always have fresh food to eat!"

We moved around the cornfield until we had reached the end where it led to a small tree. I had seen it before from the few times we had gone behind the castle and as I learned, it was the fairy berry tree. It stood, beautiful and small, with deeply impressed bark and flat green leaves. Little fuzzy berries hung from the end of every twig like ornaments adorning it. It was simply wonderful.

We continued to a place with a strip of flowers. They were white, with tall and slender stems. Their tops spread out like umbrellas, looking like bunches of little flowers all grouped together to form a large one. They resembled the snow so much that I wouldn't have known they were there if Sheena hadn't shown me.

"They are royalty flowers," Sheena explained, "only royalty can harvest them. You harvest them by magic. Touch the top and when they recognize that you are royalty, they will come up out of the ground. The roots are edible and many fairies enjoy the rich taste. This is what you will be harvesting."

Rob and I gazed in wonder as we passed them. Sheena wandered far ahead of us as we stooped to gaze at the royalty flowers. When at last we looked up, Sheena was gone.

"It's ok," Rob said nervously, "let's call her and she'll answer us."

So we began to shout. At first we heard nothing, then a faint voice floated over the wind. It was Henry! Rob and I dashed wildly through the woods, thankful that he'd heard our cries and before we knew it, we had reached him. Henry stood on the snow, smiling and waving at us, but something didn't seem right. The snow around him was sharp and pointed, not at all like the snow doves. I could tell that Rob sensed something also by how he nervously tapped his foot.

"Kay," Henry said calmly, "could you go pick some fairy berries for me?"

Rob and I exchanged confused glances.

"But harvest day is tomorrow," I explained questioningly, "besides, Sheena barely showed us where the tree was just a moment ago."

"Then find it," Henry screamed, anger flaring in his eyes. Rob and I stepped back at his harshness.

"Henry," Rob choked out, "what's wrong?"

"Hee hee," Henry chuckled with a smile.

"I guess that I kind of lost my temper," he roared, but it wasn't him. Henry grew taller and taller until Rob and I silently, inwardly screamed. That was when we realized that we were in E-ville and right in front of us stood King Monster. His cape flapped behind him in the wind like a banner. His nostrils steamed in the cold and his mouth was turned upwards in a grin.

"Stupid flies," he laughed, "you actually followed me! Don't you know that monsters can change into anything or anyone that they want to?"

"That's not fair," Rob yelled. King Monster laughed even harder.

"Haven't you ever been fascinated by fairies," I asked. King Monster stopped laughing.

"No," he said quickly, "I don't waste my time on flies!"

"But look," I continued, flying into the air, "isn't the melody beautiful, just listen! Don't you ever wish that you could fly?"

King Monster watched in wonder, but then took on his cold stare once more.

"I don't care," he screamed angrily, "you have no power! Why should I care about you?"

"I'm getting a little hungry, Kay," Rob said slowly for effect, "I think that I would like some fairy berries for lunch."

King Monster growled as we laughed.

"Why aren't you afraid," he yelled in fury. We explained that fairies lived forever, didn't monsters? But I could tell that monsters did not live forever by the way that King Monster's face twisted in pain and he stood, slumped, saying nothing.

"You do not know as much as you think," he finally replied.

"You're right," Rob cut in, "there are many things we do not know, and we need answers."

"In return for fairy berries," I quickly added. King Monster considered this for a moment, then his eyes glazed over with anger once more.

"I do not make deals with powerless beings," he hissed, "you will not control me! I am not weak!"

"But we want to learn from you because we are so weak," Rob replied, trying to convince King Monster to give us answers, "and to give you what you want; fairy berries."

For once, King Monster's face looked soft and his eyes became calm.

"On one condition," he replied, "that one of you bring me the Rainbow Crystal as well." Rob gasped.

"Agreed," I quickly answered. Rob glared at me, his mouth gaping in total shock.

"We'll escape tonight," I whispered, "back to the Human World and he can't get us there." Rob nodded and grinned.

"Agreed," Rob answered. King Monster smiled and grasped the end of his cape as it flew around him. He whispered something and soon, lifting the cape off of his hand, he held a book. It was just like the Book of Fairies, the same colour and pattern, but instead it read 'The Book of Monsters' and was large enough to stretch the length of his hands.

"How did you do that," Rob and I both exclaimed.

"I'll answer that and more," King Monster replied, opening the book, "so, what do you want to know?"

"You have told me before that you needed fairy berries so that you could live forever," I began, "I guess that monsters cannot naturally live forever, can they?"

King Monster's face was unreadable.

"Let me ask you a question," he scowled, "could *you* live forever before you ate fairy berries?"

Rob and I exchanged glances, shaking our heads. King Monster flipped through the pages of the Book of Monsters.

"For every question that you ask, I get a berry," he stated.

"Only if you answer our questions," Rob argued. King Monster let out a growl and his eyes flared red.

"I make the rules," he yelled in fury. Rob and I stepped back in fear. King Monster growled so much that I became upset and began to cry. One single tear touched the snow and turned its sharp edges soft. I stared down at it curiously.

"No," King Monster cried out in a shrill yell. He threw the Book of Monsters at me and I jumped out of the way fearfully. It grazed my wing before landing beside me. Rob stood completely speechless. I looked at the book with its pointed black lettering and as my last tear fell, it touched the black letters, running along them until they turned golden.

"No," King Monster raged, and I suddenly realized that he was covering his ears with his hands, "stop! Stop!"

"Please stop," he yelled, and I stood up quickly from where I had been kneeling on the ground. Please? He had asked kindly? His words surprised me.

"Dear, dear fairy! Don't cry, don't cry, I'm-" he paused, "I'm sorry."

His face became tight as he finished with, "I will not do that again."

"It's a trap," Rob whispered hurriedly, "all a trap! The book's letters turning to gold was only a trick of the light!"

I looked up at King Monster's tense body and smiled.

"Rob," I whispered, "it's the noise! He can't stand the sound of crying!" Rob stared at me with a puzzled expression upon his face.

"You mean, that noise we make," he asked, "that kind of sounds like 'bizz-buzz'?"

"No," King Monster cried, covering his ears again, "do not say that awful word! Stop!"

Rob and I both grinned. King Monster cautiously uncovered his ears as though, at any moment, Rob and I would begin to make that sound again.

"So," I began the conversation again, "how are you today King Monster?" He growled again, thinking that I was being rude to him, that I was trying to control the situation.

"You cannot control me," he shouted once more. Rob and I looked onwards in fear.

"If I am a King also," Rob said slowly, "then you need to show me respect."

"When you have shown me none," King Monster questioned. Rob grew silent.

"Stupid fly," he laughed again. I interrupted, taking Rob's side.

"Actually," I exclaimed, "his name is King Rob, or King fairy. How would you like it if we called you 'stupid monster'?"

"I shall not show respect for flies! You are pesky little beings," he replied angrily. I could tell that this conversation was going nowhere.

"Why," Rob questioned, "what have we ever done to you?"

King Monster focused intently on him.

"I had a friend once," King Monster explained quietly, "who was not a friend at all."

Then it was as though the missing piece had been put into place; not a friend at all, friend all, *Frendall*!

"Well, we're your friends," Rob stated. King Monster growled again.

"No you're not! You're out to trick me, all of you," he snarled. I realized that he saw fairies in the same way that the fairies saw monsters. 'They trick you,' Sheena had told me. Had someone told King Monster that fairies were the enemy? I shook my head.

"Why is your cape white," I decided to ask.

"It is because I am pure evil, I am King," he quickly answered.

"You have no good in you at all," Rob asked. It was the same way, a quick, short answer, 'no'.

"I have a good question," I shouted excitedly, "do you have the Lost Book?"

Rob nodded to me with a 'that's- a- good- question' look.

"No," King Monster replied, "I did once, but I no longer do."

"If you don't have it, then who does," Rob asked with a twinkle in his eyes.

"Someone, the one I gave it to," he answered. He gave it away, I thought to myself, just rid of it like that? All of the secrets that would probably be hidden inside and someone was walking around with it carelessly? Even when King Monster was calm, I noticed, there was still a hint of anger in his voice from somewhere deep inside. Are you angry at me, I thought to myself quietly, wondering why he always seemed upset when I was around. Unfortunately, King Monster had seemed to read my thoughts and his green eyes snapped to the left until he was looking right at me. I dropped my gaze, but could still feel his burning stare upon me. Slowly I looked up at him again and his eyes softened.

"No," he said slowly and quietly, somehow having read my mind, "I'm not."

Rob sensed my thought and seemed to understand King Monster's answer. It was as though, at that moment, our thoughts all seemed to connect.

"Why are you angry," Rob asked sorrowfully, "I wish that you weren't."

"You cannot wish, stupid fly. Wishes are useless, wishes never come true," King Monster stated.

"Yes you can," I cut in, "wishes do come true. If you could wish for anything, what would it be?"

"The Rainbow Crystal," King Monster laughed, "but now I don't have to wish because you gave it away!"

Suddenly I remembered the Fairy Game, the one that Rob and I had played behind the castle. Wasn't the number one rock for wishes? I was almost certain.

"Hey, Rob," I whispered to him as he stood there at my side, "let's convince King Monster to play the Fairy Game. Remember how the board runs itself when you throw the silver piece onto it? Maybe one of us would win a wish and then we could wish the evil out of King Monster!" Rob smiled.

"King Monster," I called, "come with us and play the Fairy Game." He stared at me blankly.

"Have you ever won anything? It's all a big joke, I refuse to play," he argued.

"Yes, I won a free pass into Monsterland, but-" I began.

"-Oh did you," King Monster interrupted. He tipped his head thoughtfully.

"Then you shall come with me instead, to Monsterland, and we shall see who wins."

Rob looked at me fearfully.

"Don't worry," I said, "I'll be fine, we just need some more answers."

§

The forest was dark, black like night although it was day. The sky had turned a threatening grey-green colour. Finally, we had arrived at the cabin bordering Monsterland. I noticed a nearby row of trees where the snow had melted away, revealing a row of stones. With a clawed finger, King Monster pointed to the blackened earth and said, "the Monster Game."

It was made of grey moss covered rocks, each deeply pressed into the earth. They bore numbers in thick, pointed black scroll and there were ten of them all aligned in order as they had been in the Fairy Game. I walked forward with uncertainty, fearing the invisible force field that had thrown Rob and I back away from Monsterland before. But I had a pass to enter, so it must have lifted the force because as I neared, I felt nothing until I had finally crossed the border into Monsterland.

The first thing that I felt was the cold. It was a bone chilling, biting cold and along with it, blades of sharp snow not at all like the doves in Fairyland, floated through the air. My eyes ran along the ground, up the gnarled branches and thick trunks of the bending trees and then into the distance. The black castle stood as eerie as ever with points jutting out in every direction. I cringed at the sight. Looking back at King Monster I could see that he was staring forward, concentrating on the game until at last we were standing there beside it. King Monster shrank the stones to the size of the Fairy Game so that I could play. Then he stooped and picked up a smooth silver stone, dropping it into my hand.

"Throw this at the board and see what it lands on," he quickly explained.

"But, what do the numbers mean-," I began.

"-Just *play*," King Monster screeched, cutting me off. With a shaky, uncertain hand I half closed my eyes and thrust the stone forward.

§

Rob paced back and forth, flattening the snow with every step. He glanced around, his eyes darting from place to place.

"Rob, what's wrong? Where's Kay?"

Rob jumped and spun around.

"Oh, thank goodness it's you," Rob sighed, "I thought that it was King Monster again."

"Again," Sheena asked, bewildered. Then, with desperate determination, she demanded, "where is Kay?!"

§

King Monster howled with laughter as the silver stone landed on the number one rock. I tensed, not liking his attitude towards what I had landed on.

"Number one," he cried excitedly, "stupid fly! The rules of the Monster Game state that a fairy cannot win! Number one means that you are my slave and can only use your powers when I give you permission! If you don't obey me, every time you use your powers without my permission, I become more powerful!"

"No," I screamed, "you're lying!"

"Ok, then," he laughed, "try to use your magic."

I pointed at King Monster and concentrated on flying up over his head. Startled, I realized that no matter how hard I tried, I couldn't fly and suddenly King Monster's hands grew green with light. It was power, *my* power, and he was taking it.

"You're a cruel monster! You lied to me, you tricked me," my voice cracked more with every word. King Monster's smile widened.

"Yes, I am cruel," he cackled, "and yes, I lied. But you fell for it, didn't you?"

I was so shocked that I couldn't speak. I should have listened to Sheena when she told me never to trust monsters. Now I not only felt guilty for letting myself down, but also Fairyland. How would I ever be a suitable Queen if I made mistakes like this?

"I will keep you in a room in my cabin until I decide if I want to let you go or not," he explained. Suddenly, I remembered another thing that Sheena had said, monsters could be tricked if fairies were clever enough to trick them. I smiled.

"Ok," I calmly stated, "so, I guess we had better get a move on then."

King Monster looked shocked, the smile fading from his face.

"What," he exclaimed in a shrill voice, "where?" I gave him a confused look.

"To the cabin of course, where else? I am your slave, aren't I?" King Monster looked dumbfounded.

"Well then," he said slowly, "let's go." Then, with the grin coming back to his face, he lowered his hand to the ground.

"Climb on," he said menacingly, "or are you too afraid?"

He laughed. I traced my eyes over his red hand with scales lining his skin, and at the long, black, sharpened claws lining the tip of each finger. He could crush me in an instant, I knew, and I wouldn't be able to stop him because I had no powers. Then my mind went back to when Rob and I had travelled back in time and how gentle King Monster had been as a baby. His hand was not very different from mine, other than the colour and texture of the skin and claws. Besides, he wouldn't hurt me I figured, because then, how else would he get the berries? Rob wouldn't give the berries to him then. So with uncertainty I lifted one leg onto the edge of his hand and then the other, until I had made my way into his palm. At this, King Monster gasped, shifting his hand. I fell into a sitting position because of how he jerked back.

"You," he said quietly, half to me and half to himself, "you trusted me."

His face showed disbelief, then his green eyes glowed brightly and he burst into laughter. I cringed at this action. Again he had tricked me, again I had fallen into his trap, but this time it was too late to escape.

"I remember," King Monster cried in total delight, "fairthee, I used to call them fairthees!" I looked up at him quickly, wondering if he was joking.

"When I was a baby," he continued, clarifying his thought, "I caught my first fairy and called it a fairthee, and look at me now! I caught a fairy again, I caught you!" He laughed in delight, then his eyes softened.

"Why did you trust me, I could have crushed you," he asked seriously.

"I didn't think that you would hurt me," I stated, quickly adding, "you wouldn't, would you?"

King Monster's face grew serious, with his mouth drawn into a straight line and his eyes focused on me. I tensed, regretting that I had asked.

"I won't hurt you if you don't hurt me," he answered softly, his mouth curving back into a smile. At once his hands glowed green again and light surrounded me. I curled into a ball, hiding my head, afraid of what was happening. When my eyelids grew dimmer I knew that the light was gone. Slowly I opened my eyes to find that everything was just as it had been before, nothing had seemed to change.

"What happened," I asked slowly, still dazed. King Monster looked away.

"I gave you your powers back," he whispered without expression in his voice, "if you trusted me, then I will trust you."

"Trust me? With what?"

King Monster's head swung back in my direction.

"You are still my slave," he explained, "and I trust that you will come to the cabin once a week to do work for me. You may go home now."

I was shocked, why was he letting me go? Was this another trap? I decided not to ask.

"Thank you," I exclaimed, unsure of what to say. King Monster snarled.

"It is nothing to be thankful for," he growled, "I only restored your powers so that you can work for me! I only let you go because otherwise, all of the fairies in Fairyland would come for you and I don't need a bigger problem than I have now! Don't you understand? I'm an evil, selfish monster. Now go away!"

I flew from his hand at this statement, overjoyed to be able to move my wings again. I stared forward, going past the cabin standing like an old faded structure from some history book. It did not occur to me until that moment how old the cabin was.

CHAPTER TEN

"There you are," I heard someone shout as I looked towards Fairyland. Sheena was flying towards me quickly, her face tight with concern.

"Rob told me everything," she called, then sadness filled her eyes and she looked away.

"Sheena," I asked quietly when she was close enough to hear me, "what's wrong?" She grasped my hand and we slowly lowered to the ground.

"It's over," she said hopelessly, shaking her head, "over, all over, done." Her bright blue eyes dimmed and at that moment she seemed to be older than ever.

"What," I pushed her on frantically, "what's wrong?"

"Frendall was right," she replied quietly, suddenly looking up at me, "I knew that we could never trust humans. I knew that they would be too foolish, too selfish to save us."

"What," I gasped, "save who, what humans? What is going on Sheena, you're making no sense!"

"You," she cried angrily, "we gave all of Fairyland to you! Every year, the weather worsens. Every year, the fairies grow older. Don't you see, don't you understand? We don't know how to stop it! That's why we called upon you. The Rainbow Crystal is our only hope of survival and now it's gone. We are doomed, all doomed." Her voice trailed away with the wind. I stood in shocked silence.

"What happened to the Rainbow Crystal," I exclaimed. Sheena stood very still with a desolate look overshadowing her face.

"You promised it to King Monster," she spoke quietly, "and when a fairy makes a promise, they cannot break it."

Suddenly a cold fear set into me, a slow realization making itself known. For the first time in my life, I had made a mistake so horrible that nothing could correct it.

"Here," I heard a voice behind Sheena. It was Rob, holding the sky map. He handed it to her, then looked up at me. As our eyes met, we felt our guilt and looked away from each other.

"Thank you," she said flatly, spreading it out with her hands.

"I'm sorry," I blurted out suddenly, deciding to tell the truth, "we found the passageway to the Human World and-" I was too choked up to continue.

"-And you forgot us," Sheena concluded, still staring at the sky map, "as soon as you saw the Human World, you forgot us. That's why you so easily gave the crystal away." I hung my head down.

"It is time for an application test," Sheena piped up. Rob and I exchanged confused glances. Hadn't I heard that somewhere before?

"I explained the different kinds of tests when you were first learning," Sheena explained, "an application test means that you have to tell me what you know, in words." Rob and I nodded. Sheena seemed to be calming down...slowly.

"What are the layers of the sky map called and how many are there?"

I remembered faintly what she had taught us. I answered, recalling three; the flying zone, the upper level and the furthest reaches. Rob remembered that we flew in the flying zone and that only experienced fairies ventured into the upper level. No one had ever gone into the furthest reaches.

"Correct," Sheena stated, then she eyed us very carefully and seriousness came into her voice, "there is a way out, but it will only last for three days. We are going to give King Monster a fake Rainbow Crystal."

Rob and I gasped but Sheena did not seem to have noticed, as she continued to talk.

"You will fly to the very top of the flying zone. There you will find a rainbow, that is where they stay," Sheena pointed to the flying zone on the sky map, "you must catch a rainbow, that will be your reality test where you will do something in real life. Do whatever you must in order to catch it, even if that means twisting sideways and throwing yourself at it, you must catch it! Then, when you have captured it, hold on tight and bring it to me. I will turn it into a crystal when you return." Rob and I stood, staring at Sheena in confusion.

"You mean," Rob said slowly, "that rainbows *move?*"

"Yes, and you are going to catch one." Sheena thrust the sky map forward and Rob took it into his nervous hands.

"Go on," Sheena urged, "and good luck."

§

"Do you see one yet," Rob asked and I shook my head. I had, just moments before, discovered that Rob knew how to fly. He explained that he had been watching enough fairies to figure it out. Now we were flying at the top of the flying zone. It was beautiful, with puffy white clouds littered across a bright blue sky. The air was soft, pure and beautifully scented like roses.

"Look," Rob blurted out, pointing to a cloud. Behind it I could see the tail of a brightly coloured object and knew at once that it was a rainbow.

"I'm going to go get it," Rob shouted excitedly. I bit my bottom lip nervously as he drew closer and closer to it.

"Got it," he yelled. At that very moment there was a burst of light and the rainbow shot into the sky like a shooting star. It twisted and danced, flipping and twirling, flowing on the breeze like a delicate ribbon. There at its end Rob held on, bewildered, with a shocked look coming over him. He was being tossed and twirled with the rainbow!

"Rob," I screamed, "let go, let go! I'll catch you!"

"N-o," I heard him answer back, his voice fading in and out as the rainbow tossed him about, "th-is is the on-ly wa-y to sa- to save Fairyland!" Finding an inner strength from his words, I flew fast and hard until I had grasped the other end of the rainbow in my hand.

"Rob," I yelled as I was being jerked back and forth, "on the count of three, pull back on the end, ready? One, two, three -now!" I tore at the rainbow, tugging and pulling back, and Rob did the same. Finally, with a 'twang' we had pressed it into a flat, wide band like a giant ruler. We sighed, it had stopped moving and we had it! Rob and I smiled at each other. Our job was done, we were heroes! We had saved Fairyland…well, at least for the next three days.

When we arrived back on the ground, Sheena rolled the rainbow from end to end until it looked like a fragile, colourful scroll. Then, her hands glowing, she crushed it into a crystal and handed it to me. I could not see a difference between it and the real Rainbow Crystal.

"Take this to King Monster," she instructed us, "he will think that it's the real crystal. In three days, it will crumble to dust."

I knocked on the cabin door. Rob stood beside me and I was thankful that he had come along. Under the snow around the cabin the roses peeked up, their thorns large and sharp. A cold shiver ran through me as I looked at them. The giant cabin door opened, its hinges creaking painfully, and King Monster stepped outside.

"Who dares to disturb my peace," he bellowed. I flew up to him so that I was in sight. Rob joined me and, catching sight of us, King Monster grinned.

"Two little flies," he chuckled, "harvest day is tomorrow, I must prepare for it. Go away, come back next week!"

"Wait," I called, and his eyes focused on me, "we've brought you the Rainbow Crystal." King Monster's face showed disbelief, then turned joyful as I dropped it into his hand.

"At last," he cried, "it's mine, all mine! Ha, ha!" He danced around singing 'mine, mine, mine' over and over again until he came to a dead stop and glared at us angrily.

"It's fake, it's all a trick isn't it," he demanded. Rob and I exchanged nervous glances.

"Of course not," I answered quickly, "when a fairy makes a promise, they must keep it." King Monster believed me. His eyes softened and his mouth turned upwards into a grin once more.

"Why do you want it anyway," Rob questioned, "to take over Fairyland?"

"Why would I care about fairies," King Monster laughed, "I am using it for my own purposes. You can keep your worthless land." After this statement, King Monster waved us away.

"You're not going to thank me," I asked. King Monster shook his head.

"How rude of me," he replied, "not to show my thanks." Then, opening his hand, a seed appeared.

"Come alive," he whispered. Suddenly, the seed sprouted and the stem grew across his hand. Green leaves burst out of their stubs and the prize at the top, the silky red petals, came out and wrapped around each other.

"For you, my dear," he stated, extending it towards me. It was small, just the right size to fit in my hand and it was real!

"Oh, how beautiful," I commented in awe, then I turned my gaze upward to see a beaming King Monster, "you're not truly evil. If you were, you wouldn't have been able to grow such a lovely rose." King Monster stepped back at my statement.

"I am evil," he argued, but was too baffled to say any more and fell silent.

"Wait," he broke through the calm suddenly, "you promised me fairy berries. Where are they?!"

"Harvest day is tomorrow," Rob spoke up, "we'll gather some for you."

With this, we wished him a goodbye and flew away. Before we had entered the castle we heard King Monster's voice come trailing over the wind, "I am only evil because no one has cared about me."

"Rob," I said hurriedly before we had entered inside the castle, "I keep having this feeling that we made a huge mistake."

"What," Rob scoffed, "come on, Kay, you're being silly about this! We're going back tonight, then we'll never have to see this place again." Those words hurt me. Never see this place again, never know what the fate of the fairies would be, never remember?

"I can't," I said, "at least, not now." Rob turned away, disappointed and saddened.

"We have three days Kay, that's it," he assessed the situation, "I'm sure that King Monster will be ok with the fact that we lied to him."

"Oh, Rob," I cried, "what are we going to do? We can't abandon the fairies. We can't give the real crystal to King Monster, but if we don't give him the real crystal, he will find out and then what? The fairies are doomed because of us!"

"I think you're right," he exclaimed, taking a step back, "we can't go back to the castle now. If we do, we will have to face the fact that we lied to King Monster and we'll have to pay for our mistake." I began to nervously pace back and forth.

"Or maybe," I said, cutting through the awkward silence, "we need to take our place as King and Queen no matter what the cost, even if we never see the Human World again."

§

Night was falling. Looking out my window I could see the forest, dense and powdery white, stretching on and on. In front of the castle, all of Fairyland would be preparing for sleep. Lights in the houses would grow dim and fade, and ploughs would line the fields waiting to be used come tomorrow. Somewhere very far away would be the Human World where people, the ones that I had once come from, would be looking at the same moon and even the same stars. They would have no idea where I was.

I was glad that Rob and I had returned to the castle earlier. It had become cold outside and I was thankful for the warmth. Everyone; Sheena, Henry and Frendall, had all acted as though nothing had happened but I still felt uncomfortable. Somehow I slept that night, but it was a rough sleep. I tossed and turned until I finally settled into dreaming. In my dream, I was out by one of the fields. I was alone, startled and horrified to find that the field was not green… it was brown. Then something caught my eye; it was the monster in the black cape standing at the edge of the field, smiling a cold, grim grin…

"Kay, Kay! Wake up!" Someone was talking and nudging me in the side. Upon opening my eyes I realized that it was Sheena, the morning sun beaming on her silver-edged chestnut hair.

"Come quickly, it is harvest day!"

I sat up in bed, still unsure of my surroundings from being suddenly awakened, and looked out the window. All of the snow that had fallen the day before and all that I had been gazing at just the night before was gone. The land was green, just as it had always been, just as Sheena had told me it would be.

Rob and I sat at the table in the kitchen for breakfast. Henry had made his famous chew bread again with fairy berries on the side. Henry, Sheena and Frendall had left the castle to us while they went out to prepare for the festivities. I glanced down at my fairy berries in dismay.

"Rob," I spoke aloud, since no others were around to hear me, "this is the second day. King Monster will find out that the crystal isn't real tomorrow. We don't have much time! We promised that we would bring him fairy berries from today's harvest, we have to do that tonight." Rob twiddled his thumbs, puzzled.

"There's no way out of this," Rob agreed, "he's going to find out. He's going to be very, very angry..."

"Great news," Sheena bustled in the door excitedly as Rob and I fell silent, "harvest day has arrived! Come see, it has begun!"

We rose from the table and rushed outside at Sheena's words. The street was filled with busy fairies rushing to and fro, dressed in brilliant fall colours. Some were pushing overflowing wheelbarrows, others were gripping hoes and shovels. The shop windows had been crammed with new items and some fairies had decorated their houses by hanging up strings of bright flowers. It truly was a wondrous sight!

"There will be festivities by starlight," Sheena spoke at our backs, "with dancing, singing and a large feast for everyone!" She ran out in front of us after this exclamation and ushered us to the royalty flowers in the field behind the castle. In the fields around us the fairies were harvesting and plowing, working busily under the shade of the trees.

Rob and I were left on our own after Sheena showed us, once more, how to harvest the crop. We would place our hands over the delicate, lace-like flowers and the stem would uproot itself. The field wasn't as large as the others, so it wasn't long before we had uprooted all of the royalty flowers. Looking around, I watched as other fairies stooped over and bent down, picking oats and other crops, while all that we had done was used magic.

"Rob," I mentioned quietly, "let's go help the others." So we did. Rob and I bent down, picking off every grain by hand and dumping them into a pail. This type of grain was gold and in long pellets with pointed ends. We left the long, thin stems in the ground for the fairies behind us coming up with the plough. We worked in that field until the large moon had risen and the stars were clearly visible. The moon was deeply golden in colour, almost orange, and was so called a 'harvest moon'.

Finally, after a day of exhausting work, Sheena came to lead us to the celebration in the heart of Fairyland. A large festival was taking place and a large table had been set up, running down the length of the small village. A feast was underway, the table slowly filling with fruits and vegetables, and the harvest which many a working hand had picked. All was worth it for this night. The stars twinkled overhead and the full orange moon sat up in the sky watching us down below. Lanterns with painted walls emitted yellow, blue, pink, orange and green light.

Soon the fairies lifted from the table and the ones that could fly flew, while some that could not were carried upwards until all of the fairies had risen into the sky. We danced on the midnight air while the gentle melody of busy wings kept time with the beat of the music. Some fairies began singing in sweet voices while others took out tiny instruments constructed from wood and woven grasses. Caught up in the excitement and seeing the joy reflecting in the eyes of all who attended, I forgot about the false crystal that I had presented to King Monster. In fact, I had even forgotten the berries that we had promised him from the harvest. So that evening, long after all of Fairyland was sleeping and the castle became silent, I laid awake for a long time. I could sense an awaiting doom, but as

I said, I did not know why. So, unable to think, I decided to sleep but my sleep was uneasy and the pounding of my heart resounded in my ears so loudly at one point that I awoke quickly and sat up to welcome the unfortunate morning.

I had in fact heard drums and it was not my heartbeat alone. They became louder and louder, thundering, seeming to shake the entire ground. I ran out of my room and down the stairs, joining Sheena, Henry, Frendall and Rob. Together we went outside to witness the fate that would await us.

There he was; King Monster, towering high above us, above everything, so tall that his face could barely be seen way up in the sky. With every step he took a thunderous boom shook the ground like an earthquake. Behind him, appearing like little ants compared to his size, a slew of hundreds of monsters followed him. There were ghosts, mud monsters and scale skins, so many that the scene was indescribable. I felt so faint that I fell to the ground in a dazed confusion.

"You lied," King Monster yelled sourly, his voice shaking the earth and rolling across the clouds like thunder. Rob clutched onto me and we both shook.

"We cannot have a conversation if you are so tall," Sheena called upwards as loudly as she could. King Monster seemed to ponder this, then slowly he shrank back to his normal size. His eyes glared a burning red as he looked at us.

"Kay," he hissed, "and Rob, my soon to be slaves, you will pay for this. When a fairy makes a promise they cannot break it, so because you have broken the rules, we must make a wager. My wager is this; you will both be my slaves and I will take over Fairyland. Accept this offer or let us go to war!" King Monster's face curved into a horrible smile.

"You cannot legally do this," Sheena replied, the Book of Fairies suddenly appearing in her hand. She leafed through its ancient pages.

"It says here that if a fairy breaks a promise to a monster, a compromise must be reached. I believe that you are being too harsh. It clearly states that you cannot take over Fairyland, so you must choose another way to gain what is yours. After we agree to your terms we will have our say and you must agree to ours." King Monster's face became twisted in thought and for a long while he was silent.

"You must let us dwell among you and we, the monsters, must be allowed to set up our own houses in Fairyland and enter any shops unharmed. You must not use any magic to fight us," King Monster finally responded. The monsters behind him nodded in agreement. Rob and I exchanged shocked looks and Sheena took his proposal into consideration.

"We accept your offer," she spoke, "now the King and Queen will speak. Rob and Kay, what is your offer?" Soon all of the fairies in Fairyland were looking at us from inside of their houses, too afraid to come out. All of the monsters had their eyes on us also. At that very moment, the very fate of every fairy was resting on us to decide.

"Umm…" Rob began, "it would make sense that if you're going to live in Fairyland, you have to follow our rules. You cannot use any magic against us unless we use ours against you first." There was a moment of silence.

"Is that all," Sheena asked. Suddenly, I had a brilliant idea.

"Not quite," I said, and every eye turned on me. I looked at the crowds of monsters towering above us and smiled.

"If in fact we are living together, we should be equal. The only way to be equal is if…" I paused. The monsters and fairies leaned forward, anticipating my next words. I finished, "…is if the monsters shrink and become the same size as fairies." Suddenly there was a great burst of joy as all of the fairies shouted 'hooray' and threw their arms into the air.

"The day has come," Sheena spoke, addressing the fairies, "that the monsters shall be our equals and we have no need to fear them anymore." Another burst of applause followed her words.

"No," King Monster screamed, "you can't do this! We are big, you are small, it cannot be done!" The monsters behind him were in an uproar, hissing and yelling in total disagreement.

"It can be done and will be," Sheena argued, turning to Rob and I, "now you both have the power to do it. Point to the monsters and if the ancient laws are not broken they will become our size, their castles and cabins included, from now until always." Then, for the first time, I saw King Monster shake with fear. He was afraid of becoming small.

Rob and I raised our hands, pointing to the monsters. Miraculously, they shrank smaller and smaller until they were the size of fairies. The black castle way off in the distance became the size of the white one and King Monster's cabin became the size of a fairy house. King Monster stepped forward, a King Monster who was my height, and his eyes were able to meet mine straight on for the first time. All was silent as the monsters looked around at what had before only been tiny miniatures on the ground. Then in the eyes of all the monsters there appeared a small glow, much like the glow of a fairy's. A new understanding had developed between us, a bond, and now that the monsters were our equals they did not seem so different after all. King Monster continued coming forward until he stood right before Rob and I. He looked at us carefully, then he surveyed our wings closely with his eyes.

"We are not yet equal," he stated, "because we monsters are forever banished to the ground and you are able to fly." Rob and I regarded each other once more.

"I guess it wouldn't hurt if we didn't fly, we could just walk everywhere we go and only fly with permission from a monster," he half asked and explained. I nodded, the monsters nodded and even the fairies agreed.

"Ok," I spoke, "then this is how it will be from now on."

King Monster returned to Monsterland for the evening with the promise to return the next day. Tomorrow we would decide where they would live, as only a few decided to make Fairyland their home. The rest would remain in Monsterland and pass through whenever they pleased. That night, Rob, Sheena, Henry, Frendall and I sat down to a delicious feast.

"I am pleased with your judgement, Rob and Kay," Sheena explained in her sweet voice, "we compromised our ability to fly freely and the monsters compromised their size. Now we are truly equals. Now maybe, for the first time in the history of our worlds, we will be able to live in peace with each other. When the monsters were banished from Fairyland in the beginning of our time, we would not allow them back. But, because you broke a promise, this law could be replaced by a compromised one." Rob and I could not find the words to say, so we simply nodded and continued to eat. I realized that I would no longer be King Monster's slave, no fairy or monster would ever be a slave again since we were equal.

I fell asleep that night and dreamt that we were living in peace, completely unafraid, but soon my pleasant thoughts were interrupted by another dream, an unpleasant one. The monsters were banished from Fairyland again and grew into evil, terrible creatures again. In the middle of it all, standing outside of King Monster's cabin, was a monster that appeared to look like him. But instead of wearing a white cape, it was black; so very black that even a night without the moon or stars could not equal its colour.

CHAPTER ELEVEN

I awoke and the five of us ate a breakfast of berries and, of course, chew bread, then we walked outside and awaited our visitors. Twelve monsters came forward; six mud monsters and six scale skins like King Monster. At once, I recognized one of them and sprang forward.

"Cookstone," I called happily. He grinned and came up to me.

"I'm moving here," he exclaimed cheerfully, "so we can see each other every day!" All of the monsters were advancing slowly after him with large black sacks upon their backs in preparation for the move to their new houses. King Monster rushed up the path from his cabin to oversee the operations.

"You may use the land between the fairy houses to build your own," Sheena explained to the monsters warmly, coming to my side, "and may we welcome all of you to Fairyland." The monsters smiled shyly and nodded, each hurrying to find their small portion of land. King Monster addressed the fairies, some of which were pouring out of their houses to see what was happening.

"We the monsters will build our houses in the same style as the fairy houses, but because many are used to living in the dark castle and deep woods around it, we will make our houses black." The fairies agreed with King Monster and as soon as everyone had found a place and Sheena approved it, King Monster would snap his fingers, making black houses suddenly appear. They were exactly the same as the fairy houses, with a sloped roof lined with tiny shingles and a rounded front door with square cut windows. The only real difference was in the colour; fairy houses would appear in earth tones of brown, grey, white, or a hint of mint green.

Soon the monsters had occupied their houses, placing their few belongings in their rooms. The twelve houses stood amidst the others, nearly making a black and white pattern. It looked so very different at first that I feared we had made a mistake but soon, as I saw how delighted Cookstone and the others were, I became happy also. As we stood looking out over the land, Cookstone and four other monsters approached us.

"We all wish to make a living in Fairyland and to assist the fairies," Cookstone spoke, "therefore I wish to set up shop and make rings and other such things, like bowls, out of stone."

Another mud monster stepped forward, stating, "I am a blacksmith and wish to set up shop."

A scale skin spoke up, his red cape flapping behind him, "I am a baker and would like to work in the town's bakery."

Another approached, also with a red cape, "I could put on puppet shows and plays if there were a theatre."

Finally, a shy scale skin stepped forward and quietly said, "I am a doctor and have the power to heal the sick." At this comment there were excited and questioning whispers from the fairies. Frendall stepped out before us, his eyes glaring.

"We do not need your services," he cried angrily, "that's impossible! All monsters are evil and none of them can do any good! Besides, only monsters become sick. It clearly states in the Ten Rules of Fairies that fairies will never become ill-"

"-But we do," Henry shouted, cutting through Frendall's words, "we do and we don't know why! Maybe he could help us." There was more whispering, fast and confusing now.

"All I can say is that no good can come of evil. If you are willing to risk yourselves and your children at the expense of monsters, then that is your choice, but I will not stand for it!" With this, Frendall stormed back into the castle. Rob and I made an agreement that if all went well, we would allow the monsters to set up shops. The change of them moving in was so great that it alone would take much effort to get used to, and the monsters agreed. Soon they settled into their houses and so had all of the other fairies as evening was upon us.

There was so much to think about that night. How would the monsters and fairies get along? What if Frendall was right, what if Rob and I had jeopardized everyone? Was it really possible to live in peace? Sheena came into my room, sensing that I was troubled. She believed that we could live in peace because we had made an unselfish decision. Her words comforted me but a part of me was still unsure, how would everyone else feel about these uncertain neighbours?

When I ventured outside the next morning I found that there were mixed feelings. Some fairies spoke to the monsters while others would not go near them. Even the monsters seemed uncertain of what to say, so they kept to themselves. King Monster had just come into Fairyland and was speaking to the twelve monsters when I walked over.

"Good morning, King Monster," I called and he regarded me. I decided to talk to all of them.

"How are all of you feeling today," I asked, "I hope that you do not see yourselves as strangers here. How do you feel about this decision?" At first they were all silent, then the doctor spoke.

"I like my house," he said. I smiled as the others nodded. King Monster turned and left at that point, but I followed him.

"King Monster," I said quietly once we were in front of the cabin, and he looked at me, "will there ever be peace between us, or will we always be enemies never trying to be friends?" He stared at me with a blank expression. I stared back at him but soon turned around knowing that he did not want to talk to me.

"Wait," he said, and I turned towards him again, "can you bring these roses back to life?" He pointed a clawed finger towards the tangled thorns and leaves, long since brown, and the brittle black petals hanging by threads. Watching him, I saw sadness in his eyes that I had not noticed before. He looked longingly at the roses, almost wishing them to life in his mind. I leaned down and gently held the crisp petals in my hand until they went from black, to brown, to light pink and then to a lively, burning red. Life spread up through all parts until they were green once more, much to my amazement.

King Monster's eyes brightened more and more until they glowed with joy like a fairy's, then he clapped his hands and laughed with childish delight. His fingers stroked every delicate petal and leaf gently, and the widest smile his face could hold came upon it.

"How very nice," he said, then his face took on a straight expression once more, "but don't be confused. This doesn't mean that we can live in peace." He fell silent once more.

"Then Frendall is right, we will never understand each other," I said sadly. King Monster's face twisted with anger.

"Frendall is always wrong," he explained bitterly, "it is the fairies who wronged us. We could have been friends, we could have helped the fairies, but Frendall could never believe that. We are only evil because we have been shunned and unloved."

Listening to King Monster's speech and seeing the pain in his face, I finally began to understand the monsters. For the first time, I realized that they weren't different, perhaps they *looked* different but inside they were the same and they experienced happiness and sorrow just as any fairy would. Suddenly, a thought came to my mind.

"King Monster," I began once more, puzzled, "once, you grew a red rose in your hand. Why couldn't you just bring these roses back to life yourself?" King Monster pondered this for a moment, or at least it appeared, and he did not seem to have an answer. Finally he spoke in such a quiet voice that I had to strain my ears to hear him, "I wanted you to do it, so I know that I can trust you."

Suddenly Sheena's voice pierced through the air, calling me back to the castle. So I walked back, watching King Monster over my shoulder leaning down, smiling beside his bush of living red roses.

§

Another night had come, filled with millions of sparkling stars and a burning silver moon. I sat at the window for a long while that evening and soon my thoughts turned to a distant memory of the

Lost Book, the one which came from the rose when the Book of Fairies and Book of Monsters entered into existence. I had asked if King Monster had it and he told me that he did once, but gave it away. I wondered who owned it now.

Then my thoughts shifted once more, this time to Frendall. Where had he come from? No one had explained. Was he human once like Rob and I, or did he come from the rose? Why did he and King Monster dislike each other so much? Thinking of their disagreements, I began to wonder if the monsters really would make Fairyland a better place. What if they secretly took over? How would there ever be peace if the monsters and fairies didn't trust each other?

Slowly I began to realize my importance as a leader. I not only had to listen to the needs of the fairies but now I had to tend to the needs of the monsters as well. I, most importantly, had to help the monsters feel comfortable and yet assure the fairies that there was nothing to fear... or was there? I must have gone on this way thinking these thoughts all night, because I couldn't sleep. Questions without answers flooded my mind until I felt dizzy. As soon as I could regain my senses, it was the start of another morning.

It was snowing outside, heavy wet flakes fell not quite with the beauty of snow doves but each was delicately and intricately patterned. The monsters, as I saw, were in wonder. In Monsterland the snow fell only in the shape of blades with sharp edges. They had never seen such beautiful snow and in fact, neither had I. I stood at the window watching it fall, laying on the ground, resting on the rooftops and creeping in the small crevices of the shingles upon every house. Soon Rob was at my side as mesmerized as I was. As we looked onwards, we saw the fairies slowly gathering around the monsters, showing them the snow and no doubt explaining the other things, such as the summer's blooming wildflowers, that Fairyland had and Monsterland didn't. Sheena came up behind us, smiling with that warmness only she could have and her eyes glowed.

"I believe that there will be peace at last among us. The monsters and fairies can now live together as neighbours because of you. I never thought I'd see this day," Sheena told us joyfully, then she called us to the table to eat breakfast. Henry was waiting in the kitchen with two steaming plates of chewbread, one for Rob and one for me. We took our seats at the table and began to eat.

"I am the only one who can make chew bread," Henry commented, "so whenever you eat chew bread, it could only have been I who made it." Rob and I nodded and continued eating. Soon we were done and as we rose from our seats, Henry nodded at us approvingly. Then Sheena, her eyes glistening with a hint of tears, pointed outside and said, "here is your land, these are your people-now go, go to them."

Rob and I looked at each other, then at Sheena and Henry who were gazing at us. For an instant, I could almost feel them drifting away, their looks almost saying goodbye. I could tell that Rob felt it too. We stood there locking eyes with them, sending silent messages until finally we turned around and closed the door of that giant white castle behind us.

Fairyland stretched out before us like a blank white sheet of paper just waiting to be filled. The fairies were touring the monsters, now equally divided into two groups, through the stores. Once more the monsters were fascinated, their eyes greedily taking in everything that they could see. Smiles came to their faces as they listened intently to everything that the fairies were telling them. The fairies seemed to be enjoying the tour also, paying careful attention to the monsters as they spoke about Monsterland.

"Kay," Rob said suddenly, his voice startling me as it broke through the calm, and I turned in his direction quickly, "didn't it seem like Sheena and Henry were acting oddly?"

I agreed, but not finding a reason why, we decided to ask them when we returned. King Monster entered into Fairyland again, looking as though he had picked up the snow and wrapped it around his shoulders because of his white cape. He had wrapped his rosebushes in gauze the day before as could be seen by the small bits of it peeking out through the fresh snow. He was wandering around inspecting the monster's houses but he didn't stay as long as he had the day before. As soon as he came he walked away slowly back to his cabin and shut himself inside of it.

Fairyland was buzzing with activity late that morning as many of the fairies were speaking quickly and excitedly about the monsters living among them. As the tours for the twelve monsters came to an end, they approached Rob and I once more.

"Winter has come and we are not aware of what it will be like," Cookstone said in his deep grumbling voice, "are the temperatures as extreme as they are in Monsterland? Does as much snow fall?" Rob and I explained that it was our first winter also and the monsters chuckled. As we had come to find out, the monsters had lived deep in dark forests and in the black castle. They had not been part of a community and often fought for survival. In Fairyland they had quickly been accepted, they didn't have to fight for survival and their houses were safe and warm. In fact, the monsters wanted to repay us for our kindness but they weren't sure how.

After the monsters had returned to their houses, Rob and I decided to go back to the castle. As we moved in that direction, we nearly decided against going inside. Something didn't feel right about going back but at the same time something compelled us to walk inside. There was something empty about it, a certain sense of loneliness, but at the same time there was something new and exciting about it that I had not noticed before. Rob and I stood in silence. The castle appeared the same as it always had, with its grand staircase leading upwards, full of what had once been unexplored rooms that we had discovered. Everything was quiet and unmoving so when Rob's voice broke through the silence and echoed off of the walls, I jumped in surprise.

"Sheena, Frendall, Henry," Rob called. A noise drew our attention to the kitchen where Frendall sat at the table sipping a sweet drink from a shiny cup. When he caught sight of us, he dropped his eyes sadly.

"They're gone," he said quietly, "Sheena and Henry have left, they live in the palace now. You have passed through the first stage ruler and young ruler. You are now full leaders and all is yours."

§

Not much was spoken that night as all of us were in deep concentration about the recent events. I laid awake that night wondering why Sheena and Henry had left us so soon, wondering if we truly were ready to rule Fairyland by ourselves. Just as I had closed my eyes, a burst of bright light filled the room and I opened them quickly; it was the ring that Cookstone had given me. Once again, as it had done a time before, tiny letters in fine scrollwork began appearing on the ring, burning onto the wall. 'Christopher, the one who planted the rose, is...' there was a pause, the light flickered but finally the last word appeared barely visible, '...alive'.

I gasped out loud. How could it be? How could Christopher be alive when the Book of Fairies clearly stated that he had died?! How would Cookstone know, was it true? What if Christopher was walking around somewhere, the one who planted the rose which began the two lands and the magical world, living and breathing and no one knew? What a crazy thought! But if it were true, just imagine finding him and talking with him! I began to think of all of the questions that I would ask, knowing that he would have the answers to all of them. Maybe he could explain why the fairies were growing old and becoming ill. Where would I begin to look? I would have to go back to the Human World and then what? There's an entire world to search! Even if he were alive, I'd never find him anyway. With this, my excitement left and I rolled over and closed my eyes once more. This time the light did not come again. No more words played their way across the smooth surface of the ring and only darkness met my eyelids until I had fallen asleep and began to dream.

PART TWO

CHAPTER ONE

The winter set in, cold and snowy but still fairly mild. Some days the sun would become very warm, melting all of the snow, and Fairyland would once again be green and colourful. The monsters would come out on these days, staring in amazement. Rob and I came to learn that in their land, the snow would continue falling until all sources of food were buried and harsh storms would prevent them from venturing out. As Rob and I looked off into the distance the castle, standing in a menacing black, would be hidden by a blanket of swirling snow until it appeared to be swallowed in its depths. The monsters also told us of snow tornadoes which would blind them with white then lift them off of the ground and throw them. Monsterland truly sounded like a horrible place.

The monsters began making regular visits into the stores to gather food and look around, but as the winter set in the fairies began to become nervous about the monsters living among them. Frendall had explained that monsters had more power in fall and unlimited power in winter. When spring returned, the fairies would become more powerful and have unlimited power in the summer. If the monsters decided to overthrow Fairyland they could do that easily since they were already here and because of their power strength in winter. The monsters did seem to have more power, they must have had enough magic to keep themselves warm because as the fairies walked around in heavy fur coats, the monsters only wore their capes.

All of Fairyland seemed duller since Sheena and Henry were gone. We had planned to announce that they had left for the palace yet somehow, perhaps through some ability to sense change, the fairies already knew. Sometimes on beautiful days when the sky turned blue Rob and I would watch the palace from a distance, not yet ready to visit, and without saying a word we could both sense the emptiness. Even Frendall had become silent, roaming through the castle thinking about them.

Many times I would sit on my bed, cradling the red diary in my palms, reading over and over again the note in pointed lettering, 'some day you will know what to do with this book'. Who had sent it? My mind suddenly recalled the day when Letterman had delivered it, my birthday, seeming now as though it was so very long ago. 'You will know what to do' I read once more, the lettering burning off of the paper, but I didn't. I didn't know what to do now since Sheena and Henry had left. I didn't know how words could express my sadness so I tucked it away once more with the old brass pen, appearing more ancient than ever, to wait for 'someday'.

Everything had somehow become older; the fairies, the land, even the cabin which once stood tall against the horizon now seemed to lean and appear almost tired. King Monster continued to visit the monsters, although less frequently than before. Most times he would lock himself within the aging walls of the cabin, the only proof of his existence being when the curtains covering the windows would part and he would look out with sadness in his deep green eyes.

I met Rob in the kitchen leaning over a steaming cup of tea. We regarded each other for a moment, a quiet smile coming to his face.

"What are we going to do," I asked curiously.

"What is there to do," Rob replied with a question, leaning back comfortably in his chair, "everything is wonderful! There is peace between the monsters and fairies. Everyone is happy."

"But what about the fairies becoming sick and growing old?"

"Relax, Kay," Rob told me, chuckling, "we'll figure it out later. We are true leaders now, we have a whole land-it's all ours! Aren't you excited?"

"Well, of course, but-" I began. Rob cut me off.

"-Great! Wonderful! Let's just sit back and relax, ok? Enjoy being royalty!"

I smiled. It was exciting to be the leader of an entire land and its people. After all, the opportunity was a once in a lifetime and to be a fairy, a magical creature that could live forever, was an amazing feeling! It was true that there was peace now between the monsters and fairies, there was no threat from them or from anyone.

"Right," Rob repeated, prompting me, his smile growing wider. I couldn't help but agree.

"Ok," I said, trying to be enthusiastic, "right!"

"Great," he repeated, making another steaming glass appear on the table across from him. I sat and drank the sweetness of it.

"You know what this means," he stated, and I shook my head.

"We," he explained matter-of-factly, "can do whatever we want to."

I set my drink down, realizing the truth of his words. No problems, power, the ability to fly, a diamond castle. These were all of the things that made Fairyland wonderful. We could have it all and make anything happen with only the point of a finger.

"You're right," I marvelled, "we can! It's a dream come true!"

Somehow the dreariness of Sheena and Henry leaving had turned into the joys of becoming a leader, making our own decisions and having fun. Maybe the illness and growing old would stop on its own. Maybe Rob was right, maybe it could wait until later.

"But how do we help the fairies to be happier," I asked, coming out of my thoughts. Rob considered this.

"Maybe we could have some type of celebration," he suggested, "a winter carnival."

"Like a party for everyone," I added excitedly. Soon we began to make plans deciding where we would hold it, what would take place and when. Every detail began to fall into place until it became official.

"What's going on?" We looked to the opening of the kitchen to find Frendall there, wrapped thickly in his coat, the tops of his wings dusted with snow. He shook them off and shivered. Rob told him of the winter celebration.

"It is to help everyone be happier and for the monsters to feel more accepted," I explained. He smiled.

"The fairies would appreciate it," he commented, "but the monsters do not need to feel welcome. This is not their land." The room fell silent for a moment until he added, "would Sheena and Henry have allowed the monsters to come?" I pondered his question; yes, no?

"They're not here," I explained quietly, deciding it to be the best answer. Frendall dropped his gaze.

"It's only fair," Rob piped up and Frendall looked up at us once more. He sighed.

"Well," he began, "it is, after all, only fair to be fair. I guess it wouldn't hurt for them to come." So we spent one week preparing and planning and all the while I could just imagine King Monster there, dancing around and around, his white cape like a blanket of new snow swirling about him.

The week passed quickly until the time came when we announced that we would be holding a winter celebration. We all agreed to surprise the monsters, as they did not celebrate anything in Monsterland. The fairies were reluctant to this as the word quietly spread around the town. They were afraid that the carnival would be ruined if the monsters were allowed to join. As Rob and I visited with the people, however, we were able to convince them to change their minds. If the monsters lived in Fairyland, they should have as many rights as any fairy would.

Fairyland became a bustle of activity as the winter carnival approached, much like it had been at harvest time. Fairies dashed in and out of the shops, gathering food and baking supplies. The bakery was especially busy as new colourful and interesting desserts were being scooped up in handfuls. Little cakes with bright white frosting and coconut represented the winter season. White mint sticks, which resembled candy canes but were without stripes and didn't curve at the end, seemed to be a popular treat to the little fairies.

Outside, fairies were talking and shaking hands. The houses were glowing golden from lanterns and the chimney openings revealed spirals of grey smoke. Good smells filled the air as harvest crops were brought out and cooked, and homemade pies and cakes were a specialty. Young fairies were outside of their houses making miniature houses out of snow called 'forts', which they could play in and call their own. Snowballs flew back and forth, seemingly coming from nowhere, hitting unsuspecting victims.

The twelve monsters took notice of the activity but did not say much. They didn't know that the celebration was soon to take place and were unaware that we were going to include them in it. There was an eager anticipation about the event but also curiosity about inviting the monsters. Every fairy seemed to have developed a new glow in their eyes and faces, and when they spoke, a sweeter noise came out than had before. The monsters noticed this also and when no one seemed to be looking, they themselves could not help but smile.

At last the event began to take place. Fairies came out of their houses and laid flat in the snow leaving their imprint, which came to be known as 'snow fairies'. The monsters watched from inside their houses until I decided to invite them. I wandered up the path to King Monster's cabin and knocked on the door. Soon it opened and he stood before me.

"We're having a winter carnival," I explained to him, "you and all of the monsters are invited." He stood silently, looking intently at me.

"I'm…invited," he asked in disbelief. I nodded, taking his hand in mine. The scales felt bumpy beneath my palm and his claws stretched up my arm a ways, but it was a hand none the less. He looked down at it in shock.

"You weren't afraid to take my hand?"

"No," I said kindly, "it's not very different from mine is it?" He glanced up at me, his eyes taking on a glow appearing as a fairy's. Slowly he folded his fingers over mine and shook it gently.

"No difference that I can see," he answered delightfully, running past me and knocking on the doors of the black houses, proclaiming the beginning of the carnival. Their reaction was of surprise and then of joy. The festival took place with just as much merriment as we had seen on harvest day and the monsters were amazed at the variety of foods. They listened and clapped their hands to music that they had never heard before and danced like the fairies. Rob threw a snowball at me but missed and instead hit King Monster, ruffling his cape, slamming into his back. Silence fell as every eye looked upon the King, many in fear. He turned slowly, facing us, his face crunched in anger.

"Who hit me," he asked menacingly, darting between Rob and I, "admit it!"

"It was me," Rob confessed, his voice quivering, "I'm sorry, I didn't mean-" But before Rob could finish, a ball of snow exploded on his shoulder. King Monster watched, grinning, laughing a deep hearty laugh like thunder.

"I got you," he choked out between laughs as I knelt and crushed the snow in my hand, throwing it and hitting him again.

"You," he cried, this time at me, as he gathered the ball into his hand, "will pay for this!"

"Snowball fight," Rob cried and everything erupted into action. There was a flurry of movement as excited monsters and fairies began to grab handfuls, throwing them in all directions. Shouts and laughter filled the air and for once the line blurred, the line which separated monster from fairy, good from evil, and the two lands seemed to become one just as Fairyland Old had been. King Monster came to us, smiling a wide toothy grin.

"Thank you," he commented sincerely, "it has meant so much to the monsters to know that they are accepted."

"We are at peace," Rob broke in, "but can we ever be friends?" The King regarded him with a warm softness coming to his eyes.

"Aren't we friends already," he asked mischievously.

Soon the evening came on and slowly everyone returned to their homes, including Rob, Frendall and I. Coming inside the castle, we looked out over the land in great happiness. King Monster and in fact all of the monsters, were now our friends. The lands truly had joined together again.

"Isn't it wonderful, Frendall," we commented. He eyed us glumly.

"We cannot be friends," he stated simply, "they are the enemy. You don't understand, Rob and Kay, you don't know what they're really like! Once you are here as long as I have been, you'll realize."

"How long have you been here," I asked, and Rob added, "and where did you come from?" Frendall rose out of his chair and left the room. Rob and I exchanged confused glances, shrugging.

That evening I took the Book of Fairies into my arms, setting it on my lap and tracing my finger over the row of golden roses outlining its border. What mysteries would it reveal or would it close every page inside of it, hiding them away like secrets? What did I need to know, why had I taken it off of the dresser? 'Once you are here as long as I have been', Frendall's words echoed in my mind. Why couldn't he tell us, what did he have to hide?

"Where did Frendall come from," I questioned the book in a whisper. It didn't move.

"How long has he been here?" Nothing happened.

"Why does he dislike King Monster so much?"

Suddenly it flew open, the pages flipping faster and faster until it stopped long enough for me to read *a broken promise*. This confused me; a broken promise, what promise? There were never promises made by either of them. But soon the book continued to more pages, nearing the back now, the letters all appearing like lines. At times the pages moved so quickly that they seemed to bear no writing at all. My breath caught within me when I came upon the last readable words before, once more, it closed tightly; *black cape.*

CHAPTER TWO

"Friends," Sheena cried joyfully and I could almost see her wrinkled face curl into a gentle smile. Rob and I stood by the palace wall listening to the rustlings inside of three generations of royalty, explaining our newly found friendship with the monsters.

"I never thought that it was possible," it was Henry this time, seeming amazed at the news, "you have changed the history of the lands and accomplished what we never could." Even George and Marianne seemed shocked, hardly speaking, perhaps deep in thought. Frendall came up beside us.

"I have missed you Sheena, Henry," he spoke softly to the wall, then looking upon us added, "we all have."

"Oh, you'll be fine," Henry assured him, "after all Frendall, you've done this before, remember? When Paul and Mary left and we came into power." These words were met with agreement.

"And," Sheena added, addressing Rob and I, "you two are doing wonderfully! Surely you don't have time to miss us!"

"But we do," Rob stated, choking back tears. I nodded, dabbing my eyes as they assured us that we could visit anytime. They weren't far away after all, and just because we couldn't see them didn't mean that they weren't there. This thought comforted me and we slowly walked away down a little worn path leading to the castle.

"Wait," I suddenly called to Rob who stopped and turned towards me, "I have one more question for them." Running back quickly I came to the plain structure again, looking so empty and desolate that it almost seemed as though no one was there.

"I have one more question," I broke through the silence, sensing many pairs of ears straining to hear my words and many pairs of eyes, invisible and hidden to my view, watching me from behind the barren wall that divided us.

"Have you seen a monster with a black cape?" There was a pause, a moment in which silence pressed into my ears.

"No," was the answer, "we haven't. Why do you ask?"

"I don't know," I half whispered, looking around me, turning around to gaze upon the black castle appearing as a black mansion towering and wrapped in thorns. I saw him in my mind as vivid and real as in my dreams. Rob and Frendall waited a little ways off, half hiding the view. I went forward and left the palace, joining them. As we came upon the front door of the castle, Rob and I turned and looked out over the land as we had so many times before.

"Beautiful isn't it," I exclaimed, taking in the richness of it. Rob nodded.

"It's very nice," he commented, thinking deeply, and his eyes seemed distant, "but…"

"But what," I asked in alarm. He did not look at me.

"But it's missing something," he told me finally, "it's ok, but somehow… I think it could be better." Better? I stood silently, sadness coming over me. *Better?* Better than the place I had come to love and the people who made me so happy? Better than seeing all of the little houses take on a warm glow and slowly wink out their lights every night? What could be better?!

"You, you want to change it," I finally got the strength up to ask. At this Rob turned to me, his eyes meeting mine, the glow dulling ever so slightly, so slightly that I questioned if I even noticed a difference at all. He seemed to sense my sadness.

"Just a little, what would it hurt?" I turned away.

"Come on, Kay," I heard him say, recognizing the tone of his voice. Hadn't he said that to me before? Yes, I remembered, suddenly recalling the dream I'd had before we came to Fairyland, before we'd ventured into the woods even. When I had told him about the monster in the black cape. 'Come on Kay', he had said, 'you know that it isn't real'. But it was real, maybe not the monster in the black cape- or was it?- but Fairyland, all of this, and he didn't believe me.

"Just a little," he continued, "you'll hardly notice it." Taking a stick he began to draw pictures in a section of soil where the snow had melted away, back and forth, making lines which ran alongside each other.

"Roads," he explained, "some alternate paths to take. There is only one road in and out of Fairyland but if we had more, the fairies would be able to have easier access to the fields and woods."

"There are already paths," I argued.

"Yes," he justified, "but they are overgrown. If we made new paths it would be less confusing. The fairy children would have less chance of becoming lost." He pointed and I followed his direction to see a group of children frolicking about, chasing each other. It was possible; if one of them chose to go off alone, without a path they would have no way of finding their way back. Maybe it was a good idea.

"Where will the paths go," I asked as Rob pointed to a group of thick trees.

"Through there and a couple over there." But all I saw were trees.

"How will we get through the trees?"

"We won't," he answered seriously, "we'll have to cut them down."

The last words hit me, dizzying me, making me suddenly sick to my stomach. I watched the trees that stood there in disbelief, the trees that had occupied the space for hundreds of years with thick trunks growing together. In my mind I could nearly hear the sickening 'thwack' of axes killing them, leaving grey, ringed stumps in their places. They weren't just trees; they were my trees, our trees, Fairyland trees. A cold fear set into me at the realization of his words.

"What," I cried in fear, "Rob, are you crazy?!"

"Just a couple," he responded, "ok, only two, how about two? We can make new paths and have enough firewood for everyone to last the rest of the winter. We will begin construction in the spring."

"But the stoves run on wood from fallen limbs," I explained, "they would never agree to, or need to take trees down!"

"We have the monsters to think of, Kay," he rebuked, "think; firewood for everyone, paths for safety, it's worth it! We'll take out small trees, we'll leave the old ones. We have to think of our land, of our people. Don't you feel that way?" I did; under the snow it would be difficult to find branches. We did need paths and the monsters needed our help now. Maybe Rob was right; there was an entire forest and it would only be two small trees, surely it couldn't hurt, right?

So we announced it with heavy groans of disapproval and shocked silence from the fairies, yet the monsters seemed unfazed. After fighting for survival in Monsterland it was a welcomed idea and they agreed happily. King Monster came with three other monsters carrying saws to do the work. Two monsters tended to one tree, pushing and pulling the blades back and forth. The trunk swayed with every cut until it split with a final 'crack' sending a few crisp leaves, still clinging to the branches, scattering. They cut them into logs, loading many pieces into their strong arms and carrying them back to the little black houses. We offered a few to the fairies who rejected them icily, turning their backs in pain and sadness, although a few took them reluctantly.

"Thank you for your kindness, Kay," Cookstone said sincerely, coming to my side. I nodded but still the guilt remained liked a shadow over me. I decided to change the subject.

"I received your message from the ring," I explained, suddenly recalling the night that Henry and Sheena had left, "is it true, Cookstone? Is Christopher really alive?!" He smiled, the mud creasing at either side of his mouth.

"Yes," he answered excitedly.

"But how," I questioned hurriedly, "how do you know?"

"I found it within the Book of Monsters," he told me, "I held it, just for an instant. One day I crept into the cabin when King Monster was away and it opened. The page read 'Christopher is alive'. I just had to tell you, no one else would believe me! Now we just have to figure out who he is." I was baffled at his last statement.

"No, *where,*" I corrected him, "*where* he is, not *who.*" He opened his mouth to speak when Frendall came over, interrupting us.

"What are we discussing," he asked and we both fell silent, sensing that he had heard by the look on his face. Should I tell him, I wondered, would he believe me? Probably not, he would never believe something written in the Book of Monsters. What if I lied, what if I told him that we were talking about something else when all along he had heard us? As he set his fiery green eyes on me, I looked away nervously.

"It's about Christopher," Cookstone piped up and I caught my breath, beginning to feel panicked, "he's alive, it says so in the Book of Monsters, and Kay believes it too." Frendall shot a look towards me as I paced nervously, pivoting back and forth on my feet, daring to glance up only for a moment to see his eyes burning with curiosity.

"Do you," he asked. I swallowed a lump rising in my throat.

"Well," I stammered, "you'll just think I'm crazy."

"Do you," he repeated. I nodded.

"Yes," I finally admitted, expecting him to lecture me.

"Even though the Book of Fairies clearly states that he died," he went on, "you still believe in the possibility that he could be alive?" But his tone was gentle, not angry, and I looked up in surprise.

"Yes I do," I concluded. Frendall nodded at my words, his face glowing.

"If you believe in these things," he told me, "then you must consider this; if Christopher is alive, he must not want to be found because you don't know where he is. Maybe it would be best not to look, maybe he wants to remain hidden. He may not be who you think he is, you may be disappointed to find that he is not willing to tell you all that you desire to know. Kay, maybe there's a reason that you're supposed to think he died. Some things are not meant for you to know." I stood in shock, my legs feeling like rubber. That's it, just give up before I began? Just forget it?

"I'm supposed to *think* that he died," I asked in disbelief, then I paused.

"So he didn't die," I concluded, staring Frendall full in the face. He stared back with a surprised expression, his mouth gaping open. Suddenly he turned away, walking slowly back to the castle, ignoring my pleas for him to come back. As he shut the door he turned to look at me, beyond me, gazing into the distance. His look was a mix of sadness and resentment, one which I did not understand and would not understand until much later.

§

King Monster remained in his cabin for the longest time that winter and somehow I feared he would not emerge until spring. I watched the crooked stone chimney puffing out smoke and peered closely, desperately watching for some movement, some parting of the curtains, but all was still. When he finally did come out one snowy day he knocked on the castle door, Rob and I opening it in amazement to find him standing there. The monsters and fairies became still, watching him, wondering what would happen next.

"Hello King Monster," I said nervously, "what brings you here?" He stared at us thoughtfully, snow swirling up all around him.

"Is Frendall gone," he asked impatiently.

"Yes," Rob answered, "he is visiting the palace, why?"

"Could I come in?" We gasped in surprise. A monster wanted to enter into the Fairyland castle! The villagers gasped behind him until all was quiet once more.

"Why," Rob questioned, and King Monster answered, "I wanted to talk to you." Rob and I glanced at each other fearfully. 'No good can come of evil', I heard in my head, hadn't Frendall told us that?

"Yes," I answered and a smile came to his face.

"Kay," Rob whispered angrily, "what are you doing?! I know we are supposed to be friends with the monsters, but they are still evil. He's going to try to destroy us all!" But somehow I trusted him and as crazy as it seemed, he stepped inside and we shut the door cautiously behind him.

King Monster marvelled at the castle's beauty, at the gold and white and diamonds dangling from the chandeliers. We led him to the kitchen where he sat at the table, still gazing around him in wonder. I made a honeysuckle drink appear before him which he took and quickly drank thankfully. Turning his attention towards me, he pointed a clawed finger and a glass of steaming hot chocolate appeared.

"Kay, he's trying to poison you, don't drink it," Rob whispered, beginning to sound like Frendall. King Monster watched me closely.

"He could have been afraid that I would poison him but he took the honeysuckle anyway," I argued quietly.

"He knows that fairies can only use magic to do good," Rob whispered, "so he knew it was safe to drink!"

I suddenly recalled a time when I had been King Monster's slave, had trusted him by climbing upon his hand and he had given my powers back to me. So, still with a small doubt in my mind, I tipped the cup back and drank the delicious sweetness until it was gone. Rob was shocked, folding his arms in disgust until King Monster placed a glass in front of him. Rob sighed.

"Well, Kay, I still don't trust him," he explained at last, "but I'll trust your judgement." With that he drank it, smiling when he was finished.

"That's the sweetest, most delicious cup of hot chocolate I have ever tasted," he exclaimed. King Monster grinned.

"Thank you," he answered genuinely, "I can make a delicious feast, you may come for supper sometime." We both nodded in agreement.

"What brings you here," Rob asked, and King Monster's face grew serious.

"I need something," he explained in a low voice, seeming to address me, "more precious to me than it is to you, more valuable to all of us, not just yourselves. I need-"

"-Nothing," Frendall scowled, entering the room. He was back. King Monster's face took on a twisted expression of anger and desperation.

"You'll be getting nothing," Frendall yelled.

"No, please, you don't understand," King Monster cried, shifting his gaze quickly between Rob and I, "the Rainbow Crystal, I need it, we all need it! It must stay living, it's the only way!"

"No," Frendall screamed, "get out! Leave!" At this, King Monster jumped from his seat and ran out the door, down past the houses, back to the cabin where he imprisoned himself once more.

"Why do you hate him," I cried, tears coming to my eyes, "he told me that he's only evil because he has been shunned and unloved!"

"He's a deceiver, Kay," Frendall explained icily, "a liar, all of them are! They trick you, even Sheena and Henry could tell you that!"

"They're not here now," I reminded him sadly, "we are the rulers now, we make our own choices. There will never be peace, Frendall, because you will always want them to be gone." I opened the castle door, walking past the rows of houses with Rob at my side.

"Wait," called Frendall behind us, his voice trailing over the wind. We continued to the cabin door and opening it, walked inside. At first we saw nothing but finally, there in a dark corner sat King Monster all alone.

"Go away," he growled, his eyes burning red. We shook with fright.

"I am evil, I tricked you, now leave!" Rob turned towards the door.

"I don't believe you," I called over his growl, "you aren't evil, you're not!" He sneered and hissed. I went towards him, taking his clawed hand in mine and a reluctant Rob did the same.

"I don't care what Frendall says," I explained, "I trust you. We know that you wouldn't do anything to harm the fairies. Please don't trap yourself in this cabin; we already had to say goodbye to Sheena and Henry, I don't want to lose you too." His eyes came back to their normal green irises and his hands wrapped around ours.

"I won't," he promised, "I was being honest. I really do need the crystal."

"I believe you," I replied, "but we can't give it to you. I'm sorry, it's too precious." Rob nodded and King Monster hung his head. Finally we decided to leave him to his thoughts. We began to walk out the door.

"And," he added, causing us to pause before we left, "I guess I'm not so evil after all." At his words, my attention turned towards the little door in the cabin wall, encased in a glow all around its edges.

"What's in there," Rob asked and I realized that he had seen it also. King Monster jumped from his chair, thrusting the edge of his cape over it, concealing it within its folds.

"Nothing," he snarled.

"Is it a crystal like the rainbow one," I asked. He shook his head.

"No, and it is none of your concern!"

"But why," I questioned him, "why don't you tell us? What are you hiding?"

"It must remain hidden," he explained quickly, "it has always been hidden and it must always be hidden."

"But what is it," Rob pried, "what do you have behind that door?" King Monster looked over us carefully, his eyes slowly beginning to glisten with gathering tears. When he spoke his voice wavered, tinged with sadness.

"Everything."

Maybe it was; he guarded it like it was everything and spoke with sincerity in his voice. What was 'everything' to a monster? Power, maybe. Maybe behind this door was ultimate, unlimited power and all that he needed to take over everything was the Rainbow Crystal. After all, hadn't he said it was more precious to him than it was to us? But soon I remembered the winter celebration and our newly found friendship. Why ruin it with assumptions? So I pushed the thought from my mind and decided, once more, to believe him.

"I have but one more request," he explained, breaking me from my thoughts, "the monsters wish to set up shops in Fairyland. You once promised that if all went well, you would provide them with these. Are you willing to stay true to your word?" Rob and I agreed. Everything was going well and we were planning construction in the spring anyway. With the agreement made, we left feeling good about our decision. We stopped alongside the row of stores all pinched together. Where would the monster's businesses go? Everything was already so settled that there would not be room for them.

"A shop for Cookstone's stonework," Rob mumbled, thinking aloud, "a blacksmith shop, a theatre, a doctor's office and one willing to work in the existing bakery."

"Four more shops," I concluded in dismay, "but we gave them our word! How are we going to stay true to it?" Rob explained that the only possibility would be to extend the land out further and tuck them in behind. Extend the land, I wondered, how? Stretch it by magic to make it larger? We couldn't, it was just a patch of grass and then… the trees. Oh no. My sickening feeling returned. Not the trees! I watched them towering like beautiful giants and saw Rob staring at them, wishing them down in his mind.

"We could use them," he said suddenly, "to make more land and build the shops out of wood. Just a couple more, just two more." Two more? Two more would be enough to build four shops? Two small ones, just two more, just two? His words circled around in my head. Then we'd stop, right? Then no more would have to come down! It was just two and we'd only taken two for the paths. Ok, just four, but everyone cuts down trees, don't they?

'No', a voice within me cried, 'you can't! You mustn't! The forest; Kay, think of the land! Even two is a loss, where will it end?' I didn't know. All I knew was that it wouldn't happen until spring. Spring, when Fairyland would become new again and beautiful, and I would take delight in the season. I didn't have to worry, not until spring and spring was far away. Winter was upon the land now like a frigid blanket, sleeping a long nap until the warm season would come upon it again. Spring was only a far off memory buried beneath the snow. It would be a long time until it returned, wouldn't it?

CHAPTER THREE

A flower had bloomed. Fairyland was in a hustle as all of its inhabitants rushed around finding other little blue, pink, purple and yellow flowers.

"What is this," I asked to no one in particular.

"Spring," Frendall replied, coming up beside Rob and I who stood in the melting snow.

"What," I cried, "but it was just the beginning of winter, and now it's already over?!" Frendall nodded.

"Of course. Winter in Fairyland moves very quickly, it only lasts a long time in Monsterland." The monsters began pouring from their houses in amazement at the sight, bending down and gently stroking the icy petals. Even King Monster seemed cheerful, skipping about and uncovering his roses, rediscovering them as though they were new gifts. Rob glanced at me, smirking, and I could tell what he was thinking.

"My friends," he announced, addressing the monsters, and every head turned towards him, "we will build shops for you so that you can earn a living in Fairyland, according to our promise when you first came."

The monsters cheered, flailing their arms in the air. Soon they had taken up their axes and saws once more, rushing to the stretch of trees eager to begin work. The slush sprayed up around their feet as they walked with heavy steps. I stayed among the fairies admiring the blooms, while over the fairy shops I could see the treetops swaying and falling in harmony with the 'thwack' of tools burrowing into their trunks. I looked away, swallowing a lump rising in my throat. The fairies noticed too, giving me a sorrowful look. I could only look back in dismay.

"You don't have to cut them down, Kay," Frendall whispered apologetically, "you are the Queen, you can make a difference. You have a choice." I took his words into consideration.

"It's only two," I responded, looking up at him. His face showed worry and he shook his head sadly.

"By the looks of things," he commented, "it's far more than two."

"What," I exclaimed, rising from my stooped position. I ran around the row of fairy stores until I found myself standing in a new clearing with a backdrop of trees, appearing sparse, with many grey, barren stumps upon the ground. A pile of massive logs had been stacked in rows with enough rings that I knew they were nearly ancient.

"No," I screamed, "stop! Why didn't you listen? You were only supposed to cut down two!" The monsters turned towards me in confusion.

"Rob told us to take all of these down," they explained. I watched Rob approaching me. He set his eyes upon me, taking on a very serious look, his face becoming pale.

"You," I cried, "you lied!" No more words came out, I was too shocked to speak and Rob looked away with guilt. I turned and started to walk back down the path that led to the castle when I realized that King Monster was still in his cabin. I ran to the front door and knocked.

"King Monster," I cried breathlessly, "you've got to stop them! You have to bring these trees back to life!" He opened the door.

"I can't," he told me, "I'm sorry."

"But you brought a rose to life once, remember," I argued frantically, "why can't you?!"

"I can bring only a few things to life, but these trees are ancient and I cannot restore hundreds of years. Once they are gone, they are gone forever."

"I didn't know," I bawled, "I didn't know!" King Monster pulled the edge of his white cape into his claws and dabbed glistening tears on my face. The fabric felt like fine silk against my skin. His other hand fastened itself over his ear.

"Don't cry, Kay," he assured me, "I can't stand to see you cry and my ears can't stand to hear you." I laughed lightly at his comment.

"You may come in," he ushered, "if you wish, and we will talk."

I took his offer and once more stepped into the quaint structure, taking a seat at the table. The Book of Monsters sat in front of me and I eyed it in wonder.

"Could I look at this," I asked, pointing to it. He nodded.

"Yes, but it will not open because it knows that a fairy holds it," he answered.

I took it into my arms. The weight was the same as the Book of Fairies and the cover was smooth. I traced over the spine, coming upon a groove. It was a hole, a keyhole.

"What's this," I asked. King Monster shrugged.

"I don't know," he answered, "I've never found a key and I don't know what it would open." Hmm, I wondered. I gazed at it, a fuzzy memory coming to my mind. Hadn't I seen a key somewhere, a little golden key on a red ribbon? Maybe not, maybe I had just imagined it. How was I to know?

"Who wrote the Book of Monsters," I asked and he concentrated on me.

"I don't know," he gruffly explained. I was surprised, wouldn't the book have told him? Wouldn't someone know? He was the King, believing in some book by some unknown author?

"Do you have another name," I asked and he looked at me quickly.

"You know," I continued, "like me. You could call me 'Queen fairy' but that's not my name, it's my title. My name is Kay."

"No," he answered quickly, "I don't have another name." Yet he stumbled through his thoughts and somehow I began to wonder if he really had been given a name.

"But before you were King," I questioned, interested now, "what did they call you before you came into power?"

"Just 'monster'," he answered, "many monsters do not have a name. They are named once they have a title. Cookstone is called Cookstone because he cooks stone." I giggled, it sounded like a tongue twister! Even he smiled.

"That's kind of sad," I replied, "to not have a proper name." He nodded in agreement.

"Yes, but names are not important to monsters," he explained, "we are all the same; equals, nothing divides one from another." It was a comforting thought. Soon I decided to leave, thanking him for his kindness. He stood at the doorway and watched me venture back to the castle, waving goodbye. It wouldn't be long before I saw him again. Rob entered awhile later looking apologetic.

"I'm sorry Kay," he spoke, "we needed more trees, but we're done now. We won't cut anymore down, I promise." I remained silent until at last he walked away.

That evening I sat awake as I had so many nights before, in a chair in the living room, watching the glow being taken from the houses one by one. The emptiness of the trees was evident on the horizon. Suddenly, a light came on in the cabin. I watched it pierce through the night, shadowed by King Monster's silhouette. The door flew open and I watched him run out into the night.

"Rob," I instinctively called and he ran to my side in alarm. The King came to the castle door, knocking.

"Come quickly," he hollered excitedly as we opened the door, so we followed him to the cabin with haste. Stepping into the warmth of the cabin we gasped to find a small monster tucked into the corner. He was a baby, like a little miniature of King Monster himself, with the same scaly red skin and shiny black horns. He grinned a full, sharp-toothed smile and reached out his clawed hands helplessly. King Monster stood beside him, beaming.

"He has come from the rose, the sharp thorn of it," he explained, "and I have decided to take him in and raise him as my own." Rob and I approached him excitedly.

"Wow," Rob exclaimed, "how exciting! Wonderful!" I stooped down and lifted him into my arms, cradling the infant close to me. He stared up at me with sapphire blue eyes and gurgled, wriggling enough that I had to hold him tighter. As he moved his hand suddenly, the claws dug into my arm, leaving little pink scratches.

"Ouch," I cried, nearly dropping him. He giggled. Looking down at the small creature I saw an edge of fabric tucked around his back. It was a cape, and as I pulled it into view, horror struck me.

"It's black," I sputtered out loud, "so deeply black that even the night cannot match its colour!" I became frantic, thrusting him into King Monster's arms, fearful to touch him. It startled the baby and he began to cry.

"Oh," I cooed sadly, "I'm sorry, I didn't mean to startle him. It was the cape, the colour scared me." King Monster understood.

"It's fine Kay," he told me softly, "that is what happened when I was born. They feared me because my white cape was different." 'But it's the dreams' I wanted to tell him, 'the nightmares'. It had to be him, didn't it; same monster, same cape?

"What is his name," Rob asked, now taking the little one upon his lap as he sat in a chair by the table.

"He is my son," King Monster figured, "so, from this moment forth, he shall be known as 'King Monster's Son'." He looked down upon him proudly.

"Some day when I am old he will take my place as King."

Rob rocked him slowly and soon King Monster's Son fell into a peaceful sleep. I watched his eyes gently close and his breathing become slow and steady. Soon my fears left me. The little one was so beautiful and peaceful, how could he do any harm? With the guidance and care of King Monster he would grow to be kind and caring like his father. Already I was growing fond of him; maybe my dreams were just silly nightmares, it couldn't be him. Rob handed the baby back to King Monster who made a cradle appear out of gnarled roots. He set him in gently as Rob and I crept out the door, careful not to wake the infant. We wandered back past the houses, now glowing with light, as the fairies learned of the event and excited voices spread the news of the Prince.

"Now that Fairyland's expanding," Rob explained as we walked, "and the monsters are here, we should have a way to communicate other than by speaking alone, a way to proclaim the news. Remember when we went back in time to see King Monster as a baby? They had a newspaper back then, so why don't we make a newspaper now?" I agreed, a paper would be a great way to spread the news and document events!

So we sat at the kitchen table into the wee hours of the morning planning a story and making many copies to hand out. Finally, once the sun had risen and everyone began to trickle out of their houses we ventured out, handing a letter to everyone we met.

'A Prince Is Born', the headline read in bold letters at the top, with the story of the arrival of King Monster's Son beneath it. Fairies and Monsters read it eagerly, lining up at the cabin door to see him. We watched as more monsters travelled in from Monsterland as well. It was official; Fairyland would have a newspaper. Everyone enjoyed having their own copy of the event, so we put the monster who was working at the Fairyland bakery in charge. In the mornings he would create and hand out papers, and in the afternoons he would work in the bakery. He accepted the job happily.

After the excitement had died down I went back to the castle, up the grand staircase and to my room. Sunlight streamed in through the curtains and onto my face as I laid down to take a nap. My sleep was soon disturbed; over and over the image played of the black cape, that crazy black cape! I could not seem to escape the thought. Opening my eyes I looked at the scratches on my arm, fading now, barely visible. An accident, perhaps, by a baby who didn't know any better? Or maybe he was plotting against all of us already, seeming innocent when really he was secretly planning to take over? I decided to befriend King Monster's Son but I would be cautious, just incase.

§

Thunder roared across the sky with sparks of lightning jumping across the clouds. The snow had melted away and as the rain came down, the road became muddy and flooded. Fairies trudged through the slop, staining their clothes and ruining their shoes. As I walked through the water it flooded between the rose petals of my shoes and pulled them apart. I watched them float away on a little stream as I stood in bare feet watching the bottom of my dress turn brown.

Crack! The ground shook and the fairies ran inside their houses. The only ones who remained outside were a couple of scale skins holding soggy pieces of paper, shouting, 'get your newspapers here'. I took one, watching the ink bleed together, ruining it. All that remained was the headline, 'Severe Weather Hits Fairyland'. Suddenly the mud gurgled up, bubbling and rising to form a figure. I screamed until I heard a familiar laugh. It was Cookstone! He flowed through the mud, raising his head up sometimes with only the gap of his eyes and mouth showing before he disappeared once more into the swirling pool. He enjoyed the rainy weather! I watched him swim away until I could see him no more. Frendall called to us and we rushed inside where it was warm. The windows looked like waterfalls as the rain slipped down, blurring the outside world. I smoothed the newspaper out on the table, pointing to the headline.

"Is this weather normal," I asked Frendall with concern. He shrugged his shoulders.

"It storms sometimes in the spring," he answered, "so I guess that it is normal." But by how his forehead wrinkled and he bit his bottom lip nervously, somehow I guessed that it wasn't. The wind whipped wildly. I heard a tapping from outside, sounding quiet at first, then becoming louder until it began banging and slamming.

"What is that," I called above the sound, watching white spheres knocking on the windows.

"Hail," Frendall cried, backing away and pulling Rob and I into the middle of the room with him.

"Ok," he sputtered, "*this* is not normal!" His eyes began to dart from window to window, keeping time with the twiddling of his fingers.

"Just try to remain calm," he bellowed, his voice rising higher with every word.

"Why is this happening," Rob questioned frantically.

"I don't know," Frendall cried out quickly, making the sentence sound like one word rather than three. He shook with fear and his face went ghostly white as the castle grew darker. Panic had set in. The book, I suddenly remembered, the Book of Fairies could tell us what was happening! I ran up the stairs to the dresser and snatched it, running out of my bedroom as I heard the window crack behind me.

"Hurry," a voice called from downstairs and I ran faster, nearly tripping over myself.

"Why is this happening," I asked the book. It didn't move.

"Come on," I urged it, tapping the cover, trying to get it to tell me. The little key on the side spun as I shook it, desperate to pry it open. What if the diamonds came crashing down on the outside of the castle? What if they shattered into millions of little slivers? What if the castle itself, the entire building, came crashing down? What if…

It stopped. As quickly as it began it ended and the sun came through the windows, making the little drops of rain sparkle. We ran outside. Above us a rainbow had formed, moving and flowing across the blue sky like a ribbon. Frozen white marbles of ice lined the ground and rested on the windowsills beneath the cracked panes of glass. There was damage to the houses, mostly the windows, but also to the little shops. Water trickled down the rooftops and poured out of the eves as everything became strangely still and silent. There he was, the only living being outside, clapping his hands and joyfully playing in the ice. King Monster's Son looked up at us, smiling mischievously as though he were guilty. Soon King Monster came out of the cabin, scooping him up into his arms.

"What, why," I could hardly collect my thoughts.

"He went out during the storm, then the sun came out," King Monster exclaimed, "my boy saved us from the storm!" As the fairies and monsters heard the news, stepping outside, they cheered for the baby.

"Storm," King Monster's Son cried joyously, "storm gone!"

Everyone laughed and went forth to admire him. I folded my arms; something didn't make sense here, something didn't add up. The storm, as I'd learned from overhearing conversations, was the kind of storm that was only seen in Monsterland. So, only a monster could have brewed it and if a monster caused it, a monster could stop it.

"Come on Kay," Rob suggested, "let's go thank him!" But I didn't go. I stayed behind, watching the scene from a distance with a bad, sickening feeling rising in me. The black cape swirled around the baby in an unseen breeze. He was growing more already, even from the day before when he was just new.

"How quickly does a monster grow," I asked myself quietly. Frendall heard me.

"About two weeks and he'll be an adult," Frendall answered, walking past me. Two weeks, I thought, that's it? In two weeks he would be grown and become more powerful than he was now.

"Frendall," I gasped, "where are you going?!"

He was heading towards King Monster's Son as though hypnotized and for an instant I feared that he, too, believed that the baby had saved us. Frendall who believed that all monsters were evil, who trusted no one, *he* was going to see the little Prince?! But he didn't, instead, he fetched Rob and brought him back. I sighed in relief.

"I think," Rob explained slowly once he stood before me, "that we need to pave the dirt roads. If we have more weather like this, the flooding will cause the fairies to be caught in the mud."

Already I could see them becoming stuck and pulling hard to walk, and the ground was full of holes, impressions of feet and bits of torn shoes. I agreed with him, we needed to lay down some hard, smooth material, but first we needed to fix the damage caused by the storm.

We walked over the uneven ground, pointing at the windows of the houses and removing the cracks by magic. It was amazing watching them repair before our eyes as though the scene were playing backwards. The monsters repaired their houses and eagerly returned to their shops, finished now like little log cabins, to begin setting up. They made advertisements appear in the windows and large, colourful banners above the entrances to announce the grand opening.

Rob and I ushered everyone onto the grass as we paved the road over with asphalt, the thick smell of tar rising up in the air. We filled everything in simply by moving our hands and making it appear. It dried instantly and when we were finished the monsters and fairies hurried onto it. They had never seen such a material, but were thankful for it.

"What about sidewalks," Rob questioned. It was another good idea, we could have sidewalks running the length of the stores and the houses, so we placed a long stretch of concrete slabs on either side of the road and in front of the monster's shops. King Monster joined in helping us, liking the idea so much that he built the sidewalk into Monsterland, pointing into the distance, making it run all the way to the black castle. An eerie feeling met me watching it and I shivered despite the warmer weather. A sidewalk, hadn't I had a dream once of a sidewalk somewhere and the castle? The castle with points jabbing fiercely out of the walls in all directions. Who had been walking on it, was it really King Monster's Son? What had they been carrying? Something, somewhere…

CHAPTER FOUR

Two weeks passed by very quickly. I watched King Monster's Son go from a helpless baby to a laughing, happy toddler who held his father's hand and followed him wherever he went. I watched him trample the roses by the cabin and saw King Monster's head shaking in disapproval as he made them grow again. I watched him grow to the height of King Monster, becoming a spitting image of him, with the only difference being in the eyes and the cape. He walked among the fairies, ignoring them, growling and speaking in a deep voice like his father.

The only shops that he would enter into were the monster's shops, frequented by the fairies. Nearly every household had stoneware by Cookstone, metal pails and silverware by the blacksmith and herbs to prevent and treat illnesses, given by the doctor. The children would flock to the theatre to watch puppet shows, mostly about the history of the lands, and the bakery was filled with new delicious pastries baked by the monster who worked there. As King Monster's Son passed by he glanced over at Rob and I, locking his gaze upon us, his cold and unfeeling eyes burning into us.

"Rob," I whispered, barely moving my lips incase he could read them, "don't look at him!" I feared that he would come towards us if Rob locked eyes with him.

"What," Rob questioned, "why not? Why can't you accept him? Didn't you tell me that the only way there would be peace is if we rely on each other?" I had believed that and I felt guilty judging him because I'd had a nightmare about a monster. Maybe it wasn't him after all. Maybe another monster would appear, a second one, who had a black cape and it would be that one. King Monster's Son approached us.

"Queen Kay," he addressed me, smiling, his bottom teeth protruding slightly from his lip, "and King Rob, let me formally introduce myself. I am King Monster's Son." He hunched forward slightly in a bow. Rob bowed back and I curtsied.

"Welcome to Fairyland," Rob trilled cheerfully, "welcome to the community! As a friend of King Monster you, his son, are our friend as well."

"Thank you," King Monster's Son replied, then sensing my discomfort added, "am I not your friend also, Kay?"

"Oh, yes, of course," I hurried.

"But you don't trust me?"

I looked away, unable to find the words to say. When I finally looked up again I saw disappointment forming in him. He extended his hand, making a seed appear as King Monster had once done, trying to make it come alive. All that it produced was a barren brown stem lined with thorns.

"Oh," he exclaimed, "my mistake. I'm still learning about my powers." It turned to dust and crumbled in his palm, sifting between his fingers and falling on the ground.

"So, you came from the rose," Rob asked. He nodded, questioning where we had come from. We described the Human World but not to his understanding because he had never seen it.

"Isn't there a way into the Human World from here," King Monster's Son asked, highly interested. Rob nodded.

"Yes, maybe we could show you." I nudged Rob. Open the portal?! Let, of all things, a *monster* look in? Was he crazy?! He seemed to get the point and fell silent. The subject changed.

"You have the Rainbow Crystal," King Monster's Son asked intently at which Rob nodded again and he continued with, "you know, it is of more value to the monsters than it is to the fairies. It would make sense to transfer it to us."

Hadn't King Monster said that once, I thought to myself; 'more precious to me than it is to you, more valuable to all of us, not just yourselves'? The Book of Monsters appeared in King Monster's Son's hand and opening it, he turned it towards us so that we could read the scrollwork. It read, *the Rainbow Crystal holds its greatest value with King Monster.*

"No," I cried, "it can't be! It's ours, the Rainbow Crystal is ours! If it were meant for King Monster he would have had it all along instead of us! It's all lies!" He quickly shut the book and made it disappear, his face looking pinched.

"I'm sorry to have upset you, Kay," he apologized remorsefully, "and I'm sorry to have asked for something that does not belong to me. Perhaps it has been placed with you for a reason, perhaps you are meant to keep it."

"Thanks," I offered gratefully. Maybe he understood us after all. He bid us goodbye, turning before he shut the cabin door. He stared with a confusing look which I did not understand, one mixed with anger and joy which, unfortunately, made light of itself early the next morning.

I awoke early, when the sun had barely touched the horizon, to see monsters moving through the shadows. I could see their silhouettes gathering near the cabin, gathering around King Monster's Son who stood slightly taller than the rest of them. I stepped out into the crisp morning air, hearing faint rustlings and whispering voices. What was happening? What kind of secret meeting was being held? More importantly, where was King Monster? Suddenly I realized that I had not seen him for awhile, a couple of days perhaps, and I searched the horizon frantically, looking for any sign of the white cape in the dim light. At last I caught sight of him inside the cabin, peering out the window in concern. Why wasn't he part of the meeting? Why was he inside alone?

I caught his eye and he gazed at me, lifting a hand to the pane of glass and motioning me away. I stepped back just as King Monster's Son turned his head in my direction and I froze. He would see me any moment! I suddenly remembered the spell of invisibility and used it, feeling myself fading from sight, but he marched forward anyway extending a clawed hand.

"You may be invisible, Kay," he said grimly, "but I can still see you." Fear pulsed through me. How was it possible?!

"Curiosity got the best of you, didn't it," he laughed, "you just had to see what was going on, didn't you? Shouldn't have done that, Kay. Now you're all alone and no one will know what happened to you."

What *happened* to me, what was he talking about?! The sinking feeling met me again as I felt his claws dig into my wings. I winced, struggling against his strength, realizing that I was no longer invisible. He pulled me backwards and I watched the castle moving away from me. He dragged me through the group of monsters who watched helplessly. Cookstone lunged forward trying to help me and with a nod of King Monster's Son's head, he turned him into a statue, into a smooth stone just like the stone he carved.

"Cookstone," I screamed, "no!"

Those were the last words that I spoke before being thrust into the cabin and locked inside. I ran to the window desperately, seeing... myself? I gasped and cupped my hands over my mouth. There I was, standing out in the cold laughing a terrible laugh, but how?! As Kay turned towards me I saw her eyes and discovered that they were blue. But wait, mine were hazel! There was only one person I knew with such deep blue eyes... it was King Monster's Son disguised as me! I ran to the door, kicking and wrenching the knob as I watched myself, like some nightmarish mirror image, walking to the castle door and entering inside.

"No," I screamed, warning Rob, "no, Rob! It's not me! It isn't me!" A hand gently rested on my shoulder.

"He can't hear you, Kay," King Monster explained quietly, "no one can. We're trapped in here until I can find out how to get out."

"Why can't you just open the door," I cried frantically.

"He has locked us in with a particular type of magic," he explained calmly, leafing through the Book of Monsters, "I must find out which type he used and do the opposite to open it." I began to pace back and forth nervously, watching the sky lighting in the pastels of dawn. In the houses the fairies began to stir and with horror I realized that King Monster's Son could do or say anything and the fairies, thinking it was me, would follow the command.

Oh, Cookstone! I watched him standing there, a frozen figure appearing grey and smooth in the sunlight, still with a determined expression on his face. My friend, who had done so much and helped me in so many ways; would he ever talk again, walk again, *live* again even? I buried my face in my hands, walking away. I had failed him. Slowly my ring began to glow and the letters appeared faintly on the bare wall of the cabin; 'it is only temporary. I will only be stone for a day. Are you ok?' I ran to the window joyfully, nodding. I was ok now, knowing that he was.

Surprisingly, the castle door opened and Kay came out alone, changing back into King Monster's Son with every step closer he came. It was too quick; he had barely entered the castle and now he left again, beaming victoriously, passing the cabin and flashing me a cruel smile. That's it, I thought, he just wanted into the castle for a moment and now he was leaving? Where was he going? The hinges of the cabin door creaked open painfully and air flooded in from outside.

"I've got it," King Monster cried happily, "now go, Kay. Run back to the castle, tell everyone the news!" I did. I ran hard, my legs aching and my lungs burning so that when I finally arrived at the castle and was questioned by Rob, I was almost too breathless and startled to answer.

"Kay," he asked seriously, "why did you take the Rainbow Crystal?"

"What," I exclaimed, growing faint, then the horror of the reality set in. That's why King Monster's Son had disguised himself as me, so that he could enter into the castle and take the Rainbow Crystal without being questioned!

"He took it," I whispered under my breath, hardly believing it was that easy for him. It was gone and now we were all doomed! I couldn't believe it; ultimate power in the hands of a monster, a highly evil monster. I had been right all along, he was the one from my nightmare! After telling Rob the whole story, his face grew very pale and he lowered himself into a chair.

"I think," he said slowly, "that it's time to leave."

"Leave," I asked. He nodded.

"Go back to the Human World," he explained further, "because it's all over." I shook my head.

"We can't give up, Rob! We have to follow him and get it back!"

"Where did he go," Rob asked. I thought about it for a moment, I had seen him walk behind the cabin and behind the cabin was... Monsterland. I ran up the flight of stairs to a high window and gazed out. Sure enough, I saw the black cape moving slowly towards the distant castle. I ran back downstairs to a wide-eyed Rob.

"Monsterland," I said quietly, my voice sinking.

"We can't follow him," Rob cried frantically, "we're doomed!" It was true that we were doomed. King Monster's Son had outsmarted us and now that he was in Monsterland, he had escaped.

"No," I said, suddenly determined, "Sheena told me once that a fairy can enter into Monsterland. It will be dangerous but we have to, the fate of Fairyland depends upon it." Rob was bewildered.

"It's already too late," he told me, "he won." I crossed my arms.

"The day a monster wins is the day I give up," I told Rob, "and I will never give up."

"I'm going into Monsterland, are you coming with me or not," I concluded. There was a bang and we both turned our heads quickly. Frendall had returned from the store and dropped the shopping bag. He stared at me, obviously having heard my statement, appearing very concerned and shocked. After we explained the situation he hid his face in his arms and shook his head.

"Rob's right, Kay," he explained sadly, "it's over. I can't blame you if you want to leave, you should. Go back to the Human World, you'll be safe there. This is the end and you can't follow him. There's no use in risking yourselves."

"But nothing could happen to us, remember," I said, "fairies have eternal life." Frendall shook his head.

"Only by the power of the crystal. Now he could destroy us all, we're defenseless! If you, the most powerful fairies in Fairyland go into Monsterland, he would take your powers and become so powerful that his magic would be unlimited!"

"Then why don't we give all of our power to the fairies," I suggested, "so that they can protect themselves while we go after him?" Frendall shook his head again.

"You would go into Monsterland," he assessed the situation, "with no power, no protection; like humans, but even worse off. You'll never see Fairyland again, you'll never see the Human World again. You would spend forever in Monsterland as prisoners!" I looked out the window at the fairies, my people, all lost, alone and afraid. I felt their pain, I understood what it was like to lose almost everything, but not quite everything. There was still hope and if only for that, there was a chance.

"Ok," I took a deep breath and finally said, "I'm willing to do it." Frendall rose to his feet at my statement with a small smile forming on his face.

"It's you isn't it," he half whispered and I strained my ears to hear him, "you're the one with the pure heart that the Book foretold of. You can save us." We gazed at each other until, at last, he nodded.

"Then go," he spoke confidently, "and good luck." He took my hands into his and squeezed them, and for the first time I saw his eyes fill with tears. Rob cautiously followed behind me.

"I don't have a good feeling about this," Rob sighed, talking to me, "but I will go because you are my friend and I can't let you go alone." I thanked him with sincerity. We walked past the houses to the cabin. I threw my arms around Cookstone, the stone bitterly cold against my skin.

"Goodbye, friend," I said quietly, then turning away, we entered into the cabin and told King Monster the bad news. He sat for a long while silently, staring into the distance deep in thought.

"You would sacrifice all of that for the fairies," he asked when he finally spoke and he turned his eyes up towards me. I nodded. Then, as Frendall had done, King Monster began to cry, sobbing and dabbing his eyes.

"That means everything to me," he choked out and I was confused. It meant everything to *him*? But he was a monster, why did the fairies mean so much? He looked up triumphantly with hope in his eyes.

"You are the one, aren't you? The pure heart, yes, it makes sense now!"

"What do you mean," I questioned. Frendall had told me the same thing.

"A fairy cannot open the Book of Monsters," he said, "but the Book tells of a fairy, one pure of heart, who will sacrifice everything to save the land. They will not only care about the fairies but will hold a place in their heart for the monsters as well. The Book will open when held by the pure of heart." I listened carefully and shook my head.

"No," I said simply, "I held it the other day and it didn't move."

"But you didn't tell it to open," he argued, pressing it into my hands. I looked down at it, stuck shut, unwilling to open.

"Open," I said with uncertainty. It didn't move.

"See," I said, "it's probably Rob."

"It's you," he insisted, "but it won't open because you have to believe in yourself. You have to know who you are, do you know who you are?" I looked at the Book again.

"Yes," I said confidently, "yes I do and I believe in myself. I believe that I can do anything if I put my mind to it. Open." My face felt the fanning of air as the pages of the Book of Monsters sprang to life, much to my surprise.

"Take it," King Monster explained, "it will guide you." I ran to him and hugged him. He wrapped his arms around me and I could feel warm tears landing on my shoulder.

"I'll see you when you return," he said happily. I nodded once more.

"I will return, I promise." But I couldn't promise anything, I knew. I couldn't promise that I'd ever return.

"Here, Rob." He handed Rob a pendant, red and shiny like a hologram.

"If you need me," King Monster explained, "just speak to the pendant and the message will arrive back to me." I felt safer knowing that we had a way to communicate with him.

"And here, Kay," he told me, removing the cape from his back, "wear this and the monsters will think that you are the King. Hide your face and speak in a deep, gruff voice." I pulled the cape around my shoulders, hiding my wings in its deep folds. We both thanked him and left.

"Wait," he called, stepping outside, "I will lift the force field which will drive you out, so that you may enter. After that, you're on your own." We nodded.

"Ready," Rob asked, and we looked at each other.

"Ready," I answered. We turned towards the castle and the houses, letting the magic flow from us until we had covered the land. The monsters were included, who still remained at peace with the fairies, until everything was closed in an invisible dome. We stood, as Frendall said, like powerless humans with wings. Then, with uncertain step, we crossed the border and entered into Monsterland.

CHAPTER FIVE

The eerie darkness loomed over us as we moved forward into the strange shadows.

"Rob," I spoke in barely a whisper, and suddenly I could nearly feel hundreds of ears listening. Dead silence pressed into our ears and as we walked along slowly, the blades of frozen grass snapped under our feet, the noise bouncing off of everything. I shivered, wrapping the thin cape tighter around my shoulders, realizing that our only warmth came from the fur coats that Henry had given to us when we first came to Fairyland. I was glad that we had remembered to wear them but even so, the cold cut through us. We had no ability to become invisible, everything and everyone could see us in plain view. I gulped.

"Yeah," Rob asked shakily, whispering as I had. I looked into his brown eyes mirroring the same fear that I felt.

"I'm afraid," I concluded. He nodded, answering, "yeah, me too."

We entered the woods cautiously. It was pitch black, the treetops nearly shutting out the grey sky and only little specks of light here and there peeked through the branches. Rob's pendant lit up, spreading red light illuminating the forest floor, creeping around the rocks and skidding off of slimy leaves littering the ground. Sheena had told me once about entering Monsterland, what had she said? 'A curse surrounds Monsterland,' she had told me, 'a curse drives you out. The first curse is a force'. We had made it through the first curse because King Monster had lifted it.

"Let's take the sidewalk," Rob suggested, pointing out between the branches to the faintly seen path of concrete slabs, but I knew that we'd be in unlimited view if we took the sidewalk. As dangerous as it seemed, the woods did give us shelter and a place to hide. Sheena had explained that the only way to enter was 'on the outside, deep into the forest where strange and dangerous creatures live'. We would fly for three days and… but wait! We couldn't fly, we had to go by foot. Now we couldn't escape if we were caught because we were trapped on the ground. Slowly, as the bleak reality set in, I too began to lose hope.

"I don't like this, Kay," Rob commented quietly, "it's too quiet."

I gazed at the treetops. It was so silent, so very silent that I wished for a noise, some type of sound, anything! The trees! I turned around. The trees were blocking our path, they hadn't been there before. We couldn't go back now and as I turned to face forward again, I saw the tall thistles planted in rows that would not let us out of the border of the woods. We were trapped! Somehow the scene was becoming all too familiar. We had been in these woods a long time ago, when we first came, before we found Fairyland. Rob remembered them, I could tell by the look of recognition coming upon his face. Now the thistles bent and bowed slightly, coated in thin layers of snow and ice.

I grasped the Book of Monsters tightly, a pressing question repeating in my mind. If the cabin were in the centre of Fairyland Old when Fairyland used to be the entire land, then why did it take three days to arrive at the Monsterland castle from the cabin, but only a few minutes to arrive at the cabin from the Fairyland castle? I asked the Book this and when it opened and I read the words printed there in the dim light, I began to shiver with fear; *the black castle moves further away as you near it. It is a mirage and part of the curse. It takes three days to arrive in hopes that the monsters can rid of you in that time, for you are considered an enemy.* Showing Rob, we stood in silence for a moment staring at the page, reading it over and over, hardly believing it.

"It's just three days," I spoke aloud, assuring myself more than him, "we can do it. Just one step at a time."

But three days in Monsterland might as well have been forever and something inside of me whispered 'we'll never make it'. We entered into a patch of evergreens densely meshed with entangled branches. Even the thick boughs and deep green hues made it feel as though we were sinking further into darkness. Little quick sighs could be heard, sending spirals of steam up in front of my face. My own breath was beginning to frighten me! We wandered further, feeling the weight of the suspense rising. Something was in the woods, I could sense it following us, watching our every move, ready to strike.

"Fairy," the rumbled voice rocketed through the afternoon, piercing into my ears. Rob began to run blindly and I followed him, hearing the quickening feet patter behind us.

"Capture him, don't let him get away," the monster yelled and as I turned to face our captor, I realized that he was talking to me.

"Trespasser," he cried, "King Monster, seize him!" I stopped, feeling the chill in the air tingling the inside of my nose. He thought that I was King Monster!

"He is my prisoner," I lowered my voice to a growl, hiding my head and grasping onto Rob's arm, "I am taking him to the castle."

The branches were more sparse here and the forest was now filled with grey light, a welcomed change from the darkness. The monster eyed me suspiciously, I could tell behind the mask of the white cape. He was a young scale skin with slightly shorter horns and a deep pink cape. Not a child, somewhat older, but not yet an adult. He noticed my hair. A strand peeked out and I quickly tucked it away behind my ear, but it was too late. His eyes opened wide.

"You're a fairy too," he gawked, then began to yell again, "over here! Fairies!" I stood up straight.

"Please," I begged him, "don't! I have the approval of King Monster to be here, see? This is his cape and I have the Book of Monsters." He fell silent for a moment, then continued, "trespassers, fairies, get them!"

The entire forest came alive with noise, bustling and roaring, and heavy breathing. It was too late; we had been discovered! Rob and I exchanged a helpless glance.

"Bizz-buzz," I called in despair. At once I heard shrieks of pain and the monsters in view covered their ears in agony.

"Run," I yelled, and Rob and I raced blindly through the trees hearing heavy feet trailing after us in all directions, cutting through the snow.

"Bizz-buzz," we yelled breathlessly over and over. It was our only defense, I realized, the best way to slow them down and our only chance to escape. But even as we hurried along, we realized that all they had to do was follow our footprints. They were on our trail, how many of them was uncertain, and I cringed as I heard their forced breathing and wheezing at my back, not too far away. They were easily gaining on us! So we would just run on and on, exhausting ourselves from effort, screaming 'bizz-buzz' until we collapsed and were taken as prisoners? It was useless, there was nothing we could do. We were powerless, unable to fly, unable to do anything. At any time the monsters could use their magic against us! I felt the energy draining from me quickly and as I gasped for air, the cold filled my lungs and I couldn't catch my breath at all. At last the chase ended as my foot hit something hard and I stumbled to the frigid ground. I rolled onto my back and shut my eyes, thankful that the pounding of my heart drowned out the noise of the outside world. I did not want to see or hear what would become of us.

I laid there for awhile until I began to feel cold prickles on my face. Cautiously I reached up and brushed it. Realizing that it was snow, I opened my eyes and let the image fade in. It fell towards me, drifting over my face in flakes appearing as white blades. I lifted myself up and stood to find Rob leaning over the red pendant, talking to it. I heard the faint murmuring of King Monster's reply coming back to him. He looked up at me with a pale face.

"They just ran away, Kay," he told me, "I don't know why."

I looked behind us at the drifting wisps covering our tracks. The wind was picking up and the flakes were slanting towards us. Very slowly, so slowly that we hardly noticed, the temperature began dropping dangerously low. I wrapped the thin cape tighter, pulling it across my cheeks, burying my hands in its folds. The sky turned burnt black, we could see bits of it in breaks and spaces beyond the overhang of twisted grey branches above us. Was it night? It felt as though it had only been a couple of hours but perhaps the passing of time was different here.

As I continued to watch the ominous clouds towering, building and merging, I felt the pit of my stomach turning. It wasn't evening; these were snow clouds, storm clouds, twisting clouds. I blinked and focused harder, gazing further. They were rotating slowly at the bottom, growing longer, being sucked down by some invisible force. They were tornadoes, but how?! It was winter so it couldn't be possible!

"Rob, Rob, Rob," I repeated frantically, trying to think, running the words through my head and trying to get them out of my mouth; twister, vortex, tornado! The whistle in our ears became deafening, shrieking like a broken train. Ahead of us a giant spinning wall raged through the forest, snapping thick trees in half like simple toothpicks, uprooting others violently with sickening wrenches. It came barrelling towards us with a monstrous roar.

"We have to find a hollow," I screamed, and the Book of Monsters opened to reveal a small map. There was a dip at the bottom of a steep hill nearby, but we would have to venture even deeper into the woods. I raced towards it and Rob followed, bewildered. We struggled forward against the suction ripping at us, threatening to pull us back into the swirling depths. We mounted the hill and when we knew that we had reached the peak we jumped, hitting the hard ground and rolling over and over, watching up and down blend dizzyingly together, spinning and spinning! Suddenly, everything stopped. I regained my senses and listened carefully to nothing more than the shaken snow and ice sliding off of the branches and shattering. It was over and we were ok.

"Bizz-buzz," I asked and there was no answer. We were safe and our tracks had filled in so no one could follow us. The snow stopped just as quickly as it had begun. Rob and I sighed in relief, chuckling lightly to ease the tension.

"You ok," he asked. I nodded, the event that had just occurred playing over in my head. We had almost been taken by it, I realized, we would have been sucked up into the funnel if it weren't for this hill.

"I think that was a weak one," Rob considered, not willing to call it a tornado and I agreed. Had it been stronger, we would not have been able to even begin to run. I had a feeling that we had been very lucky to escape it. We remained on the side of the hill for quite awhile waiting for the sky to appear calm before travelling further. Rob explained that when he had spoken to King Monster earlier through the pendant, he had advised us to stay low and wait out any storm that came our way. His suggestion had come just in time.

We stayed there through the night taking turns staying awake to watch for enemies, but even when it was my turn to sleep I struggled to shut my eyes. Every minute I could feel some hidden gaze upon me, some invisible creature waiting to pounce, lurking in the shadows. I was just waiting for Rob to yell and shake me from my dreams. So I was awake nearly all night staring fearfully in all directions, scaring myself more than being startled by anything else. Finally after an evening stretching on forever, the sky took on the pale greys of morning and we entered into our second day.

As we came around the hill, we realized the extent of the damage from the day before. Trees laid flat on the forest floor with massive roots spiralling out of the trunks. Some were broken in half painfully with sharp points of wood sticking out here and there. Large limbs lay mingled and interwoven with a soggy pile of strewn thistles wilting over them. The torn trees had made an opening leading to the main clearing. I looked out and in the distance I could see that the sidewalk had blown clear. We were on the right path! The newly formed clearing allowed us to see into the distance. The black castle came into view, seeming further away than ever.

I moved forward uncomfortably, my legs aching and my clothes frozen stiff. I was so bitterly cold that I could not speak because of the chattering of my teeth. We went on further and as the day dragged on, we began watching branches dripping and deepening in colour from the warming air. The temperature had begun to rise and I was thankful for the warmth. The slush gathered around our feet in pools yet still the deep drifts remained solid.

Suddenly the drifts began to move as I watched in surprise. Were they supposed to do that? Rob watched in fascination as they rose and then sank flat until we would never know that they had been there at all. They would reappear right beside us one moment later, just to sink and disappear again. I came to the horrifying conclusion watching them rise and fall around us, more and more beginning to form, that they were not drifts at all. Something was beneath the snow, many things actually, and they were alive. A large head emerged with beady eyes and a flicking tongue; it was a giant white snake directly in front of Rob!

"Rob," I gasped in barely a whisper, "don't move! Hold still!" He shook, trying desperately not to move as the snake wound around his feet and regarded him curiously. He grasped the pendant in one swift movement and it took notice of the action.

"King Monster," Rob hissed between closed teeth, "there are snakes here! What do we do?!"

Snakes, I thought, but I had only seen one! Another curled around me and I watched my helpless reflection in its eyes. The tongue flicked, causing me to grow nervous. As a third emerged my nervousness turned to panic. King Monster didn't respond. We were trapped! They slithered smoothly back and forth with their icy scales shining, met with small hisses like vibrations from deep within them.

They looked at each other, communicating somehow in some secret language. They rose and nearly came to the height of our faces, still with much of them buried beneath the snow. How large were they?! I barely dared to breathe. One was right in front of me, I could almost reach out and touch him. I did; very slowly and carefully I raised my arm, extending it, clamping my hand over his head… I caught a handful of snow and the remainder of him fell in a blanket of soft flakes and was carried away in the breeze. I ran and did the same to the two others until it was as though they had never existed in the first place.

"They were a mirage," I exclaimed as Rob turned towards me, "a trick. They weren't real!"

"How did you know," he asked. I shrugged, answering, "the tip of the nose was dripping as though it were melted. I knew from its appearance that it was made of snow."

"Right," Rob agreed, still shaken. We walked on for most of the day, becoming weak. We had gone over a day without food and I realized fearfully that we had brought none with us, and no water. How were we so unprepared?! I had been so preoccupied with the danger of our journey that I had overlooked my own hunger and thirst.

"Who dares to trespass on monster territory," a deep grumbling voice hollered and we saw a mud monster step out into our path. His face grew tight with anger and he growled.

"I'm-I'm Rob," Rob stammered, then his attention turned to me. I was so weak and afraid that I tried to keep my voice steady as I spoke to him.

"I am Kay," I announced, "I have permission from the King to enter and travel through Monsterland. I have the Book of Monsters and his cape." The mud monster took this into consideration for a moment, then his grim face returned.

"I do not believe you," he stated, spreading his arms wide and coming towards us with menacing steps. I held my hand to my cheek in fear. He caught sight of my hand and his arms dropped to his sides.

"What is that," he asked out of curiosity now. I looked upon it, holding it in the air for him to see.

"It is my hand," I answered nervously. He shook his head.

"No," he corrected, "what is upon your hand?"

"A- a ring," I told him. He nodded, squinting to see it more clearly.

"Fine craftsmanship," he commented and I wondered why we were out here in the forest discussing rings with a monster, "made by my kind, a mud monster." I nodded.

"Cookstone," I explained, calming slightly. He took on a look of recognition and his face softened. He came to me and took my hand in his, the mud was cool and moist beneath my palm.

"It is a friendship ring," he explained, adding, "you are a friend of Cookstone." I nodded in agreement again. He stepped back.

"What are you two doing in these woods?"

We explained our situation and he listened carefully, shaking his head in dismay.

"It is very dangerous here," he told us, "and already you look starved."

"We have no food," I commented regretfully. He opened his hands and they were full of dried nuts, seeds and fruit.

"Not much," he explained, "but used sparingly, they will last."

We took it thankfully, tucking the morsels into our pockets. He offered both of us a large canteen brimming with clean water which we hung over our shoulders. Finally, with a quiet farewell, he wandered away until we lost sight of him. We ate and drank joyously, eager for more but we had to save some for later. It was another stroke of luck, I realized, what were the chances that we would meet a mud monster who knew Cookstone and could help us? Perhaps the monsters were not so evil after all.

"Wonderful," Rob trilled as we continued along, "now we have food and-" He screamed as he broke through the ice. I watched in stunned horror as he sank into freezing, rushing water up to his shoulders.

"Rob," I screamed, running to the edge of the melting ice. We had reached some sort of body of water and we hadn't known of its presence under the drifts until he took a step and plunged in. I leaned down and extended my hand further, further, setting the Book of Monsters at my feet. He reached towards me, fighting against the current but I couldn't grip his hand. He drifted a little ways.

"No," I cried, "please Rob, no!" He caught the edge of the ice on the other side of the bank and pulled himself up, drenched and dripping. He shot me a crazed glance.

I was moving. The ice beneath me split, swaying back and forth, threatening to tip. I was stranded on a small frozen island, intense fear setting into me. Cautiously I dropped to my stomach, rowing fiercely with my arms. The water numbed my skin as I fought the current. Oh please, I silently begged, please let me make it to the other side! I struggled as the water lapped over me. For an instant I would sink under, then be thrust up again until my clothes were soaked as well. Once more I went down then… it crashed. The block shook and I came to rest at Rob's feet.

I pulled the Book of Monsters out from under me and Rob tugged me over beside him. Quickly we both fled away to solid land and collapsed by the trunk of a great tree, breathless and shivering. Night was falling. When we had gathered our strength we searched for branches, stacking them in a tidy pile. I read a spell from the Book of Monsters and the sticks burst into flames. Although we had no powers, I realized, the Book's words were powerful enough that when spoken, they had created fire. Rumble. I looked up at the sky. It was beginning to storm.

"Shh," Rob whispered, "what was that?" I listened carefully.

"Thunder," I hardly got out before he silenced me again.

"No," he said, "something else."

Behind where we sat, footsteps echoed off of the ground. The night was warming very quickly, oddly enough, but still it remained damp. The ice and snow melted away revealing flooded dark yellow grass and mucky soil.

"I'll go take a look," I said, grasping the Book in my hand; it would protect me, I had faith. I followed the sound carefully, masked in thick shadows, cautious not to be seen. When I reached the sidewalk at the main clearing, the sight before me was disheartening, yet encouraging and very familiar.

CHAPTER SIX

It was him, the one who wore the black cape. We'd somehow caught up to King Monster's Son! He walked quickly along the sidewalk, his cape flapping silently as he carried the Rainbow Crystal. It was my dream but now it was really happening, it was coming true. I watched the scene play out before me as expected and once more as I had in the dream, I hid behind a bush being slammed by rain. The light came again as it had at the end of the dream… it was Rob, carrying a burning torch, blinking as it tried to burn out in the heavy weather.

"Come on, Kay," he yelled over the noise. I grabbed his arm and we ran towards the woods. The lightning hit the ground near us, the intense noise rocketing through us, shaking the ground and blinding us for an instant. I blinked, watching a green line strike through my vision, the after effect of the bright light. We darted crazily as it continued to pierce the earth all around us. I became dizzy with fear. Get to the woods, I told myself, you'll be safe there! We entered under the canopy of the trees. They slowed the rain and blocked the wind well because of how closely together and tightly interwoven they grew. We leaned our backs against the trunk again by the warmth of the fire, eating a supper of now soggy food from being submersed in water.

"We've caught up to King Monster's Son," was the last thing I spoke before exhaustion overtook me and I fell asleep.

§

"Kay, wake up!" Rob's excited voice rang through my dreams and when I opened my eyes, in my state of sleepiness, at first I didn't know where I was. As Rob's beaming face looked down at me I suddenly remembered.

"It's day three," he squealed happily, "look Kay, the castle- it's not far!"

I wiped the sleep from my eyes and squinted. There it stood, more ominous and frightening than ever, pointed like a giant burnt thistle. Rob was right, we'd be there in a couple of hours. I lifted myself up slowly, sore from leaning against the rough bark. We trekked through thick mud, soggy moss and dead grass. We were nearing a monster town and I noticed a white square sign on a leaning post.

Suddenly, invisible hands shoved Rob to the ground, dragging him away. I could see more footprints approaching me in the soft earth as I covered my mouth to stifle a scream. They were the invisible guards that Sheena had told me of once. We had to get past them, but how? I had to think fast while Rob was still within reach! I hid my head in the folds of the cape.

"Unhand him," I spoke in a deep voice, "he is my prisoner, I will take him!" The rustling and footsteps stopped. I tucked the cape around my hands so they couldn't see that they belonged to a fairy and pulled Rob to his feet, hoping that they would believe I was King Monster. They did.

"Our apologies, my King," one spoke, "we did not realize." I watched the footprints walk away through the sheer white of the cape. I threw it over my shoulders, relieved and astonished that it had actually worked! We ran onward joyfully until we were there.

"We're here," I laughed in delight, "we made it! Just one more town to pass through and we'll be at the black castle!"

In the town we had come to, ghosts, mud monsters and scale skins hurried to and fro busily. It reminded me of the busy downtown of Fairyland with its little shops and bustling people. The reminder of Fairyland brought with it a certain sadness. I felt so far away from them. Looking behind me, I saw King Monster's cabin like a fuzzy outline on the distant horizon and the castle even further like a shining white pillar. It was sunny in Fairyland.

We left the woods and entered into the clearing. I felt jittery and uncomfortable as many eyes watched us and all activity ceased. Everything became eerily silent and still. A scale skin with a red cape encircling him stood at the entrance with seriousness. He caught sight of us and his blank expression turned to surprise.

"We request entry into this city so we may venture to the castle," I explained. Everyone held their fixed positions.

"You actually survived," he commented in wonder, "how fascinating! If you have come this far, we will allow you into the city, but you must answer a question first." He paused, then continued. "What is the name of this city?"

I looked at the sign bearing pointed black letters; J-A-Y-P-O-N, I spelled it out in my head, Jaypon. Wait! The startled thought jerked through me. This was a curse! My mind brought forth a memory from a long time ago. 'Answer Jaypen', Sheena had warned us, 'for that is the name of the curse in fairy language. Never answer or speak the name in monster, or they will imprison you for speaking their tongue. They will let you pass into the city if you answer Jaypen'. Rob looked upon the sign. No, Rob! But I didn't have time to warn him.

"Jaypon," Rob announced and instantly two monsters captured him. I yelped.

"You are hereby being imprisoned on the charge of speaking our native tongue," they decreed and a bewildered Rob soon disappeared into thin air.

"Rob," I cried, turning to the guard still standing before me, "what did they do, where did he go?!"

"They took him to the castle," he explained.

"Jaypen," I answered frantically, "I'm in Jaypen!"

"Enter," he grumbled, stepping aside. I began to run fast and hard as quickly as my aching legs could carry me. I dodged through the crowds, moving along at such a speed that they all seemed like blurs. Rob was gone. It echoed through my head, repeating, driving me onwards. Already I felt like a part of me was gone and I was alone and afraid, but I couldn't take the time or energy on my emotions. I had to focus on saving him! At last I made it, resting my hands on my knees and gasping for air, waiting for my dizziness to subside. When I regained my strength and stood, the view was beyond description.

It towered above me like some menacing depth of darkness in pieces carelessly thrown together to form a castle. It was the same size as the Fairyland castle yet its hideousness made it appear taller somehow, but there was no time to assess its structure, I had to save Rob! So with that, I bravely approached the leaning front door and came face to face with the mud monster who stood there.

"What is the password to enter," he asked in a rumbled voice. I froze, a password?! A secret word to enter the castle? No one had told me!

"What is the password," I repeated, asking the Book. The mud monster stared at me impatiently with sunken hollow eyes. I shook the book frantically; oh please, I begged it, please open! But it couldn't hear my thoughts. Slowly it did open a crack and I looked upon the word '*honesty*'. I glanced back up at the guard.

"Honesty," I announced. He crossed his muddy arms and shook his head angrily. No, I yelled in my mind, the Book had lied, the Book had given me a false password! Honesty, honesty, what was honesty?! It meant telling the truth, I realized and I looked back up at the guard. The password could be a million things and I didn't know.

"I don't know," I explained, beginning to turn away, "I just don't know." He nodded.

"Enter," he explained, "for monsters often lie and try to guess the password but they really don't know. 'I don't know' is the password."

I looked at him in disbelief as he stood to the side of the open door. I went forward joyfully and entered into the depths of the Monsterland castle. At once I found myself in a long hall, curving at its end, with lit torches lining the slimy walls. My feet echoed off of the stone floor and the thick air hung moist and stale.

"Rob," I called with uncertainty and my voice echoed until I was surrounded by overlapping 'Robs'. Where was I to begin? The darkness around me was deep and gave the appearance of the ceiling stretching up and up, never seeming to end. The walls were made of thick stones and drops of water could be heard making 'bloops' and puddles in the hollows. I was shoved down and pulled backwards, a cold hand clamping over my mouth. I felt the vibration of my scream echoing in my head but the hand stifled the noise. I thrashed, desperately trying to see my captor and it was not long before I did. I was pulled outside into the rain, thrust down into the mud and pinned to the ground by the foot of King Monster's Son who towered above me. He laughed deeply, roaring with joy.

"You followed me," he caught his breath long enough to choke out, "you- you actually thought that you could win!"

"Where's Rob," I cried, "what did you do to him?!" He did not respond, he continued to cackle until his entire body shook.

"The crystal's mine, all mine," he cried joyously, "and now that I have you *and* Rob, I'm invincible!" I could see the glowing of the crystal beneath his cape and I stared at it, beckoning it.

"Wait," I called, realizing the urgent situation, "give me a chance, just one chance to get it all back!" I watched the glowing of the rainbow colours, adding, "Rob, and the crystal." He listened and took my words into consideration.

"How?"

"I will play the Monster Game," I answered. He grew serious for a moment then he burst into laughter once more.

"It will be of no use," he explained, "you will lose and I will end up with everything anyway. Admit defeat Kay, it's over and I won!"

"No," I demanded, "I will play, take me there."

Suddenly we appeared in a little clearing in the forest near the cabin. I looked out over Fairyland, reaching for it. I was so close that I was almost there, yet it felt as though it were worlds away. I saw the little people hurrying back and forth and there I discovered Frendall gazing about. Look here Frendall, I thought, look here. He did; his eyes skimmed over me, then returned to settle on me. He yelled something and soon all of the fairies came to the border of Monsterland, gathering to watch. A capeless King Monster ran out looking horrified. I felt comforted to see Cookstone, brown and made of soil just as he had always been, no longer a stone statue.

"She's going to play the Monster Game," Frendall yelled and everyone began to yell excitedly, fearfully.

"Don't do it, Kay," King Monster cried over the wind, "you can't win!"

"Well," King Monster's Son trilled, "what do you wager?" I looked out over the land, over the fairies and the monsters, over everything. King Monster's words came back to me, 'the Book tells of a fairy, one pure of heart, who will sacrifice *everything* to save the land'.

"I wager everything."

"No, Kay," Frendall screamed, as the fairies gasped and cried in distress, frantically clinging onto each other. King Monster's Son howled in excitement.

"And what are you playing for," he asked, handing me the silver piece. It rested in my palm, cold and smooth and tarnished with age. I looked out at the moss covered stones bearing their engraved numbers.

"You have no magic," he reminded me, "and I will ensure that you never have magic again!"

"Sheena told me once that the power of the mind is greater than that of real magic," I said, "and I believe that I can do anything if I put my mind to it. So what am I playing for?" I focused on the board, concentrating.

"I'm playing to win."

Suddenly I thrust the piece forward, feeling the force of it leaving my hand and listened to it skid across the chipped rocks, shutting my eyes. There was a gasp and uproar as I heard it stop and slowly my eyelids parted as the image of it met my vision.

"No," King Monster's Son screamed in agony, pounding his feet on the ground. I watched in complete disbelief as the silver piece rested upon number eleven. Eleven! But beforehand there had only been ten stones, where did this one come from? It rested in the ground bearing its number, identical to the others. The fairies began shouting and jumping and I could hear their excited laughter floating sweetly over the wind.

"You won, Kay," Frendall yelled, "you won! You won!"

"You won the Monster Game," King Monster cried joyfully, confirming it. My stomach fluttered and I danced around and around, watching colours smearing together as I twirled happily. But how, how did I win? It was impossible! I had no magic, I didn't have the fairies or Rob, I didn't have the crystal yet somehow in the history of the lands, I did it.

"No," King Monster's Son snarled. I nodded.

"Yes," I answered, "I won, I wagered everything and now nothing is yours; not Rob, nor Fairyland, nor the Rainbow Crystal." I watched the crystal float out from his cape, moving quickly towards me until I held it in my hands. Rob appeared beside me, blinking and glancing around wildly. I cried in relief, it was all over. We had been successful, we had saved Fairyland. We could return as promised.

As we stepped into Fairyland I could feel my powers flooding back. I walked slowly through the crowd, shaking hands and being pat on the back, and I could see the grateful glow in the eyes of the fairies, many of which were speechless and could only bow. All of the fairies began to bow as I passed and I stopped.

"No," I said, "do not bow to me." Then I remembered what King Monster had once told me. Names didn't matter to monsters because they were all equal.

"We are all equal," I added, looking back at him, approaching him. He stood before me, his eyes glistening with tears, in all the greatness of a King. I took the white cape from my back and handed it to him as well as the Book of Monsters. Rob returned the pendant.

"You are the one we should bow to," I commented. He appeared confused.

"Me," he asked, "why?"

"Because without you, none of this would be possible." I slowly lowered to the ground and bowed to him, all of the fairies and monsters following the action until King Monster was the only one standing. I did not realize how genuine this statement was nor how great an honour it was that we bowed to him, until much later when I discovered the truth.

§

We walked into the castle slowly, taking in the beauty of it like we had the first time we'd seen it. Again we met in the kitchen over steaming glasses. My back felt familiarity in the chair and the kitchen filled with sweet smells as it always had. I was home.

"How did I win the Monster Game," I asked, cutting through the silence, rising and placing the crystal back in the little door beside the oven. It was safe now, we all were.

"You won," Frendall explained, "because you saw beyond what existed. There were ten stones but you could only win if it landed on number eleven. You wagered everything anyway knowing that such a stone did not exist. You were willing to take a chance knowing that you probably couldn't win, for the sake of saving us all. You looked beyond yourself and saw your people, Rob and the crystal; everything, and the stone appeared. It was there all along, but it took someone with faith for it to make itself known."

I gazed upon the crystal before closing the door. Had it grown dull? It didn't seem to shine as it used to, something seemed different. Maybe not, perhaps it had been so long that I'd forgotten. How was I to know? I returned to my seat at the table.

"Where did King Monster's Son go," Rob asked inquisitively. I wondered this as well, after I had won the Monster Game, I hadn't seen him. Had he disappeared? Frendall shrugged. I concentrated and the Book of Fairies appeared before me on the table. Wonderful, I realized, now I could make it appear without having to walk upstairs to retrieve it. It opened and we read about our adventure in Monsterland right there on the paper. It was a strange feeling to experience something and then to suddenly find it there inside a book! Already we could hear excited voices as newspapers circulated with the current events. 'Kay wins Monster Game', they cried, 'Rob and Kay venture into Monsterland, return successfully!'

"Thank you," Frendall said, smiling, "I could never thank you enough for all that you have done for us." Rob nodded.

"Yes, Kay," he added, sitting straighter, "thank you for saving me. I was afraid that I'd never make it out of that place." I could only nod. I was still in disbelief and deep in thought. Where was King Monster's Son? What if he had trapped King Monster in the cabin again? I rushed to the window and looked out. King Monster stood in the street talking to a group of fairies and monsters, wearing the white cape over his shoulders again. I didn't see the black cape and all was at peace.

"Relax," Rob assured me, "everything's great."

Maybe it was. Why wasn't I celebrating? Why couldn't I relax for even a minute? Because I had a bad feeling. Something wasn't right, how could he just disappear? It was better to know where he was than to go on wondering. He could be anywhere, lurking, waiting. But why, what did he want?

CHAPTER SEVEN

Three days passed in much the same way and the longer he was away the more I could relax. In fact, I relaxed so much that when he re-emerged I didn't realize until the door of the castle flew open.

"You," he pointed a clawed finger at me accusingly. I froze, not knowing King Monster's Son's intentions. Rob rushed to my side, his mouth gaping open. Frendall had just left to visit the palace, why was he never here when these things happened?!

"How do you use this thing," he boomed, extending forth the Rainbow Crystal. I yelped, feeling my head spinning. How did he have it? All of that effort for nothing! Tears welled up in my eyes.

"Awe," he cooed with sympathy, "poor Kay, you didn't even realize that I gave you a fake crystal! Well, you know how it works don't you? I collected precious stones of every colour from the earth and made them into a fake crystal. I could have caught a rainbow but, unfortunately, I cannot fly. It's been three days, you know what happens in three days, don't you?" He leaned forward mischievously. "It crumbles to dust."

"No," I cried.

"Yes," he laughed, moving the aim of his finger towards the little door in the kitchen.

"Just open it and see for yourself," he said menacingly, "or are you too afraid?" I gasped. It had seemed different but I didn't know! How could I have known? I walked over and thrust it open. All that remained was a pile of grey dust, fine and powdery. I covered my eyes and wept.

"Bizz-buzz," King Monster's Son mocked me, "the noise doesn't bother me you know. Now pull yourself together and tell me how this works!" I eyed the crystal.

"I don't know," I choked out.

"The crystal," he demanded, "how does it work? How do I get the power out of it? Why isn't it working!" It wasn't working? I glanced at him quickly; it didn't work!

"Wait," I protested, "I won the Monster Game, the crystal is mine. You have to give it back!"

"Who's going to stop me?"

Rob and I looked at each other silently. No one could stop him.

"I don't know," I concluded, "I don't know how it works. I don't understand." He glared at me, turning away angrily, the black cape swirling around him.

"Fine," he snarled, "then we'll see, we'll see how strong the Queen is once the people turn away from her! If I can't take them by the power of the crystal I will take them by persuasion." He walked out among the fairy houses, sending them inside. The monsters came out of their black houses to listen as he addressed them. He spread his arms open as if giving them an invisible hug.

"My friends," he began, "the fairies have deceived you." This was met by much excited whispering.

"Since the beginning of time," he cried, "the fairies have continuously banished us. They claim that the entire land was once Fairyland Old, but I say no. It was our land, it was Monsterland," he stole an icy glance back at us, "and they took it." More excitement and bustling followed this.

"But they let us have homes here," Cookstone argued, "and build businesses. They are our friends!"

"No," King Monster's Son corrected him, "they accepted you so that they could take over. They let you into Fairyland so that they could befriend you and the moment you began to trust them," he formed a fist and slammed it into his outstretched hand, making a whack, "they've got you!"

"No," I cried, "he's lying! He's lying to you all!"

"Am I," he laughed, his back turned to me, "I came here to get the Rainbow Crystal, and do you know why I took it? Because it was meant to be ours! The Book of Monsters states that it is best in the hands of King Monster, but the fairies couldn't accept that. I had to take it to protect the monsters, just think! There's enough power within the crystal to destroy all of us!"

"Liar," King Monster yelled fiercely. King Monster's Son hung his head sadly.

"My own father," he choked through fake tears, "my dear, dear father taken by the fairy lies, it pains me! But, I will be the King that he couldn't be. The monsters in Monsterland have already approved of my Kingship, so who will it be? Me," his voice lowered into a grim growl, "or him?" The whispers became louder until I could hear bits of conversations. 'Maybe he's right', I heard, 'they are the deceivers'.

"No," Rob cried out, "please! We've lived in peace all of this time!" Finally King Monster's Son turned towards us, sneering.

"Peace," he questioned, "this is peace? You've cut down the trees, you've put down a blacktop and you've cleared out the land and built sidewalks. This isn't Fairyland, it's the Human World."

He was right. The forest grew sparse, the wildflowers did not bloom because the sidewalk paved them over and on some mornings when the temperature had cooled overnight, the blacktop turned to ice and no one could walk upon it. The fairies had become even older and grew sick more often since we had made the changes. Once, I stood before a land beautiful beyond description but now I saw the effects of human nature, my nature, changing it into something it was never meant to become. We had made a huge mistake.

"How do you know what the Human World looks like," Rob asked.

"Because," King Monster's Son answered with a grin so wide that it nearly split his face in half, "I am Christopher."

Dead silence fell upon the land with every eye fixed on him. Mouths gaped open in disbelief and I felt the pit of my stomach flutter. There was such a deep pause that when at last he spoke again I jumped at the piercing sound of his voice.

"Yes," he continued triumphantly, "it is I! I planted the rose, I began the land, I am the ultimate ruler!" He turned to face the monsters.

"You knew that I was alive my friends," he bellowed, "and now the day of truth has come and I reveal myself to all of you to spread this message; if you join me, we can have everything. We can take what is rightfully ours! If you join the fairies, you will pay a high price."

'Yes,' I heard, 'the fairies took our land, it really is Christopher, let us follow him'. Soon the monsters had turned into horrible creatures again. They transformed before our eyes, we could see the hatred coming into their eyes and hear it in their voices until they began to turn away from the fairies. There was a certain sense of familiarity about it and I realized that yet another dream was coming true. I had dreamt of this very event before back when we first began to live in peace. I dreamt that the monsters turned into horrible creatures again and… we banished them. I felt the warm tears in my eyes. They had turned away from us, their friends, they had forgotten all of the wonderful times we had shared because they listened to the wrong voice. One single monster had the power to persuade all of them and now, for the sake of the fairies, I knew what I had to do.

"You're banished," I called out weakly. It hurt to banish them but I just knew that it was for the best. The monsters looked up at me, Cookstone included. Cookstone was a monster, I realized, and bidding them to leave would mean ridding of him as well.

"What," the monsters questioned and even the fairies appeared shocked.

"Just go," I cried, pushing past Rob and shutting myself in the castle. I watched out the window as they made their houses disappear and gathered their belongings. They turned their backs and made the long trek back to Monsterland. The log businesses stood empty and desolate. They were gone. The thought stung me and the heaviness of the loss was so great that I began to blame myself. What had I done wrong? Why was it so easy for them to leave? Did they secretly dislike the fairies all along and it had all been a big lie? Frendall entered quietly and came to console me.

"It was for the best, Kay," he told me softly, seeming to read my mind. I looked away.

"Why would you care, Frendall," I asked angrily, "you wanted them gone all along, remember? 'Monsters are deceiving, horrible creatures' you said. Your wish came true, I hope you're happy." He shook his head sorrowfully.

"No," he said, "I'm not happy because I realize your pain. I'm sorry."

"And the crystal's gone, Frendall-"

"-I know." We stood for a long time in silence.

"What if," and my question even surprised me, "what if King Monster's Son really is Christopher?" Frendall laughed.

"He's not Christopher," he chuckled, "how could he be Christopher when I-" His eyes opened widely and he went pale, quickly looking away. He hadn't meant to say that, I could tell that by the way he reacted. Frendall, I thought in amazement, it couldn't be! Was he...

Rob entered with a blank expression.

"Kay," he told me seriously, "they are going to take over. They are gathering the armies together as we speak." I looked out the window again watching gathering shadows. Monsters were grouping together just as Rob had described. Cold fear set into me. I watched Rob's eyes dim to a dull brown at the sight.

"Rob," I questioned in concern, "are you ok?"

He spoke no words, just simply turned and opened the door. I followed him as he wandered back to the field, brown and crisp. No! I frantically ran back and forth around its edge. Why was it dying?! Why wasn't it green?! I caught sight of Rob entering the stone tunnel that led back to the remaining fields. He pulled the stones away that made up the wall to reveal a large gap. It was becoming too familiar.

"What is that," I gasped. Rob looked at me and smiled a small sour grin.

"The portal to the Human World," he marvelled, watching it, hypnotized by it. I shook my head wildly.

"No, Rob," I cried shrilly, "we've got to save Fairyland! We have to stay, we're their only hope!"

"I'm leaving," he argued, decided, not taking his eyes from the sight.

"But Rob," I shook with sobs, "you're my best friend, don't leave me! You're all I have left!" He stepped in silently, not looking back, until he had entered the Human World and was gone.

"Rob," I yelled, peering in at him. He couldn't hear me. He stood by the roadside near his house, wingless and dull, oblivious to the world I was in. We weren't just apart, we were *worlds* apart and at that moment I realized I hadn't just lost a friend, I'd lost a little part of myself that I feared I wouldn't get back. But I knew that as long as I held onto my memories, somehow he could always be with me even if he never returned to Fairyland. I pushed the stones back over the entrance, pressing rocks together to conceal it. I couldn't go back, not now, I couldn't leave them. As I stood brushing dust from my hands, laughter filled the air. I turned to meet King Monster's Son standing at the edge of the field, glaring.

"You're all alone now, Kay," he explained, "Rob left you, the monsters left you and you were foolish enough to be tricked. Now I have the Rainbow Crystal, I am the Monster King. You don't have enough power to protect your fairies when we take over your land and make them our slaves. You should have left with Rob, now you'll never escape! We strike tomorrow at the sound of the drums." With this, he disappeared and I ran to the castle as fast as my feet could carry me, bursting inside to find a joyous Frendall sitting in the living room. I opened my mouth to tell him that Rob was gone but no words came out.

"We have guests," he gushed excitedly. I folded my arms, in a trying time like this full of peril and woe here he was jolly and beaming because of some guests! He was eating too. He sat calmly eating his honey covered chew bread like some party was about to take place! How could he eat at a time like this? Wait, chew bread? I took a double take, floating back in my mind to the last words that

Henry had spoken before he and Sheena had left for the palace. 'Remember,' he had told me, 'I am the only one who can make chew bread'.

"Henry, Sheena," I whispered under my breath and as I turned my eyes upwards towards the staircase, there they stood. I ran to embrace them, throwing my arms around them joyfully.

"You're back," I laughed, watching their eyes twinkle excitedly. They hadn't changed since they left.

"Back," Henry questioned, "but we were never gone!"

"You left for the palace," I explained, "I didn't think that you would ever return."

"We were with you all along, even though we were in the palace," Sheena explained cheerfully, still in a sweet raspy voice, "we wanted you to find your own path, Kay. We left so you could make your own choices, why, imagine if we'd stayed! You would always be asking and not discovering for yourself. We were there if you needed us in that small quiet voice in the palace, and we have returned now for your time of need is greater than it has ever been. We are here to let you know that you are not alone." I found great comfort in her words although sadness hung over me. Rob left, I wanted to tell her, he's gone.

"We know," Henry answered, bringing forth the Book of Fairies and I grasped it. Know what?

"The Book told us."

It opened and I fell upon the line; *Rob leaves for the Human World yet Kay remains behind*. I shut it angrily. If I had known all along, maybe I could have stopped him! Maybe I could have changed it! No, it was meant to be because the Book foretold of it.

"I don't know what to do," I stumbled aloud through my thoughts, "I'm lost without him, what do I do? How do I go on, how will I save Fairyland?" There was a time of thoughtful silence.

"I- I don't have the Rainbow Crystal," I stammered, "hope is lost, it's all over."

"There is a power greater than the crystal," Sheena told me softly, "and it lives within you. Can you find it?" I closed my eyes and even in the darkness of my eyelids, memories played out before me. Everything from the beginning until now rolled through like overlapping images. A friend in a white cape once told me that I could do anything if I just believed in myself. I opened my eyes.

"Yes," I answered, "I can." Sheena smiled warmly.

"What are we to do, Kay," she asked calmly, "to save the fairies?" I closed my eyes and the sky map appeared in my mind. I opened and closed them, open and closed, but the picture wouldn't leave.

"I see something," I explained, "but I don't understand what it means." Henry nodded.

"That's ok," he assured me, "you will, in time."

"I have a question," I broke through and they listened intently, "why do best friends leave you?"

"I don't know," Sheena answered sweetly, "perhaps Frendall could explain that." I turned to see Frendall sitting at attention, sharing the pain that I felt at that moment. He broke from my stare for an instant and gazed out at the cabin with sadness.

"I don't know," he answered quietly before leaving the room.

§

Boom! Boom! Bang! Boom! I flung myself out of bed at the noise of the drums, but as I came into wakefulness I realized it was only a dream as the noise drifted away. I looked out at the silent stars glistening in their places and down upon the forest. I had not been asleep long, I could tell by where the moon rested in the sky. Slowly I crept downstairs to the front door and wandered out into the evening air towards the cabin. Everything was so peaceful and calm that no one would ever know we were on the brink of war. A dim candle lit the cabin with a warm glow, which overshadowed King Monster's face as I saw when I entered. He sat at the table hunched over the Book of Monsters, appearing older than ever.

"War is upon us," I whispered, sitting across from him, but he didn't move. He remained deep in thought.

"Yes," he finally agreed quietly.

"But Rob won't be here," I explained, "he left. He went back to the Human World." This caught his attention and he appeared shocked.

"Without you," he exclaimed. I nodded and he fell back into silence.

"I just can't believe this," I called, quickly hushing my voice, "I can't believe that they followed your son because they think he's Christopher." King Monster shook his head disapprovingly, still lost in the Book.

"If Christopher really is alive," I continued, "he needs to come here and help us."

"He's already here."

I jumped at his words. Christopher was *here*, here in this magical world?! But how? The candle shone upon King Monster's face etched with age and made his green eyes appear like emeralds. The suspense hung thickly in the air, pulling like a stretched elastic band threatening to break.

"If the Books tell of him," King Monster figured, "and he is alive, it makes sense that he's here. Both Books explain that he may have become a fairy. Tell me, Kay, have you ever met a fairy that seemed to have no past? Who won't tell you where he came from or who he *really* is? A fairy who seems to have secrets?" It didn't take long for me to picture Frendall. We had asked him where he was from but he refused to answer. 'How long have you been here,' we'd questioned, but he had given no answer.

"Yes," I answered, deciding not to explain further. After all, he didn't like Frendall and probably wouldn't believe that it could be him.

"How are you going to save the fairies?" The question was offered yet again and again I envisioned the sky map with its layers and intricately sketched constellations. The flying zone, the upper level and the furthest reaches; what did it all mean? I decided not to answer his question, I truly didn't know.

"Go now," King Monster dismissed me, "get some sleep."

But how could I sleep? How could I fall into dreams when every moment I would hear my heart resounding in my ears like drums? Then it really would be drums and they would come unexpectedly with little warning. Tomorrow, one night away, the beginning of a new morning. So I turned and walked out into the evening once more, watching ominous clouds drifting across the sky from Monsterland, blotting out the moon and stars as they covered everything in a blanket of darkness.

Something moved. I saw it out of the corner of my eye, some strange flowing black shadow; a cape, the black cape of King Monster's Son. My scream shattered the stillness and echoed through the clearing. His head turned and he stepped out until he was fully visible, his eyes burning red. He laughed in a monstrous roar as King Monster ran out of the cabin. Before he understood what was happening, King Monster's Son flicked his wrist and bound him in chains.

"Stop," I yelled, too frozen with shock to run. King Monster thrashed and the two began throwing red and green balls of fire at each other that disappeared when they hit the ground. Back and forth they struggled, growling and flaring their eyes red. It was my dream coming true, and horror came upon me. I had dreamt of this before, a long time ago, and the scene was playing out exactly the same. Why did my dreams always come true?!

"Save the village, Kay," King Monster called to me as King Monster's Son dragged him helplessly away. I wanted to save him, to help him, but I had to save the fairies. King Monster's Son sneered.

"I'll come back for you tomorrow," he hissed at me. I ran to the castle, bursting inside to find a startled, sleepy Frendall. He stood wide-eyed in his blue night cap, holding a candle.

"He's captured King Monster," I cried in fear. Frantically he ran to the window in concern.

"Who captured him," he asked quickly, "King Monster's Son?" I nodded. Much to my amazement he made his way to the door and touched the knob. He paused.

"Well, he can look after himself," he finally settled on.

"You're not going to help him," I shouted in disbelief. Frendall fought with himself, I could tell. He wanted to, I knew, but something was in the way, some hidden emotion was stopping him. He walked away.

"Frendall," I gasped, "you have to help him!"

"We need to focus on helping the fairies," he argued, "don't worry about him. Get some sleep, I'll see you in the morning."

In a last desperate attempt I called behind him, "is this how Christopher treats others? Just leaves them to fend for themselves?" He stopped at my words but did not turn to face me.

"Yes," he said icily before mounting the stairs. I watched the candle's light grow dimmer as he ventured further down the hall.

Soon I made my way up to my room as I had so many times before, to think. The night was very dark with only a sliver of moonlight laying beams on the windowsill. The Book of Fairies met my hands again and I traced over the winding roses that made its border. The golden key winked and sparkled as it twirled on its ribbon. So many questions, I thought dizzyingly, so little time.

"How do I save King Monster," I asked, but it remained shut tight. I placed my fingers on either side of the cover, attempting to pry it open, but it was no use.

"Open," I urged it, "why won't you open?" I stared at it, cradling it.

"What do I do? How do I save the fairies?" It opened to a page bearing the sky map, a small version of it with all of the markings and labels that had become so familiar to me.

"But what does it mean," I asked with urgency. The Book shut once more.

I set it back on the dresser. Such a stubborn thing, I could go on asking questions all night and not even have an answer to one of them! I laid on my back watching the dimming stars as the clouds stretched across them. Way up there in the sky, the sky, the sky map. It repeated in my head. Before I knew it I had drifted off to sleep. The map circled around in my head; the flying zones, the sun, the moon, the stars. Dizzyingly circling round and round, impressing themselves into my mind. Again as they had for so many nights, my dreams became vivid, seeming so real that I undoubtedly knew they would actually happen. One was about King Monster and as the image drew nearer, it became clear.

CHAPTER EIGHT

He stood upon the pathway, half sheltering the view of the cabin in his shadow. I watched King Monster from a high window in the castle, the chilling breezes flooding in from a gap beneath the pane, swirling the curtains. A collection of crisp brown leaves mixed with fluffy snow collected around his feet, spinning in the wind gusts, seeming to dance around him. He raised his gaze up to the grey sky longingly, catching sight of me for an instant, holding my reflection in his deep green eyes. I did not understand the look; it was sadness, a deep sincere sadness, but yet a glimmer of undying hope, like a golden glow.

The glow! I looked beyond him until my eyes met the cabin window. Golden beams filled the room winking between the crossbeams of the window, pure and brilliant. A candle, perhaps? No, even a candle could not give such light. Suddenly in my mind I went there; went to the cabin, in through it, and stood in the room. The door, that little door built into the wall. It was behind it, I knew now, I could sense it. I reached towards it further, further, grasping the wood in my palm. I opened it and gasped to behold…

We were moving. The castle shifted upwards with an awkward creak, pulling itself off of where it sat and the fairy houses followed it, uprooting, floating on the air. We moved higher, the land below us moving out of sight as we drifted away. I watched with panic now as he remained on the ground, his white cape beaming like a silver-lined cloud, like the clouds we were beginning to enter up there in the sky.

"No," I cried, throwing the window open, "King Monster, come with us, please! No!" He smiled a quiet gentle smile.

"This is the way it must be," he called towards me reassuringly.

"No," I argued frantically, "I can't leave you, I won't leave you!"
I felt a comforting arm around me and turned to face Frendall.

"Frendall," I cried, "we can't leave him!"

"It's already been done," he explained, "I'm sorry."

I opened my mouth but no words came out. Frendall remained at my side, peering out, watching the land shrink and fade. Then, I saw it; as he watched I saw tears coming to his eyes, a heavy loss settling in. He was looking at King Monster, not taking his eyes off of him and King Monster looked upon him, sharing his pain until at last we could see him no more...

§

Boom! Boom! Bang! Boom! This time when I heard the drums I knew that they were real. I woke up quickly and jumped out of bed, running downstairs where a worrisome trio gathered. Outside, armies of monsters marched through the street, trampling a few unsuspecting fairies. I looked out in fear to find, in the midst of them, a joyous King Monster's Son leading the march. His laugh roared across the land like thunder and the pounding of his feet kept time with the steady beat of the drums. He halted abruptly just outside of the castle and a thick, dead silence filled the air.

"Surrender," he cried, "or prepare to meet your doom!"

"Sheena," I whispered frantically from inside the safety of the castle, "I don't know what to do! I don't know how to save the fairies!"

"Oh, Kay," he called impatiently from outside, "we're waiting!"
I gripped the knob in my shaking hand. This was the day, now everything rested on my shoulders. Though my legs felt like rubber, my stomach knotted painfully and my head spun, I walked out and stood before them.

"Here she is," King Monster's Son announced sarcastically, "the Queen!" He pretended to bow, sending the monsters howling with laughter. He laughed along, mocking me, prancing around.

"Look," he laughed, "I'm a fairy! I'm afraid because those evil monsters are going to get me!" He pretended to shake with fear as the monsters around him threw comments in. 'Poor fairy,' they cooed, 'we'll protect you… not!' At last he stopped and fixed his eyes on me seriously.

"What is your choice," he bellowed, adding, "well it won't matter anyway. Either way, we're going to win. You see, slowly the monsters have been moving their territory onto yours and you didn't even notice!"

He was right. I looked around, shocked to finally discover what had been happening all along. They had moved E-ville a long time ago, but I had been so preoccupied with the needs of the people that I'd overlooked an even bigger problem emerging. As I looked around now, hidden in the cover of the trees between the newly sprouted leaves, white signs had been placed in the ground marking Monsterland villages. They weren't just thinking about taking over; they had already done it! The monsters easily outnumbered the fairies now and it would take a miracle to win. But, if we gave up before we tried, we'd be admitting defeat.

"This is Fairyland," I told them, "and you are not welcome." King Monster's Son grinned.

"That's what I wanted to hear," he called gleefully, pointing an accusing finger at me.

"Boys," he yelled to the monsters behind him, then lowered his voice to a grim growl, "get them!" They advanced forward and the fairies froze in their places out of fear, defenseless and helpless. What was I to do? How could I save them now?

"Everyone," I called desperately, "become invisible!"

They did; one by one the fairies disappeared until all that I saw before me were monsters searching wildly, baffled. I had done it! Now the monsters had no idea where the fairies were! They spoke quickly, blinking their eyes, frantically searching as capes were suddenly pulled backwards by invisible forces and they fell to the ground. The fairies could fight them and they had no way of fighting back! King Monster's Son glared angrily, looking around him in all directions.

"You can't see them," he roared with fury, "look! There's one, and another over there!" Somehow he had the power to see them but none of the others could. They began to run, blindly this time, out of fear.

"Let's get out of here," they yelped, fleeing to Monsterland in handfuls. King Monster's Son stamped his feet, sending the ground shaking. Then a calm look came over him.

"Everyone," he called to the monsters, "become invisible, because one invisible being can see another! You will be able to see the fairies!"

One by one the monsters began to fizzle from sight until an empty land remained before me. I could hear noises and see flickers of movement. Was it true? I went invisible as well and slowly the image came into view. It was a shocking discovery and I felt a lump rising in my throat. It was true and now the monsters flooded back in, angrier than ever. We had only provoked them!

"Now you will pay," King Monster's Son proclaimed, "feel my wrath!"

He raised his clawed hands into the air and dark clouds over Monsterland washed overhead until the sun was blotted out. Then I saw a wall; a white wall, so thick that it seemed to swallow everything in its depths. It was nearing at an alarming rate and as it drew closer I realized it was made of snow, millions of flakes with sharp, bladed edges being driven by a horrific wind.

"Everyone," I addressed the fairies again, "inside your houses, now! Secure the doors and windows!"

I ran inside, hardly having time to shut the door before it hit. It came, covering the windows, trapping us in a world of blazing white. Everything was becoming buried, how quickly was uncertain. I was cut off from the outside world with only Sheena, Henry and Frendall to comfort me. Had the fairies made it into their houses? Were they safe? There was no way of knowing. I paced nervously back and forth, back and forth, hardly able to hear myself think over the howling wind. We couldn't stay here on the ground with the monsters but we couldn't fly in such harsh weather. Even if we flew, we would eventually become exhausted and have to land, then all of our strength would be gone! I saw the sky map in my mind again. Please, I begged it urgently, what does it mean? What are you trying to tell me? The answer came, much to my relief.

"Sheena," I asked hurriedly, "you know how the monsters moved their land onto ours? Well, couldn't we move Fairyland?" She nodded.

"Yes, of course," she answered. I nodded back.

"Good," I replied, "but can we move it *up*?" All three exchanged confused glances. I made the sky map appear in my hands and opened it, pointing to the flying zone. They were just currents of air, I knew, but as crazy as it sounded we would be safe if we were in the sky. They agreed. Soon the snow stopped and I heard the monsters cackling outside.

"Have you had enough," King Monster's Son hollered in his growling voice, "or do you wish to continue suffering?" I went to the window and thrust it open.

"Stay in your houses and hold on," I called, "we're going to move Fairyland."

The monsters gasped in surprise but King Monster's Son simply scoffed, "there's nowhere left to go, the entire land is ours!" Even the fairies seemed confused, peering out from behind tiny windows.

"The land is yours," I stated, as already the castle and fairy dwellings began to rock and creak, tearing themselves painfully from the earth, "but the sky is ours!" His eyes darted fearfully from house to house.

"No," he screamed desperately, "stop!" But we didn't stop. We rose, leaving gaping holes in the ground below. Higher we went, very slowly and as we broke through the grey cloud cover, they parted to reveal fluffy white clouds above us. Somehow the air currents were strong enough to hold the weight and the rainbows banded together to help support us as well. We had stopped not too far from the ground but high enough so that no monster could reach us. We were safe!

A cheer erupted from the fairies as they came out of their houses now, happy to be able to use their wings again. They flew and twirled in the air, and still the shops remained open. There was plenty to eat and much to do. It seemed like the old Fairyland as I watched their eyes glow with excitement and listened to the hum of their wings produce a merry melody. I watched the monsters below us gather and make a slow retreat back to Monsterland. They were giving up, we had won! There was no way that they could get us unless they could fly and how would they do *that* anyway?!

I flew out and joined the festivities. There was song and dance and merriment. No more would we have to walk on concrete, I thought as I saw that it had remained on the ground below us. Now we could wander across the softness of the clouds! They were like cotton, I realized, pulling some greedily into my hands. Oh, if only Rob could see this!

I pushed the thought from my mind, it pained me to think of him. Yet sometimes I would wonder; what was he doing? Did he wish that he would have stayed? I could imagine my family questioning him. 'Rob', they would demand, 'where is Kay?' Then he would tell them everything, all about this magical realm, but they wouldn't believe him. How could they when they had never seen such wonders as this? If only I could show them, show everyone, if only there were a way!

"They'll be back," Frendall exclaimed, breaking me from my thoughts, "they're planning something." It did look like it, the way the monsters were gathering, but it didn't matter because they couldn't win.

That evening I watched the land below us sinking into darkness, hardly recognizing it. It looked so empty and desolate, especially the cabin; no warm candle glow filled the interior, no puffs of grey smoke rose up from the chimney. It was beginning to lean slightly to one side as though it were tired, as though it mourned the disappearance of the one who had lived within its aging walls for so many years. Where was King Monster? Was he safe, had he been imprisoned? Here we were up in the sky safe and at ease while he remained trapped on the ground. I would save him, I decided, when the time was right and the cabin could be moved up. I would move it for him!

Taking to my bed I laid flat on my back and watched the stars. They were close now, shining with such a pure white light that I could nearly reach up and touch them. What was up there in the furthest reaches? I would never know, Sheena had told me that it would tear a house apart but, of course, no one had ever flown that high to find out.

§

The ground was teeming with monsters in the wee hours of the next morning. The sun rose; a huge, fiery ball in the sky a bit too close for comfort. They gathered directly beneath us with who else but King Monster's Son leading them. I made my way to the front window and pulled it open to listen to the conversation. Little was spoken, mostly they just moved amongst each other strapping wings to each other's backs. Wings?! I looked closely; they had crafted wings in the same style and size as a fairy's, and attached heavy strings to the base. They tied the ropes around their shoulders and secured them around their waists. I laughed, they were trying to fly! They actually thought that those fake wings would lift them! The rest of the fairies laughed as well. What a silly idea!

Click, click, click. I stared in amazement at the little keys in the centre of the wings. They were winding them like music boxes around and around until they could turn no more. What were they for? I soon found out. The wings began to move, flapping steadily, becoming faster until they were a blur. The noise they produced was a mechanical whine and a swift wisp of them splitting the air. The monsters began to move slowly upwards until their feet left the ground. My grin left my face; it was working! They were flying! It was a crazy sight, insane really. How high could they fly? They came closer, reaching, nearly touching the bottom of the cloud we were on until they slowed and floated back down. Soon they would be here and once they were in the sky with us, who knows what they could do!

"Wind it tighter," King Monster's Son called above the noise, "push off the ground harder, we can make it!" He instructed them, yet he himself remained wingless.

"I'm afraid of heights," many of them complained shakily, afraid to go back up. He growled.

"I don't care," he roared, "get going!" The monsters fought back.

"I don't see any wings on *your* back," they argued. His eyes burned red.

"I am the King and you will do my bidding!" The monsters began to fight amongst themselves, buying us precious time. We had to move higher.

"They're going to make it up here, we have to move higher," I spoke aloud to Sheena, Henry and Frendall behind me.

"But we can't," Henry exclaimed, "we would enter the upper level and be pulled into the furthest reaches!" I gave him a concerned look.

"We have to," I yelled back, "it may be our only hope!" Suddenly I caught a flash of white below us on the ground. It was King Monster, standing by the cabin; he had escaped, he was ok! I laughed with joy. Slowly as I gazed upon him, dark clouds began to cover the sky below us and I knew that I would soon lose sight of him.

"King Monster," I called, "come with us!" He looked up, watching us silently and within the cabin I beheld a golden glow. Oh no, I realized with panic, this was becoming too familiar… it was my dream! We began to move upwards.

"No, please! You have to come with us," I cried.

"This is how it is meant to be," he explained and the situation ended just as my dream had, with a lowly Frendall coming to my side and watching it all fade away.

We had entered the upper level and the turbulence grew very strong. Everything was jerking wildly, tipping and shaking with vibrations of air. I was tossed to my knees, desperately gripping onto furniture but even it moved. It was a dizzying, nauseating experience and I realized now, now that it was too late, that the furthest reaches could indeed rip a house apart. Crack, bang! I heard the deep wrenching of the structure heaving and pulling as we were sucked up into some invisible, powerful force. The last thing I witnessed before we broke through was the shocked, helpless look in the eyes of the fairies and the last thing I heard was an uproar of deafening screams…

We stopped and all fell silent, nothing moved. I rose slowly to gaze out and was in absolute surprise when I beheld the depths of the furthest reaches. In one single, descriptive word it could only be called 'forever'. I looked out upon waves of silver lined clouds that continued on so far in all directions around me that I knew they had no end. The sky above us was endless as well, reaching up so high that the fairies could just keep on flying and never find the top. The sky was such a pure blue that even the deepest ocean could not match its colour.

The golden sun hung above us and the silver moon, I noticed now, laid in a black velvet sky to the right of where we sat. The stars decked the night around it, sparkling like thousands of Rainbow Crystals. It was night *and* day here, wherever one chose to dwell. Looking at the sky map I realized that it was exactly the same with every constellation perfectly matched. Clean air drifted in through the open window, meeting my face. I breathed it in, gulping it, so pure and wonderful that I nearly felt as though I had never truly breathed before I took in this air!

I ran outside; it was neither hot nor cold, but perfectly conditioned. I was in awe at it, amazed. All of this time the fairies had believed this place to be dangerous, impossible to reach, but now that we were here we had found wonders that we never knew existed! The fairies crept out of their houses cautiously, looking about in wide-eyed wonder just as I had been. They were speechless. Frendall came out, followed by Sheena and Henry who stood near me taking it all in.

"Amazing," I broke out, hearing my voice echo through the calm. I threw my arms into the air and went running, completely weightless, drifting across the vastness of the clouds. The others followed after me, laughing and dancing and sighing with relief. It was all over, the war and the old Fairyland all passed away. Now, we triumphed!

"It's amazing, like a whole other world," Frendall exclaimed, frolicking about.

"Truly magnificent," Henry added, marvelling at its beauty.

"It's so wonderful that we can all celebrate this together." It was Sheena this time and the joy gave her a glow, everyone glowed really. All together, I thought, but not complete. King Monster wasn't there and a guilt rose within me sickeningly. How could I have left him behind? Why had I left him? Now he was so far away, defenseless and helpless. The monsters would probably capture him and lock him in the black castle forever. Would I ever see him again?

"Oh," Sheena cooed soothingly, "I know you miss him Kay, but you can't blame yourself." I looked at her quickly; miss who? Blamed myself for what? How did she know?!

"Who," I asked, and she gave me a funny look.

"Rob," she answered, "who else?" I shrugged.

"Right, Rob," I agreed. Frendall stopped and came to me as Sheena and Henry wandered away to join the others.

"What's really going on," he asked inquisitively, sensing something deeper than I was willing to admit. I shook my head.

"You wouldn't understand, Frendall."

"I will, Kay," he argued defensively, "I will understand, I know it! Tell me." I turned my hazel eyes up towards him.

"I have to go back," I explained quietly, "I left him, I left King Monster. He was my friend and I abandoned him." He regarded me sincerely.

"A friend should not leave a friend," he explained, "I know how it feels." He paused thoughtfully.

"Ok," he agreed softly. Ok?! *Frendall* was ok with me going back to save King Monster?

"But I'm going with you."

This surprised me even more, he was coming with me! I made the Book of Fairies appear in my hand, sensing somehow that it would be needed and we set off, much to the surprise and concern of the others. Sheena and Henry wished us good luck and then we parted. We drifted through thick white clouds, completely weightless. Going down was easier than coming up, I realized, as we moved smoothly without strong currents. Below us lurked a thick cover of dark grey clouds smeared across the sky like a wall.

"This is it," Frendall explained solemnly, "I don't know what will await us on the other side." I nodded; it didn't matter, all that mattered was that King Monster was safe.

It surprised me that Frendall had not turned around by now out of fear or change of mind. Why had he not tried to talk me out of it? 'Think of the danger', I could picture him scolding me, 'are you crazy', but he hadn't. He not only let me go without question, yet even in the danger of such times, in all of the uncertainty, he was coming with me. We broke through the last portion of the upper level down into the flying zone until the land came into view once more.

It was empty. I surveyed the trees, the clearing, everything, but no one was there. It sprawled out like some kind of wasteland, a pitiful sight to behold. Yet even in the emptiness I could feel many pairs of eyes watching, waiting, lurking in the shadows. I shivered as we landed on the ground. Winter reigned over the lands in a frigid, blinding white. The trees bowed uncomfortably beneath the weight of the ice and snow. Slush gathered in pools within the hollows where Fairyland used to be and the black letters on the signs marking the monster villages blazed off of their backgrounds. Where had they all gone? I had only an instant to wonder before they came rushing out of the deepness of the woods.

"We'll take shelter in the cabin," Frendall screamed over the noise of pounding feet running hard and the excited yells and roars as they noticed us. They were blocking us, circling around us, closing in quickly. My eyes darted back and forth, there was no escape! Soon they would capture us and imprison us forever. What if they put us in opposite ends of the black castle and I never saw him again? If this was the last and final time I spoke to Frendall, I knew just what to say.

"I'm sorry that I dragged you into this," I apologized with urgency. As the monsters drew nearer I could feel their hot breath upon my wings. I shifted and turned away from the cabin towards where the white castle used to be, facing him. He opened his mouth to speak but I wouldn't let him. I just had to tell him.

"I know who you are," I began, and the rest tumbled out, "where you came from, what you did, it all makes sense now! Somehow I've always known." I smiled despite my fear.

"You're Christopher," I concluded, beginning to feel the sting of claws digging into my wings. I cringed, shrinking down. Frendall shook his head.

"No," and he pointed behind me, "he is."

CHAPTER NINE

King Monster stood at the cabin door silently, everything becoming still; the monsters in their places still with angry, twisted expressions on their faces and the fairies up above us frozen in their places, looking down in fear. He had stopped time!

"You," I stammered, meeting his gaze, "no, it can't be! But you're a-"

"-Monster," he completed my sentence, his red face wrinkling into a gentle smile, "yes I am, but it's not really what I look like."

Suddenly King Monster became surrounded in light and just as quickly as it came it faded, revealing a boy standing before me. I gasped and stepped back in utter surprise. He stood about the height of Frendall with the half hidden sunlight making his chestnut hair glow. His face was smooth and oval, almost moonlike, and the only way he even slightly resembled King Monster was in the shine of his green eyes and the gentle upward curve of his mouth.

"This," he concluded, "is what I look like." But no longer was his voice broken and gruff, now it was sweet and his words came out softly. Was he a fairy? No, I realized, for his back bore no wings. He was a human.

"I am Christopher," he announced, "I always have been."

"But why," I cried breathlessly, "why did you disguise yourself as a monster instead of a fairy?"

"It would have been too easy," he explained, "you would have accepted me for being a fairy, on the outside. That's why I had to be a monster. It took someone pure of heart to look past the claws and red skin to see who I really was, someone who would accept me and come to befriend me no matter what I looked like. That someone is you, Kay."

Tears filled my eyes as I realized the truth of his words. He had been a monster, had turned himself into something thought to be hideous. Had been shunned by the fairies and monsters alike; his own people, his own world that he had created, just to see who would accept him for who he really was.

"That's why I wore this old thing," he explained, lifting his white cape from the ground beside him, "if red is evil and black is ultimate evil, then it would make sense that I would wear white. White means pure, not evil, it is the colour of the right and just. No one seemed to be able to figure that out." So that was it! It made sense now and I found myself surprised that I had not stumbled upon that conclusion.

"But wait," I argued, "I went back in time and saw you. You had to have been born a monster, I saw you as a baby!" He shook his head.

"Sorry," he apologized, "it was a mind image, a picture placed into your mind to convince you. Amile and Hesman never existed, besides, those aren't even true monster names! You see, you would have eventually figured out that I was Christopher and if you realized this, you would never have left me behind when you moved Fairyland. If you didn't leave me behind the monsters would have captured everyone! In fact, it would have changed everything. That's why it was best to convince you that it was Frendall."

Frendall! I gasped, I had been so caught up in the excitement and shock that I had completely forgotten him! I turned around, hoping that he would still be standing there. He was, looking just as he had the first time I had met him and in fact remained the same, the only difference being that his wings were gone. He was a human as well.

"If he's Christopher," I asked, "then who are you?"

"I'm still just Frendall," he answered with a chuckle, smiling, but as he looked behind me his face became overshadowed in pain.

"I *was* Christopher's best friend," he added icily, "until he broke his promise." Suddenly my mind went back to the Book of Fairies.

'Why does Frendall dislike King Monster so much', I had asked and it opened to read, '*a broken promise*'. Now I would finally know.

"*I* broke *my* promise," Christopher cried in disbelief, "no, you broke yours! You promised me, Frendall, you promised that you would come see me! I was sick, you knew that, but you never came."

"I did come," Frendall argued, "I came but you weren't there! You left, you promised to wait at the house for me but you left!" Christopher pondered this for a moment, taking on the same look as King Monster had when he was deep in thought.

"You, you came," he choked out. Frendall nodded, his eyes brimming with tears.

"Of course I did, Christopher, you were my best friend."

"But you had to have been late," Christopher stated, "because I waited for you but when you didn't come I went out to look for you." Tears slipped down Frendall's cheeks.

"You were out looking for me," he responded, "in the cold weather as sick as you were? So that's why you weren't there. I had no idea, I didn't know!"

"Why were you late," Christopher asked, his eyes becoming shiny.

"The rose," Frendall explained and I could see him recalling it like some far off memory, "I was tending to your rose. I wanted to be sure that it survived so that I could tell you, I knew that you would ask me. I'm sorry that I was late, it's all my fault, I didn't know!"

"No, Frendall," Christopher shook his head, "it was my fault. I doubted you, I didn't wait for you. I'm sorry, I didn't understand!"

I stood watching both of them, feeling my eyes burn with tears as well. All of this time, all of these years that they disliked each other-nearly hated even, all because of a misunderstanding. All because they didn't take time to explain, to listen and to understand. Because of some assumption the lands had divided over it, friendships had been lost, and even what could have been a bond between monster and fairy had broken over it. The rose! Suddenly I remembered.

"King Monst-" then I corrected myself, "Christopher, where is the rose?" He turned towards me, a melancholy thought coming to his mind.

"You already know," he told me. I shook my head, *me*? How could I know? I'd never seen it, I'd never been told. All I knew was that it was in the direct centre of Fairyland Old when Fairyland used to be the entire land. What was in the centre of the entire land? Why, nothing... except for the cabin, the cabin where King Monster had lived, who had actually been Christopher, who planted the rose. That little door, the little door built into the side of the cabin wall. 'What is behind that door,' I had asked King Monster once and he had answered, 'everything'. Suddenly I rushed into the cabin and stooping by the little door in the wall, I took hold of the side of the wood and it opened.

I gasped. It was indeed the rose, though not red and lively as I had imagined. Instead it stood before me in radiant gold, burning with a beautiful light! 'You shall know it if ever you see it,' the words of the Book of Fairies came back to me, and I did, but as I looked more closely shock met me. It was crumpled and bent with drooping leaves and petals, many of which were missing. I gulped.

"What happened to it," I gasped. Christopher and Frendall entered, coming up beside me.

"It's dying," Christopher explained simply. I rose to my feet.

"Why," I cried, but it couldn't die! It was impossible! It wasn't just any rose, it was a *magical* rose!

"Everything that begins has an ending, Kay," Christopher explained softly, "it's ok. This is how things are meant to be."

"Wasn't there a way to keep it alive," I argued. He nodded slowly.

"In the beginning," he began, "the fairies knew that some day it would come to this. So they invented something that would keep the rose alive forever and they took it into their care, passing it down through the generations in hopes that it could one day restore the lands to what they once were. That 'something' is the Rainbow Crystal."

"But I thought," I stumbled. He nodded again.

"Yes, you thought that it was ultimate power," he explained, "but it only has the power to do what it was made to do, that's why I needed it. The rose was dying and it was the only way I could save it. That's why the Book of Monsters told that it 'holds its greatest value with King Monster'. It was of no use to anyone else, I was just afraid that when King Monster's Son took it he would destroy it and there would be no hope of bringing the rose back to life at all."

"Why, I even tried pouring fairy berry juice on it thinking that it would help! It didn't," he chuckled.

That's why he wanted the berries! I recalled King Monster placing the berries I gave him behind the door and at the time I could make no sense of it. Suddenly, knowing the truth, a broad perspective came before me and I realized what I'd done.

"I'm sorry," I told him remorsefully, "I didn't trust you enough to give it to you. It must have hurt so badly when I gave you the fake crystal!" He shook his head this time.

"It helped me to realize," he told me, "that things aren't meant to go on forever. They're not supposed to. Seasons fade into each other, nights and days pass into months and years, time moves on. Don't you see, Kay? There is something greater than us that changes the seasons, that moves the time, and we have to trust in that. It's not up to us to make something surpass its time. When I planted the rose I didn't 'make' it grow, I planted it with the faith that it would and I let it." It made sense now, yet still I felt deep sadness. So that's why the fairies were growing old and becoming sick, I realized, and why the green fields of Fairyland were turning brown. It was because it had met its end.

"But why were you so cruel," I blurted out, changing the subject, "when we first came to Fairyland, you were evil." Christopher hung his head sadly.

"I was angry," he explained, "because I thought that Frendall had left me. I acted out of bitterness and I resented everything. But that changed when I realized that we could all live in peace and understanding. A life of bitterness is no life at all." Frendall and I nodded in agreement. Christopher's gaze dropped down to my hand and he smiled a wide, joyful grin the way King Monster always used to when he was happy.

"You brought the Book!"

I looked down upon it and brought it into view. I had taken it with me, why I was uncertain, and here it was. I set it upon the table and it opened to the first page. Christopher made the Book of Monsters appear on the table beside it and it opened to the beginning as well. *The Book of Monsters*, it read, *By King Monster: Christopher.* He had written it!

"I wrote the Book of Monsters from a monster's perspective," he explained, "and George, Marianne, Paul and Mary wrote the Book of Fairies from a fairy's perspective. Now you can read them and truly come to understand our lives." But there were two books both thick with so many pages, how could I get through it all? It would take days!

The pages of the Book of Fairies began to turn very quickly but instead of reading it, images and events began to flash through my mind. I watched Christopher plant the rose, watched the fairies and monsters come from it and saw the cabin rise up around it. I saw the monsters being banished, leaving and coming to build the castle. It was all before me, a mind image playing out so vividly that I was part of it. It continued through the time that Rob and I arrived and came to rest at the very moment we were at now. I saw myself through the eyes of the fairies, watching myself like a mirror image. The book ended abruptly and as it ended, the pages of the Book of Monsters turned in the same way until I found myself there once more.

This time I felt the pain that the monsters felt when they were banished, I felt their uncertainty towards a new generation of fairy royalty coming. I watched myself through eyes full of anger and joy and all of the emotions that the monsters felt. I laughed with them, I cried with them and finally, I understood them. The Book closed and the images faded until I was left there in the cabin.

"You signed a paper when you first came to Fairyland," Frendall told me as he held it in his hand, showing me.

"It reads; you must never tell anyone about Fairyland. But on the back," he flipped it over.

"If you intend to play the game by signing this sheet, if it may arise within your time, you must finish it," I read aloud. What is 'the game' I started to ask, but Frendall already began to explain.

"There is the Fairy Game and the Monster Game," he continued, "but there is another type of 'game'; our lives. The fairies live one way and the monsters live another. We call it a game because you never know what turn it will take. Sometimes it's in your favour, sometimes the odds are against you. You finished the game, Kay. You could have left but you didn't, you stayed to help us. You understood and accepted the monsters. You didn't just win the Monster Game when you played it with the silver piece that day, you set the monsters free. They were trapped, prisoners of their own fate with no free will but when you wagered everything you didn't just bet Fairyland, you bet Monsterland as well. Now they can choose their own paths because of you." I was taken aback and honoured by his words.

"What will happen to the monsters? What will happen to the fairies," I questioned with concern, "what will become of them?" He looked out the window at the monsters and shifted his eyes up towards the ceiling, towards the sky where the fairies remained even as we spoke, frozen in their places.

"The monsters and fairies are free," he commented, "but not *truly* free. Some day they will be able to leave this land and travel anywhere in the world, but it will happen slowly. To be able to be so free that they can wander the face of the Earth, someone must believe and every time one child believes, a fairy and a monster will be truly free. You set them free Kay, now it is up to others to continue that freedom."

"But who," I asked, "who will believe? Where will I find enough people to set all of them free?" Frendall looked down this time, his eyes brimming with tears once more.

"The Human World is full of people, isn't it?" I stood in shocked silence.

"You're sending me back," I questioned. Both boys nodded. We stood for awhile regarding each other, at a loss for words, and as I looked upon the table I discovered a connection that I had not taken time to realize before. The Book of Monsters had a keyhole tidily fit into the spine and the Book of Fairies had a golden key fastened to its spine by a shiny red ribbon. I went over and slowly fit them together with a small 'click'. They burned with light so bright that I shielded my eyes and when I looked again, the books were gone and a seed remained. Frendall carefully lifted it and placed it in my palm.

"When you feel as though you've lost everything, you haven't. It just means there's room for a new beginning." He folded my hand over it. I looked at Christopher.

"Thank you for everything," I thanked him with sincerity.

"You're welcome."

There was a long, deep pause and in our minds without speaking, we knew that this was goodbye.

"Will I ever see you again," I asked with urgency to both of them, half afraid of the answer.

"You believe, don't you," Christopher asked. I nodded. I did believe, I believed without even one doubt in my mind.

"Then we'll always be with you," Frendall finished and as I looked out the window up at the dark clouds, beams of light flowed through. Way up in a clearing I gazed into the depths of a blue sky that truly seemed to stretch on forever. They would be with me always, wherever I went, whatever I did and I found comfort in these words. It was more than words, it was a promise.

I closed my eyes, listening to a new wind blow. The world was alive with birdsong. I could hear every new leaf turn, every reed bend and I was part of it, part of all of it, part of *everything*. And the final, wonderful reminder of my beloved Fairyland was the sweet ringing of the bluebells floating over the breeze to my ears as they made their way up through the frozen earth.

§

It was gone. I gasped in horror, stepping back upon the sidewalk. I was back, back in the Human World as though I had never left at all. Tears blurred my vision, the shock stinging me. It was gone; the trees, the entire forest even. All that remained was a large parking lot with white lines burning off of the pavement, the stench of tar rising to meet me. Fairyland was gone, and Christopher and Frendall, all of them, vanished. The castles, the cabins, everything. I had lost everything. Warm tears flooded down my face.

"No," I cried weakly, "no, please not this! Don't take it all away from me!" The emptiness of the loss was overwhelming and I desperately began to search for some sign, some proof that they still existed.

"Kay," a gentle voice called. It was Rob, standing before me with a backpack strapped to him. He looked bewildered.

"What's wrong," he asked in alarm, seeing my tears. I shook my head.

"How could you leave me, leave all of us," I questioned sadly.

"But- but I've been here the whole time," he stammered in confusion, looking around wide-eyed, "and I didn't leave anyone else either. No one else is here!"

"It's all gone, there's nothing left," I stated angrily. Rob looked at the parking lot.

"Yeah, so," he brushed it off, "they cleared out the woods awhile ago, you didn't know that? After all, it's just a few trees." A few trees, I thought, just like the 'few trees' he took down in Fairyland, the few trees that made a difference. We suffered when he cut them down.

"You don't remember, Rob?" He stood for the longest time staring at me with a blank expression.

"Remember what," he asked.

"Monsterland, Fairyland, everything," I explained hurriedly. Finally a look of recognition met his face.

"Don't tell me you're *still* thinking about that dream you had last night," he complained, rolling his eyes, "it's not real, Kay. I told you before, monsters and fairies don't exist. When are you going to grow up?"

His words cut me. After all of that time, all of those wonderful fairies and monsters who had touched my life and filled my days with magic; not the kind where you make things happen by the point of a finger. The kind of magic that everyone has inside of them; love, acceptance and faith, even the simple moment when you decide to believe in something you can't see because inside you know it's there and real, and will always be with you.

That's why I remembered. I remembered because I believed, because I believed in them and in myself. Suddenly I felt something hard in my palm and quickly opened it. It was the seed, I realized, somehow I had brought it back with me. A new beginning, hadn't Frendall told me? 'When you feel as though you've lost everything, you haven't. It just means there's room for a new beginning'. I held it, cradling it.

"Well," Rob persisted, "when are you going to grow up?" I smiled at him, wiping my eyes.

"Right now," I proclaimed, turning away. I walked the length of that parking lot to a place where a small row of trees had been spared. The soil was cool and moist beneath my fingers and when at last I was sure the hole was deep enough, I let the seed roll from my hand pushing mounds of dirt over it, concealing it, planting it.

§

Still to this day when I walk past a patch of bluebells I can press my ear close to them and listen very, very carefully and hear them ring. Still on calm, cool evenings with thousands of stars filling the sky I can listen by the trickling river and hear the sweet tinkling of fairy laughter. And still I walk past that old parking lot; broken now, with grass growing up through the cracks and as I look upon the tree that I planted those years ago growing tall and straight, I remember. I remember everything, I always will.

When I arrived home that afternoon nothing had changed. It was as though I had never left, as though time had stood still. I even wore the backpack I'd worn to school that very morning, full of the same books except for one… the diary. Somehow I'd brought it back with me, its red leather cover slightly curling at the corners. I pulled it out and held it, still with its note; 'someday you will know what to do with this book'. My finger snagged the edge and it tore away. But wait, I thought, the cover was still intact. The leather had torn away, but beneath the red, it was blue. Blue? I looked at it in wonder. The book had another cover beneath the red.

I pulled the red cover away more and more, tugging it free until an entirely different book was before me. The cover was blue with a brilliant gold rose in the centre, like the rose that Christopher had planted which began the two lands. It was the Lost Book! I flung it open, Christopher had given it to me! I'd had it all along and never knew because it was disguised as something else just as he had been. Maybe it would be full of wonderful secrets and everything that anyone had ever dreamt of knowing!

It was empty, every page was blank. I was confused until the ancient pen rolled out and I realized I was supposed to write it in, but what? The story, my adventures, everything I saw and did and discovered. I had promised once to never tell anyone about Fairyland, but now... Now I felt that somehow, in some way, this is how I could set them free. This book, this story. I would write it and then maybe someone would pick it up and read it, and go there with me. Maybe if they read it they could have a piece of Fairyland forever in their imagination. And maybe, just maybe, someone would have the strength to believe.

But where would I begin, I had so much to write! Where did my adventure begin, when I travelled into the woods, when I ate the fairy berries, when? My dream, the dream I had that began all of it, about the monster. Everything that exists, didn't it all begin with a dream, everything beautiful and wonderful in the world? So, taking the pen into my hand I opened to the first page and as the tip touched the paper, I began.

'It was him, the one who wore the black cape. But it wasn't the normal black that you and I see, no, it was darker than the darkest night...'

ABOUT THE AUTHOR

Precia Davidson was born on September 17, 1988 in Indiana and currently lives in Southwestern Ontario, Canada. She has been writing since childhood, always aspiring to become an author. The Monster Game, based on the fantasy world she imagined as a child, is her first published book.